# The Watchmakers' Daughter

Michael Woods

To Nora

# Part One, Chapter One

A lone traveller looked out over a moonlit valley. Another journey was almost at an end. With his winter chapped hands, he drew his long cloak from his mud soaked boots before turning away from the town in the valley below. The dark stretch of road to his destination carried on ahead of him. As the moon hid behind a cloud, he started to walk. After the silver light had melted away, he needed to go on carefully. He often scuffed the ground under his feet to ensure he did not fall. Occasionally, he would think of the words he would say the next day, and they broke into the world by playing out on his lips. He could never concentrate on them for long.

The town looked as though it was untouched, but the time would soon arrive when all that would change. What he was bringing with him could destroy the lives of many who lived below, but he believed there was a slim chance he could save them.

The moon came out from behind the clouds to reveal the dark shapes of the high impassable snow covered mountains that surrounded the town. Only the pass he was on and one other that snaked through the mountains allowed the town's citizens to travel to the outside world. Despite these natural defences, the townspeople had built a wall around their collective home.

The traveller eventually found himself in front of the town's gate. The near full moon shone above, providing enough light for him to see that the walls and gatehouse were constructed of large stones carved out from the surrounding mountains. The gate was shut tight so the traveller called out into the air. He waited patiently for a while, but nothing happened. He called out again. Perhaps the guard was asleep behind the wall. He had no need to be awake, considered the traveller, not in this town.

"Who's there?" cried a drowsy voice half distorted by a yawn.

"I seek shelter and food for the night."

Silence followed the traveller's words until his patience started to wear once more. He called up to the guard one final time, just before a small door within the larger gate was opened.

"All right, no need to rush me," said the guard. "Calling out at this time of night, you'll have everyone awake. Come on in then."

The traveller crossed the threshold of the unfamiliar place and tried to make out what was around him. He could see a cobbled path, lit by a number of dull street lamps, which he assumed led to the centre of the town. However, as the moon had disappeared behind another cloud, leaving only the light of the lamps to fight off the night, the rest of whatever was out there was shrouded in darkness.

After hearing the wicket being shut behind him the traveller turned around to ask the guard if there was anywhere to stay in the town.

"Yes sir, just follow the street and you'll find a tavern. I'm sure they'll have a room to spare. Probably have all their rooms to spare. Good night."

The traveller was not surprised at the abrupt end to their conversation. He just hoped it meant he was not too late. The guard did not even wait for the traveller to respond. He just bounded back up the stairs to the room above the gate and slammed a door behind him. He was obviously not too pleased about the disturbance to his sleep.

The noise of the speedy departure of the guard was followed by silence. The new visitor was once again left alone. He wondered how welcome he would be in this hidden town. At least they had let him in.

As the traveller walked down to the tavern, he passed a number of arched porticoes which fronted many of the buildings. He noticed that many of the walls behind the pillars were covered with white paint. He moved over to one of the white patches and swept his palm across it. It was still wet. He took a knife from his pocket and scraped away some of the newly applied paint to reveal a tiny segment of a picture hidden beneath. Perhaps he was too late after all. After wiping the white off his hands, the traveller carried on to the tavern.

\*\*\*

On her way back to her father's shop, Florence noticed a small crowd had gathered in the corner of the town square. The day was getting late. Local merchant families were packing away their market stall goods and tying their red and yellow covers down for another night. Though the day was still bright, it was getting cold. Despite this, the people in the group had gathered around something. As she had no commitments, Florence decided that she would go and have a look at what was going on. She was of the firm opinion that as not much happened in Pendon it was necessary jump on whatever form of excitement presented itself: otherwise, you faced the prospect of being bored stiff for some time.

As she got closer, Florence was disappointed to notice that a few people in the crowd were already starting to leave. She picked up her pace, hoping to see at least a glimpse of what had been going on. When she arrived at the back of the group she realised that they were just listening to a man talking. 'Still,' thought Florence, 'it's best to make the most of what you can get.'

She knew that the man must have been from outside the town. No one except Andrillo, a leading councillor, would give a speech in the square, and this man was certainly no Andrillo. The speaker was dressed in a grey cloak and muddied leather boots. He looked as if he had been up all night as thick dark lines sat under his narrowed eyes. However, his movements were swift, his voice clear and full of passion.

Florence caught the end of a sentence, something to do with an oncoming evil power and how it had to be resisted at all costs. The out-of-town speaker finished this line with a clenched fist and a dramatic pause. She looked around at the faces of the people nearby, most of them familiar. None of them seemed particularly impressed or moved by the speaker's words: most carried blank expressions. A few more people started to walk away.

Florence concluded that whatever little excitement there had been had already passed. She was about to walk away herself when the traveller started talking once again. Despite herself, she listened.

"There is no time for delay. Though the threat may not seem visible here today, it is plain to see just over the horizon. This threat is to your freedom and maybe even your lives. You might think that I should keep such opinions to myself. However, I know that it is natural for all of us to turn away from the truth, and let ourselves be led away from what makes us human. So, is it not a duty for anyone who can see this happening to his fellow man to stand up? To stand up and say that this is not the only way. I say that the price of humiliation through public speech is nothing to pay compared to the cost of what will be before us if we do not act."

Florence was impressed by the speaker and was glad that she had followed her curiosity. She wondered if such speeches were heard all the time in larger towns. This thought grew into a grain of doubt leading her to take a moment to consider what the man had actually said. She became aware that it was not really that much. He had told the crowd that there was a threat. A threat that had given him a reason to stand up before them. There was little else.

When the traveller resumed speaking, Florence realised that perhaps she was wrong to think the man unlike Andrillo. All his rhetoric was just a different path to Andrillo's own favourite subject of discussion: the threat of a distant sorcerer. The topic was so worn out, so uninteresting to the townsfolk that a few more of her fellow listeners started to drift away as soon as it was raised. The speaker did not seem to be phased by the dwindling of his audience. He carried on, stating that it was wrong to adopt the sorcerer's ordinances, his suggested way of life, as they could only bring misery. This statement intrigued Florence. Andrillo, the only other person who had raised the subject in public, always said that the town should do what the sorcerer wanted. He said that if Pendon ignored this distant unknown man they would soon feel his wrath. For many of the townsfolk, Andrillo's talk about this sorcerer had led him to become little more than a figure of ridicule, despite his position on the town council.

As the speaker continued to talk about the sorcerer, more and more of the gathered group started to leave. They had heard it all before, although in a slightly different form. The entertainment, whatever there had been in the first place, was over. The crowd was reduced to a handful of people and for the first time the speaker seemed a little affected by the indifferent reaction of his audience. As the people dispersed, Florence heard a few mumbled words of "odd fellow" and "typical out-of-towner", and before long decided that she would go home.

\*\*\*

For Florence home was next to the town's sole clock tower, which like many of the other main buildings consisted of well-cut green-grey stone. It was situated on the opposite side of the square from where she had seen the travelling speaker. But, the square was small and Florence was soon at her door. She hesitated for a moment on the street. She knew that her father would be at work and did not want to disturb his concentration. He was the town's master watchmaker. A title he cherished even though it was slightly inaccurate as he mainly dealt with repairs. Not only was he her father, he was also her tutor. She had been his apprentice for many years and so knew how easy it was to be distracted by people lumbering into the workshop.

Florence slowly opened the door and peered round it to see the familiar sight of her father at work. He was sitting in front of a high worktable with a loop in his eye while the light of the dying sun shone down upon him through the large windows in the workshop's ceiling. As usual, he was tinkering with an order; building up a watch before taking it apart and then putting it back together again. He would repeat this process over and over until the piece was perfect. Florence did not want to interrupt his train of thought and walked as lightly as she could towards the back of the room. But the tell-tale sound of her father being disturbed was heard just before she reached the handle of the kitchen door. In the quiet environment of the shop every noise was amplified, and the light taps of her father's shoes on the meticulously swept floor were for her like the thunder of an overhead storm.

"Don't worry Florence," her father said with a smile, "I always gladly give up my work to see you. But, you did not disturb me anyway, the light of the sun has diminished and I must get a light for my candle. I must finish this puzzle tonight."

As her father made his way to the back wall of the workshop to fetch a box of matches, Florence started to tell him of the travelling orator she had just heard. He did not reply to her after she had finished. Florence knew that he was not ignoring her: he often went silent when considering a situation.

\*\*\*

Florence got up at six. She made her bed, washed herself with the water bowl she kept in her room and got dressed. After going downstairs, she swept the workshop floor before making breakfast for her father. Prior to starting her morning's work on her current broken timepiece, she reviewed the customer accounts. The only outstanding bills were the ones that never seemed to get paid, but a new order had come in from the town's apothecary. She would have to pay him a visit in the afternoon. She spent the morning with her father in the workshop practising the craft she thought would be her future. She enjoyed these hours with her father. They were spent in almost complete silence as they both worked on their separate benches. However, she thought of these hours as the happiest in her day, and she rarely felt closer to her father. After lunch, Florence left for the apothecary's.

As Florence did not want to waste time, she cut through the alleys that snaked between the main arteries of the town. The well cut stone that faced the street buildings disappeared from the walls as she made her way into the hidden recesses of Pendon, revealing the rough irregular shapes of something much cheaper. Though the alleys were to be avoided at night, they were mostly safe in the day. But even when the sun was up it was necessary to be wary of certain hazards. Indeed, Florence was worried that she would have to face one of the worst of these when she saw an old woman lean out of one of the windows above her. Florence breathed a sigh of relief when a rug was draped out the window a moment later. After giving Florence a neutral look the woman started to hit the tattered carpet with a wooden beater. Florence hurried through the light veil of dust that floated down.

At the end the third and final alley through which Florence had to pass was the sight of a spun glass window filled with a plurality of distorted coloured glass jars and bottles. She had arrived at the apothecary's. She made her way inside to see the shopkeeper quietly watching his apprentice turn some substance into powder with a mortar and pestle. He looked up and greeted Florence warmly.

"I suppose you've come for my watch."

The apothecary removed his repeating pocket watch from one of the many dark wooden draws that lined the walls. He regarded the plain silver case and cream face of the watch for a moment before handing it to Florence.

"It stopped working last week and no amount of winding or shaking seems to be able to bring it back to life."

"My father will do all he can to get it working again," said Florence as she carefully placed the timepiece in her bag.

"You know, I bought that watch from your father almost exactly sixteen years ago. I remember it quite clearly as I think it was the first time I'd seen him flustered. His workshop was a catastrophe and the poor man didn't look like he'd had a minute of sleep for a week. My first thought was to leave the shop as quickly as I could, but then your mother walked in and all was clear. You see, she had you in her arms, a newly born baby."

"My mother," said Florence suddenly interested. "How was she?"

"Oh, she was fine. In your father she couldn't have had anyone who wanted to do more for her. Though at the time, I think she was looking after both you and him. You look just like her, you know."

"That's what everyone says," said Florence wondering if her dark brown hair and eyes, and pale heart shaped face really were the same as her mother's, or if people just used her image to replace the one they had forgotten. "It's good to hear about her though." They both paused and for a moment tried to remember someone they never really got to know; the crunching sound of the apprentice apothecary at work the only thing to be heard.

"I better be going," said Florence, "or he'll start worrying about where I've got to."

"Thank you for picking up the watch and send my best to your father."

\*\*\*

Florence was not surprised to see the crowd gathered in the market square again. She assumed the travelling speaker was probably giving another lecture. Still, the crowd seemed a little bigger than the day before, and Florence smiled to herself as she thought about how fickle her townsfolk could be.

A gap opened up in the crowd as she passed by and revealed that it was not the traveller who was speaking. Between the onlookers Florence could see the speaker from the previous day standing still and silent. Her first instinct was to find out what was going on. But, she thought it foolish to take the apothecary's watch into the crowd. Although it was unlikely that it would be stolen, she did not want to take a chance; especially when she was already so close to home.

Florence did her best not to disturb her father when re-entering the workshop. As usual, she failed. As she had caught his attention she greeted him by holding up her bag to demonstrate that she had got the watch. She took the piece out and placed it in a chest her father kept at the back of the workshop to store their work. She repeated to her father what the apothecary had said about his watch and then asked him if there was anything else that needed to be done in the day.

"There's always something to be done, what's on your mind?"

Florence did not want to admit it, but she was burning with curiosity. Something was possibly going on in her quiet town. She wanted to find out what it was.

"Well, there's another gathering on the other side of the market place. I thought it was just that travelling speaker again. But, it couldn't have be him as I saw him through the crowd and he wasn't saying anything. I was just wondering…"

"I suppose you can have a look. There's not a lot left to do today. But, be careful not to let your wondering get the better of you. Otherwise, who knows where it'll take you."

Florence's father had not even finished his sentence before Florence was out of the door, and he let his voice trail off on the last few words. He released a sigh through a smile before turning back to his work.

\*\*\*

Florence was pleased to see the crowd was still gathered on the other side of the square. As she started to make her way over, the raised voice of a speaker could be heard on the passing breeze. The few words that reached her were insufficient to piece together what was being said, and only made her more curious as to what was going on.

The crowd was quite large, much bigger than the day before. This led Florence to make her way round the side of the gathering to ensure herself a better view. By the time she reached the half-interested passes by at the back of the crowd, the voice of the speaker was quite clear. She thought it sounded a lot like the town councillor Andrillo: no one else she knew of in the town could make themselves sound so furious. Florence squeezed herself past a number of onlookers to get to a portico just at the side of the platform where the traveller was standing. The traveller was still maintaining his silence. His arms were crossed and he held a determined look on his face. Florence turned her attention to the speaker. She had been right. Before her was a tall, slightly balding man whose face was marked with a number of long thin scars. It was Andrillo, and as usual he was wearing his heavy grey cloak. Andrillo's voice was now becoming hoarse. However, he continued to shout at the crowd and occasionally he would throw his hand in the direction of the traveller. Florence wondered why this visitor to her town did not respond. What could he have to gain by just letting his opponent speak?

Andrillo paused to catch his breath. He cleared his throat and was looked upon by a silent crowd. His eyes swept across the people gathered about him until they came to rest upon the figure of the traveller. He remained silent for a further moment before raising his hand to point at the object of his gaze.

"As I have made clear," he said in a voice that was now hoarse and low, "this man's words can do us nothing but harm. He claims that he seeks to enlighten you about the threat of the sorcerer. But, I say that he is the threat. The ideas he would have you accept and what they promote are the very things that will bring the sorcerer's wrath. Some of you have laughed when you have heard me say that we must be wary of what could befall us. But, I know many of you have traded with other towns. You have seen what has happened to those who have ignored the wisdom I am passing on to you and have paid the price. If we let this man continue to spread his malicious words in our town, he will incite a war with the sorcerer and the mist will descend. Misery will follow for us all."

Florence looked around the crowd as Andrillo spoke. The people near to her did not seem to take the speech seriously at all. It was obvious by their smirks and grimaces that they thought Andrillo was talking nonsense. She even heard the man standing next to her say, "I used to think he was a fool, now it seems he is mad. How do these people get on the council?" However, as she looked further afield, she noticed that the speech stuck a cord with some. This was especially true with regard to the merchants, whose faces had turned pale at the mere mention of mist.

"We must change our ways," continued Andrillo, "if we are to avoid catastrophe now that this man has brought the eye of the sorcerer upon our town. I will reminded you of what I have said many times before. We must get rid of ornamentation, tone down our use of colour, eliminate needless chatter, no longer play music and many other things besides to make sure that the wrath of the sorcerer is not brought upon us."

The people standing next to Florence had had enough and they started to walk away. Florence thought that like the previous day the crowd would soon lose interest and disperse. However, many of the merchants who had been affected by Andrillo's earlier words continued to stand their ground and listen attentively. But, it was not just the merchants. Many others also seemed to be taking Andrillo seriously. Indeed, after the disgruntled among them had left, the crowd had not shrunk anywhere near as much as Florence had expected. Andrillo concluded his speech.

"Most of all, in these times of great danger, we must make sure that those among us who threaten us all are removed."

Andrillo finished by pointing to the traveller once again.

\*\*\*

Florence was not impressed by Andrillo. Although she did not know what sort of threat this sorcerer posed to her town, she did not think it right that Andrillo should use his authority to publicly berate the traveller. Indeed, Andrillo had not only scolded the man, he had also threatened him. He had not explicitly said that anyone should attack the man. However, the veil under which his threat was cast was so thin as to be absurd.

Florence already thought ill of Andrillo. Though he had always been courteous to her, she was sure this was only because her father held positions of some importance: her father was not just the only watch repairer in the town, he was also a respected merchant who held a seat on the guild council. Florence had often seen others make petitions to Andrillo, or even just casual greetings in the street, only to be completely ignored by the man. Those who persisted in their attempts to gain his attention would often end up on the receiving end of his quick temper.

As she returned home, Florence tried to push all thoughts of Andrillo and what she had seen to the back of her mind. However, the sight of the ashen-faced merchants could not be displaced by anything from her consciousness. Was there really something so dangerous going on in the outside world that she did not know about? She asked her father if this distant sorcerer really was as much of a threat as some in the town apparently believed.

"I cannot really say Florence," he said. "I've heard stories of his influence in other towns, but he's never really been a great concern to people here. Why the sudden interest? Was it Andrillo speaking on the other side of the square?"

"Yes, it was Andrillo. But, it's not just him."

"Are you talking about the travelling speaker from yesterday?"

"He was there today too, but he didn't say anything. He just let Andrillo carry on and on about how he was a danger to the town because of the sorcerer."

Florence paused for a moment.

"You know Andrillo a little. Could he be right about the danger of the sorcerer?"

"Well," said her father. "I know Andrillo is an intelligent man as I've had many dealings with him while working for the guild. As far as I can tell, he tries to do what he believes is right. For instance, unlike some I could mention, I don't think he joined the council to line his pockets. He also probably knows more about the world than most of the people here. Not only does he come from a distant place, it is said he travelled through many others before he arrived here with his brother, Illarno Andrillo. You know, I heard they chose to stay after Illarno married Mary, Robert Carpenter's daughter."

Florence frowned. She could tell her father was attempting to change the subject. He smiled a little. His daughter would soon tell him to answer her question. It was better not to wait.

"But, as to whether he's right about this sorcerer, well, I could not say for sure."

Florence returned to the street. It had been some time since she left the crowd. However, she could see that a few people were still standing on the other side of the square. Andrillo and the traveller had left about the same time as Florence, but unusually there were others who wanted to be heard. Occasionally, the distant note of a voice raised in anger would float over to her.

Most of the crowed had dispersed. Those who remained wore the same dull grey cloak as Andrillo and the traveller. She knew what side of the argument they would be on. The cloak was usually only worn by those who, like Andrillo, wanted to appease the sorcerer. She did not understand them. Why should anyone in Pendon have to change their way of life just because of some distant unknown man? She had had enough of speeches for the evening. She closed the door on the remains of the day.

\*\*\*

Florence woke up with a start. She was just having a bad dream. However, the mood of the nightmare seemed to linger on into the waking world, and Florence decided to try and wash away her thoughts with a drink of water. A full glass was on the table near her window and so she got out of bed. After taking a sip she looked out onto the alley below. She noticed that a thin mist had descended. She woke up for a second time when she remembered what Andrillo had said earlier in the day. The mist of the sorcerer would descend. Even if the weather outside was just an annoying coincidence, it would not matter.

# Chapter Two

"Come on, we haven't got all day."

Edward Butcher did not turn round. He knew who had uttered the words, and he was not going to let that man disturb his moment. Instead, he paused to compose his thoughts so that he could properly judge where to place the nail he held in his hand in the wall before him. He pushed it into the soft plaster until it would go no further with just the strength of his chubby hand. A small network of cracks formed around the iron and proceeded to spit dust every time Butcher brought down his hammer. He struck the head of the nail several more times until he was happy that it would hold firm. His work done, Butcher moved over to Andrillo who was waiting with a list of edicts ready to put on the wall.

"Thank you Edward," said the councillor. "You have performed your duty well."

Andrillo did not put the list of edicts on the wall straight away. He believed the moment could only be improved by a few words and luckily he was the right man to provide them.

"We are gathered here today in the Black Swan Inn: the last of the four public houses in Pendon to receive a list of ordinances. I'm very honoured that you, the Board of Edicts, have invited me to hang up this sign which demonstrates the strength that exists in our community to face up to the great threat that has been put upon us from the outside world. A threat, now it is here, that needs to be dealt with by each and every one of us from within."

"We all know that two weeks ago a man arrived here and brought the attention of the sorcerer with him. At first, many did not believe that this was true. But, no sooner had he come than the mist arrived. Though many were not prepared for what I have long known to be our fate, we were very fortunate to have the people who are assembled here today. You, the Board of Edicts quickly responded to one of the main challenges that face those who fall under his mist: ensuring that those who are not aware of the sorcerer's demands are duly informed. So, it is with great pleasure that I now hang this list of ordinances to help our community know what must be done in this most difficult of times."

Andrillo was disappointed with the muted reaction to his speech and quickly turned to hang the edicts on the wall. Only a small splutter of applause followed. After shaking a few hands he quickly made his way to the exit. The fact that this Board of Edicts existed at all displeased him greatly. In his eyes, it was just composed of a number of ignorant, but well meaning, locals who had hastily banded together as soon as the mist appeared.

He understood their concerns. They feared the sorcerer and wanted to avoid the dangers the mist would bring. The problem was that these people had no clear idea of what the sorcerer demanded. Through hearsay, Andrillo's own speeches and a little travel the members of the Board were aware that colour, music, idle chatter and the questioning of the sorcerer were frowned upon in the cities already under the mist. They knew little else. Consequently, Andrillo thought the troop should listen to him. He could provide all the information they needed to produce a comprehensive list of ordinances to protect the town against the sorcerer. However, from the very start they had not given him the respect or attention he deserved.

When he first heard about the formation of the Board, Andrillo was pleased that people in Pendon were finally taking the matter of the sorcerer seriously. However, the first meeting demonstrated to him that this group would never provide what he wished for. Instead of a reasoned debate about what had to be done to inform the townspeople about the sorcerer and his demands, the meeting quickly descended into a spate of bickering between Butcher and John Masters. The problem was that not only did these men not get on, they were also the two strongest personalities present. Indeed, Andrillo himself had found it difficult to get a word in as the meeting went on. The battle of empty words between the two men continued for almost an hour. The only thing that was concluded by the end of the meeting was that Master could lead future discussions as long as Butcher could front the distribution on the edicts. The two main players of the Board seemed pleased with what they had achieved; Andrillo was anything but.

Andrillo had wanted to break up the Board as soon as he could. Leaving the protection of the town to such men was not only a waste of time, but potentially dangerous. If these uninformed men were given the authority to interpret the will of the sorcerer, Andrillo had no doubt that they could soon start spreading harmful misinformation. However, he was unable to make a move against the group. Despite the mist, most of the members of the council were still not convinced that they needed to address the issue of the sorcerer. Andrillo's voice on the council was also diminished by the absence of his brother Illarno, who was out of town on business. His brother was not only a wealthy and influential man, he was also a member of the council. With the combination of these two factors, Andrillo knew it would be almost impossible to persuade the council to force the dissolution of the Board.

As his reputation could further empower the Board if attached to his name, Andrillo had distanced himself from them by not attending any more meetings. Two weeks passed and he still found himself unable to act: his brother had still not returned. In the meantime, the Board had finally come up with a list of edicts. After ten days of endless meeting, they had produced a short list of rules that could have been released on day one: no colours, no music, no idle chatter and no undermining of the sorcerer. To Andrillo's disgust, this did not seem to undermine the group at all. Instead, they were lauded as the only group dealing with the issue of the sorcerer.

When the Board approached the council to ask permission to put up their list, Andrillo suggested caution and patience. A majority of the eleven present councillors did not agree. They thought that it would be good to let the edicts circulate to help reduce a sense of unease that was growing among the population. Andrillo was sickened by his fellow councillors. They did not care about the veracity of the information or who controlled it. They were just happy to let the Board go ahead on the assumption that it might reduce the rumblings of disquiet in the town.

After the Board had been given permission to go ahead by the council, Andrillo approached Masters to see if he could assist with their work. He said that he was delighted by the offer, but that Andrillo was too late to help with the list. A further meeting led to him being granted the opportunity to hang up the final list of edicts. It would have been foolish to turn this down. In hindsight, he realised his earlier treatment of the group was a mistake. He knew that if the men on the Board continued to maintain their influence over the definition of the sorcerer's rules, they would soon become powerful men. He just hoped he could repair the damage that he had done.

\*\*\*

Andrillo was heading to the market square. As he looked around, he was at least pleased by some of the changes that had occurred in the town. Quite a few of the passing citizens had adopted the grey cloak and many more of the wall murals around the town had been covered in white paint. He suspected that many had adopted these measures through fear: gruesome stories had started to spread about what happened to those who resisted the power of the sorcerer. Fear was indeed a powerful weapon, he thought, pausing for a moment and unconsciously raising his hand to a scar that stretched from his eye to his lip. If this fear could assist in the cause to save the people of Pendon, he saw no reason why it should be discouraged.

Andrillo suspected that there was still much work to be done to safeguard the town. As this thought passed through his mind, a major case in point wandered into view. From the market square, the daughter of the watchmaker appeared wearing a bright red cloak. Not only that, she was singing. While many in the town seemed to be adopting the Board's edicts, this girl seemed to be actively opposing them.

Her eyes drifted over the crowd and eventually settled on his. She stopped singing for a second, gave a smile and a nod before resuming her song and continuing on her way. Andrillo continued to watch her, happy to see she was attracting a number of disapproving looks as she went.

Florence was on her way to George Appleton's house. It was not a trip she was looking forward to even though he had been a good customer in the past. Appleton was one of the many people who had adopted a grey cloak and the Board's other edicts. He would not look kindly on her attire, but she was determined to go as she was. She was not going to alter her behaviour just because the weather had changed.

She could not understand why so many people took the edicts of the Board so seriously. It was common knowledge that they had cobbled together their idea of this sorcerer's demands from Andrillo's speeches, hearsay and rumour. They had no real evidence that the edicts they distributed were in any way connected with this unknown sorcerer. That they lacked any real expertise on the matter did not seem to make any difference: those who had recently adopted the grey cloak still gawped at her when she wore red.

Ever since the mist had descended the greys, as she thought of them, seemed to be growing in number. Every day, another gloomy fear filled figure seemed to appear on the street. But, this fear was not yet universal. Tanner, a local cloth merchant, was decidedly happy with the situation as a growing number of people bought up his grey coloured stock. He was even able to raise the price without seeing a decrease in demand.

As Florence came up to her destination, Appleton saw her approaching through the net curtains on his window and rushed to the only entrance to the house. Just as Florence was about to knock, the door swung open, revealing Appleton. He greeted her cordially, but his disgust at her red cloak was plainly evident.

"Would you mind waiting at the door while I fetch the watch for your father?" said Appleton with a quaver in his voice. He looked up and down the street before saying, "I will not be long".

Before Florence could utter a word, Appleton slammed the door. Florence was not insulted. She expected him to act in such a way. Part of her was even relieved that he had not done something worse. Only the day before, a customer had organised for her to come round just so that he could tell her that anyone who did not conform to the edicts was threatening Pendon and was therefore a traitor. Traitors were hung. She had not known what to say in response and had just stared at him blankly until he returned inside his home. Despite the experience, she was determined to carry on flouting the rules the Board had hammered into the walls of the town.

Appleton quickly returned with the watch. He hastily pushed it into her hands and thanked her before hastily retreating once more. This took place so quickly that Florence continued to stand on Appleton's front step for a few moments without really knowing if their transaction was complete. After placing his watch in her bag, she decided that there was nothing else to do but go home. The fearful eyes of Appleton reappeared at the window and maintained their steady gaze on Florence until she could no longer be seen. Florence wondered why Appleton was so worried. Did he think something terrible would happen if they engaged each other in conversation? Perhaps he believed her behaviour was contagious. As she wandered back home, she did not sing. Instead, she went over the events that had made her take up her stand.

\*\*\*

When Florence had woken up in the middle of the night just under a couple of weeks before, the mist had been very light. She had hoped it would disperse by the morning. It did not. A thin grey veil had descended over the whole town and showed no sign of leaving. As the following day went on, Florence observed the fear in the eyes of her fellow citizens continue to grow. Many saw the mist as a sign that Andrillo's prediction had been correct and that to save themselves they would have to act.

Later the same day, while returning home from a customer, Florence noticed the traveller was once again standing in the corner of the market square. She rushed over to the scene. When she got close enough to see what was going on, she found the traveller was just about to speak. However, like the time before, Andrillo prevented him from saying anything. This time it was not because he was shouted down, but because the councillor ordered a couple of the town's guard to take hold of the man. The traveller attempted to utter a word, but was silenced by one of the guards who drove an armoured fist into his stomach. Andrillo proceeded to announce that the man had done enough damage to the town, and they would not let him do more by spreading his poisonous words.

"Stranger," continued Andrillo. "The council of Pendon has ruled that you are a significant threat to this town and its people. Therefore, you will, without any hesitation, be removed from this place. I also must inform you that you should never return. If you do, we will make a proper example out of you to those that would also bring danger to our town. This example will be your death. Nod your head if you understand."

The traveller met Andrillo's gaze, but said nothing. One of the guards waited a moment before taking hold of the traveller's head and nodded it for him. After the traveller had demonstrated that he understood, the guards dragged him from the spot towards the town gates. Florence followed. The traveller showed no real signs of resistance leading Florence to wonder if he had been through something similar before. As he was pulled down the lane, many people around passed comments under their breath. Some were compelled to call out that he should be ashamed of himself for threatening Pendon, others that he should go home and leave them be. A couple of children even started to throw stones, although they mostly hit the two flanking guards. It came as no surprise to Florence that most of the people who hurled the abuse were wearing grey cloaks.

The town gate was open and waiting for the trio of the traveller and his entourage. The guards marched the man a short distance outside the town before flinging him to the ground. Florence joined a group of interested passers-by that had gathered just inside the walls. They watched on as the guards returned to Pendon at a brisk pace before shutting the gate behind them. The traveller took his time to stand. He dusted himself down and took a few steps back towards the place from which he had just been expelled. Now he was free, he started to speak.

"It was not me who brought this mist to your town, remember that. If it was, it would soon lift. But, you will see. With men like your esteemed town councillor around, it will just get worse."

After the traveller had shouted these words at the gate, a soldier told him to get lost before they interpreted his lack of movement as a return to the town. Not long afterwards the guard turned to the townsfolk who had witnessed the commotion.

"The coward walks away."

"Good riddance," exclaimed the grey cloaked woman next to Florence.

\*\*\*

Florence was not sure if it was such a good thing that the only voice of opposition to the sorcerer had been ejected from the town. It turned out that the traveller's prediction was as good as Andrillo's. As the days had passed, rather than disappearing, the mist had thickened. Every night and day for the last ten days had seen a slight increase in the thickness of the mist. Florence did not forget the traveller's words. But, it seemed as if no one else had heard them. Most of the town only seemed to have ears for Andrillo and the Board.

She was further frustrated by the many people who agreed that the traveller had to go because he had brought the mist. How could they not recognise that even though he had gone and they had adopted the edicts, the mist continued to grow? It was because of this foolishness evidenced by her fellow citizens that Florence decided that she would not follow these edicts. Indeed, as the mist thickened each and every day after the traveller had been forced to leave, Florence's determination to oppose the edicts grew.

A week after the traveller had been expelled, Florence decided that if others were going to try and force her to change, she would. Just not in the way that they wanted. Her first little act of rebellion was to sing as she made her way around the town. A couple of days passed and it was plain to her that she was not doing enough. She lay in her bed wondering what she could do when the grey cloaks that everyone seemed to be wearing came to her mind. She leaped out of bed and started to rummage through her wardrobe. Underneath some other neatly folded clothes she found it: her mother's old red cloak.

***

As she approached the market square from Appleton's house, Florence noticed that Andrillo was standing just up ahead. It was no surprise to Florence that he started to watch her as in her red cloak she stood out from almost everyone else. Still, she did not want to have to deal with his judgemental gaze as she went about her daily business. Nor did she want to turn back: that would just be another way of giving in to him. She chose to ignore him as best she could, but as she got closer he called out her name.

"Florence. Ah, I wonder if I could have a word."

Florence stopped automatically. Despite the fact that he was eroding freedom in her town, she responded.

"Yes, of course. What would you like, councillor?"

For the time being, she would forgive him the false smile and the half-hidden disapproving look and listen to what he had to say. At least he allowed himself to be seen in public with someone opposing the ordinances; unlike those such as Appleton. She thought that Andrillo was just going to carry on the way he usually did and tell her that she was leading herself and the town into peril. He managed to surprise her.

"I have a job for your father. I own a watch that I brought with me from... Well, that's beside the point. Let's just say I have a watch that I'd like your father to do some work on. There's nothing wrong with the mechanism, so I doubt it'll be a difficult job. I just need the case to be replaced. You see, it is a very ornamental piece, and I'm not sure that it's appropriate for the new world we live in."

As he finished speaking, Andrillo gave Florence a little nod. She knew he was not just referring to his watch. She chose to ignore this. She just replied that her father would be happy to take up the councillor's commission and asked if he wanted the watch to be collected.

"No, that's all right. I'll bring it to your father's workshop later today."

"I'm sure my father will be pleased to see you, councillor," Florence said with a plastic smile.

After wishing each other a good day, they went their separate ways.

\*\*\*

At first, Florence was surprised that Andrillo had been so courteous towards her. As she made her way home she recognised that perhaps he had his motives. If he really did want her father to work on his watch, then it would make no sense for him to be rude to her: her father was the only watchmaker in Pendon. Perhaps Andrillo also thought that by being courteous to her he could win her over. Unlike the traveller, Florence was a citizen. Andrillo could not just have her thrown out of the town by the guards. He would have to either suffer her presence or get the council to enforce the following of the edicts.

Florence returned home and told her father to expect the councillor. Her father could hear the half-hidden resentment in her voice and said that she could have the rest of the day off: he would have enough time to talk to the councillor. Florence understood that her father was trying to make sure that the façade of her good manners would not have to be tested within her own home. She was glad that she would not have to deal with Andrillo again that day. She thanked her father and went into the kitchen.

The kitchen was separated from the workshop by a thick wooden door to make sure that work in one would not disturb that in the other. Before Florence had fully closed off the two rooms from one another, she heard someone enter from the street. She could not be sure if it was Andrillo. She did not want to find out. However, she knew that if she shut the door or clambered up the stairs she might draw attention to herself. She just stood on the spot as quietly as she could. After waiting a moment to make sure the unknown visitor was not aware of her presence, she leant her ear to the sounds of the workshop.

"Good evening councillor, I was expecting you."

"Ah good," replied Andrillo, "so your daughter passed my message on."

"She said that you wanted to replace your watch case? Have you brought it with you?"

In response to this Florence heard a light tap and the gentle clinking of a chain. She assumed that the councillor had taken out his watch and set it down. She heard her father put down his tools, with care as always, and walk over to the councillor.

"I'm afraid that I don't think I've a spare casing for this watch," she heard her father say. "I might need to send off for a new one. It's quite a beautiful piece. Is this a city?"

"It's a depiction of my home. But, it's not suitable for the new order of things as you can well see. Sentimentality got the better of me for a while, but the time for such things has passed. We must all do our part for Pendon, even when it is difficult. Don't you agree?"

The councillor's question was followed by a short silence. Florence realised that Andrillo was no longer talking about the watch.

"Well, I suppose that we must all do difficult things. What would you like me to do with the old watch casing?"

"I would prefer to have it destroyed. I suppose that can be arranged?"

"Yes, that poses no problem," said Florence's father after a further pause.

"Good, give my regards to your daughter. I suppose she is out?"

"I gave her the rest of the day off."

"You're a kind father. I'm sure you'll do what's best for her. Now, I'm afraid I have to leave. I've just received word that my brother has returned, and I'm very keen to see him."

Before Florence's father could say goodbye to Andrillo, the man had left. Florence cautiously left her hiding place. She met her father's eyes with a look of thunder.

"How can that creep think he can just come in here and tell you what to do? What's worse is that he is trying to control me through you. He does not have the courage to talk to a young woman, but he has the audacity to try and use you like another one of his lackeys."

"Florence, I'm not sure you should talk about the councillor in that way. He may not be the easiest person to get along with, but I think he is trying to do his best for the town. Also, you have to agree, it was only after the visit of the travelling man that this mist arrived."

"It may have arrived with him, but can't you see that the stupid mist is still here. If Andrillo's ideas about this distant sorcerer are right, then surly it should have vanished by now. But, it hasn't. In fact, everyday it's getting worse and worse."

"That may be so Florence, my dear child, but I don't think many other people in the town see it that way. They're happy that the traveller has gone, but they think his influence is still here."

Florence only half heard what her father said and mumbled a response. She suddenly became concerned with her own thoughts. She realised at that moment that the last words of the traveller had now become her own.

\*\*\*

Florence lay in her bed trying to get to sleep, but she too distracted. She could not stop thinking about how foolish everyone was. They had set-up a position in their minds and closed off their ears, accosting anyone who tried to disagree with them, or make them think. Florence was caught in two minds. Should she maintain her protest and continue to try and show her townsfolk that they were deluded. Or, should she just give up attempting to persuade them. They were probably more offended by what she was doing than moved to think. She could not come to a decision. Instead, her thoughts spun around and around in her mind, settling nowhere and preventing her from settling down for the night. To break the spell of these restless considerations she sat up for a moment and looked to the window. Winter had finally started to move in, but it was still not that cold in her room. Still, Florence was glad that her window was closed as the curling frost that had grown at its edges suggested they were in for a chilly night. For a moment, her mind was clear. Out of nowhere came the observation that the mist did not seem to have any effect on the weather. This idea started a train of thought that soon led her back to thinking about the traveller, Andrillo and all the other things that were keeping her from her sleep. In frustration, she jumped out of bed and walked over to the window, muttering with annoyance as she went.

All at once, all her sleep stealing thoughts fled from her mind. She had seen something moving in the mist outside. But, she had only caught a glimpse of whatever it was. She looked again with her full attention, but there was nothing to be seen. Florence's view from her room mainly looked out onto an ally that led off the market square. But, it was also possible to see some of the square itself. It was there, somewhere in the middle of the square that the figure had stood. Although it was not completely unheard of for people to go out into the cool air of the night, it was unusual. However, it was not the mere appearance of a figure that shocked Florence, but its size. She told herself it must have just been either her tired mind or the mist creating some sort of illusion. Otherwise, the figure would have stood at least half as tall again as a normal man. Part of her was adamant she had seen something, but there was nothing to see anything anymore. She stood at the window for some time, wishing that something would emerge from the mist to explain what had roused her from her sleep stealing thoughts. But, at the same time, another part of her wished for something else, something strange and new.

Unconsciously, her arms had clasped around her chest and she started to shiver from head to toe. It was becoming too uncomfortable to remain standing about in the cold. After a few more moments she laughed at herself for freezing her body until she could do nothing but get back under the covers. She shook her head and got back into bed as quickly as she could.

The comfort and comparative warmth of the bed did its work quickly. Although Florence now wanted to stay awake a little longer to ponder over what she had seen, she was fast asleep before she got the chance.

***

Florence woke up to another grey misty day. To begin with, all she remembered was the laboured thoughts that had replaced an early peaceful sleep. Then she remembered the half seen giant figure from the market square. Despite her conviction of the previous night, she was convinced she had just imagined something as she was stressed and tired.

She got out of bed and started her chores for the day. She made breakfast and picked up the list of customers she had to visit. Since the mist had descended, the list seemed to be getting shorter. This made her feel a little guilty. It was almost certainly her actions that were causing the downturn in trade for her father. But, as she stepped out into the new day, her mind returned to the thoughts that had been spinning round her head the previous night. This was because even though the morning was fresh, the mist had become noticeably thicker. Florence could not even see the other side of the square from the alley just outside the shop.

Under her breath, she damned Andrillo and his gang of fools who seemed to be doing all they could to instil more and more fear into the hearts of her townspeople. She was also angered by her fellow citizens' gullibility. Did no one else hear the words of the traveller? She wondered why everyone was so afraid of this sorcerer who no one really knew anything about. Perhaps that was half the problem. It was easy to fear something you did not know. Your idea of its power was only limited by your imagination. If he was so important, Florence wanted to know why this sorcerer would be concerned with their little town. Like most people in the world he had probably not even heard of it. After reaching the first house on her list, she came to the conclusion that she would just have to put such notions out of her mind for the time being: she still had quite a bit of work to do.

# Chapter Three

A week had passed since the night Florence thought she had seen something in the square. There had been no dramatic changes. However, Florence often felt she was witnessing a slow dull grey procession of minor alterations that would eventually lead to Andrillo and the Board's desired utopia. Every day another family seemed to have adopted the signature grey cloaks of those who feared the sorcerer. Every day she went into the market it was a little quieter: there was less chatter, less bargaining and fewer petty arguments between the people on the stalls. People had even stopped talking about the mist. It had ceased being something new and had become the new reality of the town.

Florence made her way downstairs in her mother's red cloak. She thought it odd that this old piece of clothing that would otherwise look faded and worn appeared bright and vibrant in the otherwise colourless town. Her father was already sitting at the table when she reached the kitchen. He looked up and worried Florence with the concern in his eyes. This only lasted a moment. Despite Andrillo's recommendations, her father had not told Florence to change her behaviour. Following this form, he soon cast his concern away and with the lightest of smiles said that Florence looked just like her mother.

Florence's father had started to follow the ordinances. He had even bought a grey cloak. Perhaps this change was motivated by concern for his business more than anything else. Nevertheless, Florence was still a little disappointed. Like many in the town, he had followed the crowd to ensure his business would not be hurt rather than air his real opinion on what was happening. At least he had not said anything to her about her own behaviour. Despite the fact that what she was doing could harm his position in the town, he let her be.

Florence dawdled through her breakfast: she was not looking forward to the oncoming day. Another short list of customers was waiting for her, but it was not this that concerned her. Her problem lay in having to face up to the people in her town. Only a few weeks before, she had laughed with them, shared conversations with them about everyday life. These same people were now deathly silent in her presence and often stared at her with hate. She wanted to respond to their looks by telling them that this was her community too, but she knew they would not listen. She knew because they did not listen to anything she said. People on the street did not reply to her when she said hello; many customers did not even talk to her when she visited their homes.

She was not alone in her situation, but there were not many in the town that continued to refuse to follow the ordinances. Nor had she really been able to meet up with any of the others who tried to get on as before. Most had been argued down by their families and forced to change. Florence knew this as she had heard a number such arguments escaping from family homes as she passed by in the street. Many others who had resisted at first had been compelled into altering their ways by the reception they got in public or when they tried to do business. All of this made Florence aware that she was a member of a group that was dwindling quickly. Nevertheless, she was resolved to carry on with her little rebellion.

She picked up the list of customers her father had written and followed the block-like shapes of his handwriting. There were two names on the list that day. Still, two names were better than none. She headed out. It was still early and the sun had not yet risen over the surrounding mountains to brighten the streets. Like the last few mornings the atmosphere was dank and dark. Florence could see figures moving around in mist over in the square. A number of them would be the new merchants who had recently appeared from nearby Hesik, where the mist had fallen some time before. They were cloth merchants who sold the grey fabric that was now in high demand. These enterprising few had made their way over as soon as they heard the mist had descended. She saw these men as hardened greys. Whenever she passed near their stalls they gazed at her in complete silence. They would even stop serving their customers to follow her with their eyes until she disappeared from view. She felt that she could face up to the people in her own town as she had known them before they changed. These men were different. Despite her wish to do so, she could not meet their hard stares.

On that morning, she could avoid the market. She meandered through the streets shrouded as if her eyes were covered with a silk gauze veil until she came to the house of Alfred Alwin: an old man who was on her list every week. Florence believed he just liked the visits, but the supposed purpose of her going was to wind-up his three prised timepieces. Alfred had severe arthritis in his hands and could not perform the task himself. This led him to pay a small fee to Florence for a weekly visit. His daughter Bridget could have carried out the duty with ease, but the old man would not let her.

Florence was glad of the visit as it acted as a break from the otherwise grey ridden world. Alfred did not venture out too much from his home and was the only person Florence knew who paid no attention to the ordinances whatsoever. He was no rebel. He had just not been to the public houses or market square to see or hear about the changes. Nor did he want to hear about them. Whenever his daughter tried to bring them up, he would feign that he could not hear.

When Florence got to his door, she found Alfred's daughter waiting for her. Unlike her father, Bridget was a fervent follower of the ordinances. Florence could see the displeasure in the woman's eyes as she regarded her red cloak.

"My father will not need your assistance this morning; he is not well. Actually, tell your father that my papa will need no further assistance until I say so."

Florence had only seen Alfred the week before and he seemed fine. She was not sure if this supposed illness was just a fabrication to keep her away, but she could not argue with Bridget. This was because before she could even finish saying that she hoped that Alfred would soon feel better, Bridget had gone back inside her father's house.

Florence was furious and had to restrain herself from banging on the door to demand to see if Alfred really was ill, or if Bridget was just lying. However, the thought that Alfred really could be ill stopped her from causing any commotion. She would not want the poor old fellow to suffer because of her stupidity, or that of his daughter.

For a few moments, she just stood in front of the house teetering on the edge between anger and upset. She was soon brought out of her emotional dilemma by murmuring behind her. With her red cloak she was possibly the most notable thing on the streets. Despite the mist she was still quite visible to those who walking by. She gave herself another second to compose herself before calmly taking out the list of customers. There was one name left.

\*\*\*

Florence soon found herself back at home. The other name on the list had been that of a retired blacksmith. He had at least passed over his watch to Florence. Unlike Bridget, his only reaction to her visible opposition to the new ordinances was concern. Despite the fact that Florence wanted to provoke her townsfolk so they would review their own ignorance, she was glad that there were still some who did not scorn her for refusing to conform. She laid the blacksmith's watch on her father's workbench.

She felt exhausted. So exhausted that at first she did not think about why her father was not in the workshop. He was always there at that time of day. She soon broke out of her stupor and quickly made her way into the kitchen. He was nowhere to be seen. She ran upstairs and looked into his room. It was as unkempt as usual; the only place where his need for neatness and order did not seem to extend. He was not there either. Florence sighed to herself and wondered where her father could be. She hoped that nothing had happened. She returned to the workshop and sat at her workbench. Her eyes drifted over the old tools that he had given her. A small but essential set. She picked up a small screwdriver and started to slowly turn it around in her hand while her thoughts meandered over the situation. Finally, she decided that the best thing to do would be to go out and look for him. Perhaps he had just gone to the market to pick something up. She was not too happy about having to leave the house again and face more of those stares. A grain of anger grew within her. Why had he not left a note?

Florence carefully replaced the screwdriver into her small tool-kit box. She wanted to put off leaving as long as she could. She watched her hands lift up the leather flap on the bag and place the screwdriver back with the other tools. Just as she was about to finally get up off her stool, her father appeared. His eyes were cast down towards the ground. Even though he had gone out, he had not shaved properly. Unusually dishevelled, he looked older. It seemed that her father would keep on surprising her that day. His sight was clearly trained on whatever was going on in his head, and it was only after Florence interrupted his trail of thought that he noticed that she was even there.

"Where've you been? I was looking all over the house for you. I was just about to search the town for you."

"Back already Florence? I thought you'd be a little longer."

"Alfred's daughter said he was ill. She wouldn't even let me in the house. That meant that I only had the blacksmith to see. I've put his watch on your table already. But, you're changing the subject."

"Well, I was called to a town meeting. A man from the city guard came to take me to the council. When I arrived, most of the other guild leaders were already there. It seems..." Florence's father paused for a second. He walked over to his workbench stool and sat down. "It seems that the council has been pushed into considering what action it needs to take to secure the safety of the town."

"What do you mean? What are they planning to do?"

"Andrillo and his supporters have finally managed to persuade councillor Moss that the town really is in peril. There are now seven councillors in favour of change. The other five were happy to leave things as they were for a while, but now that Moss has changed his mind they will fall into line with the others."

The watchmaker paused. He wanted to avoid the news he had to give for a minute longer and he picked up the blacksmith's watch. Years of routine led him to automatically open the case and look inside before tinkering a little with the winding mechanism. After a few moments of silence, he put the piece back down.

"Over the last few weeks, Moss has been bombarded with demands that he change his mind. I must admit that I've not done anything to stop it from happening, Florence. I hope that you will forgive me."

"Forgive you, why? I don't know what all this means."

"The council are going to pass the ordinances into law."

Florence went white for a second, but the shock did not last long. Deep down she knew it was inevitable. The pressure from the greys had been constantly building on all the councillors' shoulders. If it had not happened that day, it would have soon enough.

"That's not all though," said her father, carrying on as soon as he saw that Florence had returned from her thoughts. "Andrillo believes that the threat is now so great it demands another, more drastic measure: he has asked the council to appoint him as an emergency leader with all of the councils powers concentrated in himself."

"Emergency what?" exclaimed Florence.

"That's what most of the guild leaders said, including myself. Andrillo pointed out that the council has been so slow to react to the crisis that things have continued to deteriorate. He claimed that this is not because his ideas are wrong..."

"What a surprise!"

"Quite, but because the town has not been tough enough on those who have not followed the ordinances. There were quite a few people who were willing to listen to his idea."

"But there's hardly any resistance to his foolish ideas any more. As far as I know, the only person who really flouts the stupid ordinances in public is me."

Florence suddenly fell silent. Her father looked at her with compassion. The reality of what they had been talking about suddenly sank in.

"The five councillors who wanted the ordinances to be passed into law have already given their backing to his plan. It's only a matter of time."

Florence said nothing. Her father dropped his eyes to the floor. The silence that grew between them was emphasised by the missing noises that once filtered in from the alley: the chatter and the noise of business that had disappeared after the mist had come.

"Florence, I don't really want to suggest this, but we don't know what dangers are ahead. I'll only ask you this once. Will you give up your protest?"

"I can't give up! Andrillo is wrong. I just know the townspeople are making a big mistake. What they're doing makes no sense. This mist has come, just like Andrillo said, but I don't see why it's got anything to do with me. I've hardly changed at all. How can I be the one bringing the mist? It's everyone else who's changed. They're the ones who've taken on these edicts or ordinances or whatever they want to call them. And what has happened since? This mist has thickened each and every day. We're doing the opposite of what we should be doing. We should all be railing against these measures rather than following them as if our lives depended on it. If those grey wearing idiots were honest with themselves they would all have to admit that they don't really know what this sorcerer even wants. How do we even know he exists?"

"Florence..."

"Everyone knows that these measures that have just been scrambled together by a group of ignorant locals. Even Andrillo avoided joining that Board of Edicts. But, none of this makes any difference. Everyone thinks that the ordinances are some sort of untouchable truth."

Florence slumped down on her stool. Her father got up and quickly made his way to his daughter.

"What does it matter." said Florence trying to hide the croak that was forcing itself into her voice. "If things are going the way that you say, how can I know if I'll be safe whatever I do?"

"That last thought that worries me the most. Ah, Florence... I have come to that very same opinion and so..." He paused again. "I think it might be time for you to leave Pendon. You can fulfil the touring part of your apprenticeship."

Florence did not expect this suggestion from her father at all. It had not even been a distant sight on her horizon. Her father waited patiently for her to say something, but the air between them continued to be filled with silence.

"Florence, you must see that your situation here is becoming untenable. Things are only getting worse. Not just for you, for all of us. This trip might not just ensure your safety. If you were to go, you could learn more about the world, your profession and even this mist. At the same time, you would be free from all the dangers you now face. It's impossible for me to tell you what you'll find out there, but I know that I gained a whole new perspective on the world when I travelled myself. You have said to me so many times that nothing happens in this town. If you go you would be able to experience new things each and every day, meet people from places you've never..."

"All right!" shouted Florence, surprising herself. She looked into her father's eyes and realised that she had shocked him too. All of a sudden, she felt self-conscious of her actions.

"All right," she said again, but the force and venom in her voice were now gone. "I'll think about it."

\*\*\*

Andrillo sat back in his chair. He had been working long and hard for people to recognise the threat that the sorcerer posed to everyone. However, now the citizens of Pendon finally accepted what he said was true, he felt no sense of relief or achievement. His speeches had made no real difference. The only thing that had changed people's minds in the end was the arrival of something he saw as evidence of defeat: the mist. The descent of this mist was something to be feared. It was a sign that the hand of the sorcerer was already at play in the town. All he could do now was to ensure that things did not get any worse. He had to ensure that the ordinances were strictly followed. If the people who chose to flout the ordinances were not stopped, they would bring death and misery.

One person in particular concerned Andrillo. One individual who still opposed the ordinances in public: the daughter of the watchmaker. There were still quite a few who wanted to oppose the ordinances, but none of them continued to show their disregard for them as publicly as her. For Andrillo, there was great danger in letting her open protest to continue. Others might start to think that as nothing was happening to her then there was every reason to suspect that nothing would happen to them if they did the same. This could lead those poor souls who were easily influenced to question the authority of the ordinances.

It only seemed like the sorcerer was doing nothing. Andrillo's experiences told him his predictions were not wrong. The sorcerer was taking action each and every day. The problem was it was just too subtle for most to see. Everyone was aware that in the weeks since its appearance the mist had grown thicker and thicker. Andrillo had witnessed this slow growth from his chamber that looked out over the market square. As the days had passed, he had first watched the clock tower dissolve under the growing grey cloud. In the time following he had seen the stalls, first in their brightly coloured canopies and then in their plane white covers, slowly disappear one by one. But, there were other things in the mist. It was these that most people did not perceive. These were the true dangers that emanated from the sorcerer and they had already arrived.

As he contemplated what he knew lay hidden in the mist, Andrillo's hand unconsciously went up to the scar on his face. He drew his finger carefully down the mark as his thoughts drifted off from his conscious mind. He continued to linger in this state for some time until the spell was broken by a rapping noise on his chamber door. Without waiting to be called, a council usher entered.

"Sorry to disturb you councillor, but councillor Moss has asked if he could have a word."

"Knock and then wait next time my good fellow," said Andrillo waving the usher away.

Andrillo was not pleased about being disturbed by this usher whose name he could not and did not care to remember. Nevertheless, he was happy to hear that Moss wanted to speak with him. It could mean that another of the barriers preventing his ability to lead the town to safety was about to be removed. If he could just get Moss to agree to his proposal, the rest of the councillors, who did not have a grain of will between them, would follow. He would then be able to eliminate many of the malignant elements in the town that still lingered.

He got up from his chair and returned his gaze to the square. It seemed another canopy had disappeared into the ever growing white space of the mist. He had to take this opportunity to seize power. No one else in town really knew what was before them except his brother. Those in Pendon did not know what had to be done to prevent what had befallen his father's home: to the place where he was born. How could they? Until recently most had not even taken his words of warning seriously. Without his direction, he truly believed Pendon would soon be lost.

When he made his way into the corridor, he found councillor Moss was waiting for him. He had expected to have to go to his fellow councillor's office. A personal visit was not necessarily a good omen. He worried he was not going to receive the news he wanted to hear.

"Ah, my dear Andrillo," announced Moss. "It takes the best of us time to judge what is right, but I finally came to a decision. I have spoken to the other councillors. You will be interested to hear that they agree with me. We will vote tomorrow to grant you the powers you need to guide us through this crisis. We accept that as you were the first to talk about these issues and seem to have a capable knowledge in the area that you are the right man for the job, as it were."

Andrillo had to suppress his feelings: he was reeling with excitement inside, but he barely showed it. All that was visible was a slight smile. He thanked the councillor and said that he was glad they had taken the right path.

He bid the councillor farewell claiming that he had to get on with the pressing issues of the day. He had to start working on the ordinances he would put into effect as soon as the vote had been cast. He returned to his chamber, happy that the menace posed by the likes of the watchmaker's daughter would soon be overcome.

\*\*\*

Florence had returned to her room. Her head was spinning. How could she leave everything she had ever known behind? Even though she was not sure if she had any, she needed time to think. The situation was bleak, but was it really so dangerous that she should leave her home, her father. She leaned her head on the pane of glass that separated her from the outside world. She followed the shapes of many grey clad figures as they slowly moved through the alley below. Eventually, they all disappeared into the mist. A tilt of her head brought into view the grey white expanse where claustrophobic mountains used to hang above her town. She used to dislike how close they were, how they cut short the day: now she longed for their return.

In a way, it was no longer her town out there. Those below were not the members of the community she had known all her life; the emptiness above them was not the landscape she had grown up with. Despite all this, leaving was still a big step to take. How could she abandon her father in this new unknown place? He might prefer her to be safe somewhere else rather than have to face the uncertainty of tomorrow's Pendon, but other towns faced the same problem: they were also plagued by the mist. If she left, she would have to give up her defiance against the ordinances.

If she were to stay, it was obvious she would have to adopt the grey cloak or, in all likelihood, lose her freedom. The first option seemed difficult to take. Could she live in her home town without carrying on some sort of fight? Even if she did give in to the ordinances, would people in Pendon believe she had really changed?

Florence laid herself down on her bed. Her thoughts continued to race around in her head as she looked blankly at the ceiling. She argued with herself into the night; her thoughts went round and round without a single new point arising and without a conclusive decision being made. In the end, she knew that she would just have to choose one way or the other without really knowing what the right thing to do would be.

\*\*\*

The next morning Florence awoke to sound of something she had not heard since the traveller had been expelled. A voice was ringing out in the market square. She could tell from the light she had overslept. As it had been very difficult to get to sleep the night before, she was not surprised that she could have slumbered for so long. However, she was not sure why her father had let her. He would normally wake her up if she did not appear for breakfast. Perhaps he had taken pity on her, knowing that she would have struggled to sleep due to the difficult decision she had to make.

The voice from the market helped her enter the day in a good mood. She bounded out of bed and a small amount of hope grew within her heart. Perhaps the mist had cleared and the normal voices of her town had returned overnight. But, before she got to the window, she could see that this was not true. The unknown speaker was shrouded by the still heavy mist. The hope for a new day in which the decision that had troubled her the night before no longer needed to be made drained away. Instead, her first real experience of the day was renewed disappointment.

Florence was still curious as to what was happening outside. She got dressed quickly and headed downstairs as fast as she could, not caring about the thumping sound of her feet on the stairs as she went. Due to the noise, her father anticipated her appearance. Florence burst into the workshop and found him waiting on his stool ready to meet her gaze. Deep dark lines beneath his eyes, his unshaven chin and damp skin evidenced he had slept even less than her. He did not attempt to hide the stress and concern he was suffering.

"What's wrong?" asked Florence.

"It seems that Andrillo has got his wish," said the watchmaker with a sigh.

He let his head fall forwards until it almost touched his chest. Florence was a little surprised that he had not even tried to deliver the news in a way that could lessen the blow. In the new order, there was no place for niceties, no matter how small or mundane.

"I've only just come back from the square," continued the watchmaker. "While you were sleeping the council passed an order that granted Andrillo the powers he claims he needed. The council's usher, Felton I think, has been announcing the measure ever since. He must've already repeated it at least four or five times. I went to listen. Many of the people gathered around were asking questions, but Felton did not respond: he just repeated what he had already said. It was strange. For the first time in a while people were speaking freely. Everyone wants to know what Andrillo's going to do."

He paused for a second and looked directly into Florence's eyes.

"Going to do," he continued, "to those who fought against the ordinances.

43

I will not tell you what those fools were saying. For something that most were not even aware about a few months ago, their demands were ridiculous. They see any protest against the ordinances as a crime so terrible they call for..."

The watchmaker's voice faded away. His silence lasted longer this time. When he continued, he did so with another topic.

"I left the square soon after. Don't go out there today Florence. I'm sure you're curious, but who knows what they might do."

It was true. Florence was curious. But, she knew that her father was right. It was lucky he had returned. Not only for herself. If those who preferred actions over words had started to join in with the day's festivities, would not the father of one of the most flagrant transgressors of the ordinances be one of the primary targets of their anger. She shuddered at the thought.

She said that she had no plants to go out, but her father was still agitated. The best thing to do would be to distract his mind with his work. She walked over to his workbench and self-consciously asked a question about the blacksmith's watch. At first he was unresponsive. Perhaps he was having to fight to pull away from what was going on outside. Eventually, he started to talk. Soon enough a familiar light returned to his eyes. The day proceeded to pass by with them both working on one thing or another. Before Florence made herself ready for bed, she looked out of her window. The crowd of townspeople was long gone, but it was difficult to tell. This would have been the case even if it was the middle of the day. The mist had thickened significantly since the morning leaving the square totally obscured. She went to bed exhausted and surprised herself by instantly falling asleep.

\*\*\*

Florence thought she was aware of something. She opened her eyes. After a moment, her thoughts slowly turned to the fact that she was still in bed. She was glad of it as she could feel the chill of the air upon her face. She looked over towards her window and saw that she had left it open. The sheen of a dull sliver of light cast by a full moon through the mist stretched out across the floor. She was still not fully awake and instinctively started to turn over in an attempt to get back to sleep. But, as she did so her eyes fell upon something in the corner. It was difficult to see anything: apart from a few silver floorboards, everything was a dull shade of grey. These greys merged and altered their form in her mind's eye as she moved. Her body yearned for sleep, but she could not shake the feeling that something was there. There was no sound, no real form to confirm her feelings, just an obscure, unfamiliar shape. As she lay still in the bed, the feeling continued to grow in the pit of her stomach. It soon grated against and agitate her rational thought. Despite her efforts, nothing could dampen it. Fear seeped into the back of her mind.

"Is someone there?" Florence said tentatively. There was no reply, no movement. She tried to push down the growing panic in her chest. She told herself that there was nothing there. Her body would not listen.

Suddenly, she was fully awake. Fear was pulling at her chest; her breathing was rapid and the grey formless room around her still held the sense of menace that she hoped a second before was just the remnant of some nightmare.

Her bed lay straight on to the window, but on the opposite side of the room. She knew that the form was in one of the corners opposite the window. Since gaining her full senses, she had been looking straight ahead towards the window. She drew her hand across the cold damp skin of her brow. She had to get a hold of herself. There was nothing in the room. She was just going mad. This town was driving her over the edge.

The corner had to be faced. Her breathing was still rapid. She tried to take control, but she only succeed in making it even harder to breath. She resolved herself to look. She pressed her fingers into her temple and quietly whispered that the fear would drop as soon as her body saw that there was nothing there.

However, when she looked over towards the darkened corner, so familiar in the daylight, so unknown to her now, she saw the grey of the space shift and move. An explosion of fear burst through her rational defences and made her react without thought. She grabbed at the matches that she had at her bedside table and struck one quickly against the rough wood of a table leg.

The grey of the room melted away from the light of the match. She lit a candle. As the flame grew on the wick, the room returned to familiarity. There was nothing in the corner. Though her brow and chest were still wet through fear, her rapid breathing had fallen away. She held the candle out like a sort of weapon to light every dark recess. There was nothing unusual to be found. As her unrest subsided, her thoughts turned to a night some weeks before. The feeling had been the same. The strange figure in the night. She was not sure if she was going mad, but she felt sure that her fear was not just the result of some terrible nightmare. She sat back down on the bed with the lit candle still clutched tightly in her hands.

She continued to sit still on the bed for some time with her eyes shut tight. She wondered if the stress of recent weeks was just getting to her. Perhaps the people in the town had finally worn her down to someone who could not even face the dark of her own room. She felt sure that this was not true. The presence felt real. While her mental functions were previously disturbed by fright, she now felt quite calm and capable of reasonable thought. She considered that she knew of no other time in her life before this when she had imagined strange entities which kept her from her sleep. She had not even suffered badly from nightmares as a child.

Slowly, she rose from the bed and walked over to her window. She looked out, but saw nothing except the dark silver-blue mist illuminated by the moon. She closed the window before quickly getting back under the covers: the chill of the night was spreading rapidly over her skin. She mopped her brow and chest before blowing out the candle. No figure or form returned to disturb her. She closed her eyes. Prior to falling asleep, she made her decision.

# Chapter Four

The watchmaker let his daughter sleep in again. It was the first time for as long as he could remember that he had let her be for two days in a row. But, he knew that work was thin on the ground for her, and the world outside was becoming ever more hostile. While he had taken a cautious path himself, he wanted Florence to determine her own. Unlike his own father, he had always wanted his child to select her own destiny.

He never expected to regret what he had done for Florence. It seemed inconceivable that giving her a little freedom could have enabled her to endanger herself. He could not blame her. She was standing up for what she thought was right. In many ways he had encouraged her. As she grew up, he had often told her that a person should stand up against what they thought was wrong and care for the sake of others. He had not really lived up to these sentiments himself, nor did many in the town. Most people only thought of their own protection, and if they could, their pockets. If he was honest with himself, he had thought of these ideals as bland truths. People just spoke about them to make themselves feel better.

He looked down upon his now cool breakfast of porridge. He had dragged his spoon through the viscous substance a dozen times without bringing any of it up to his mouth. Shame joined the regret he was already feeling. He briefly glanced down at the grey cloak he wore before having to look away. Just another coward. He was a known and respected figure in the town, or at least that is what his position in the guild conferred upon him. Despite this, he had given into the nonsense of the power hungry and the bewildered. All the while, his powerless daughter had continued to stand up for what she thought was right. He had believed that it would have been impossible for him to do anything to alter the course of events. Work had been his only focus. His daughter had fought her battle all alone.

Disgust of himself surged within his gut. How could he continue to keep up the charade and leave his daughter to suffer; to possibly even be taken away from her home due to the forces he and many others in the town had left to grow unchecked. He stood up with a sense of purpose and knocked the chair behind him to the floor. He threw his hands over his shoulders to grab at the grey cloth that symbolised his submission.

"Father, what are you doing?"

The watchmaker let go. He let his hands drop to his sides and did not make any effort to hide what he had been doing. He was too surprised for that. His daughter had given up her colour. She was wearing black.

\*\*\*

Florence's father picked up his chair and avoided looking at his daughter. He did this partly to avoid having to explain what he had been doing, but also to put off having to find out what his daughter had to say.

"I've decided that you were right," said Florence. "Some of the recent events..."

She paused for a moment as she considered the events that had really changed her heart. She wanted to tell her father about what she had seen, but she could not. He might not think that she was mad, but he certainly would not let her leave if she claimed she was seeing things. She pushed her desire to tell someone, anyone, about the night before to the back of her mind and continued.

"They've made me think that it'd be best to go."

The watchmaker sat down abruptly. He wanted to take his suggestion back, but he could see she was resolved. Her eyes burned with a determination that reminded him of her mother. All of a sudden, the tangled knot of emotions within him started to unwind, and he felt his mood lift. Though there were dangers in the wider world, home was no better and she would be less conspicuous abroad. His main desire for her to stay stemmed from selfishness. He had to let her go. Before him was a person who, despite all Pendon had thrown at her, had not given up. He grasped hold of that thought and held it tight. He stepped forwards and put his arms around her.

"Just keep yourself safe."

\*\*\*

Florence cried. She did so because of the demonstration of the love of her father. As she walked back up the stairs, the strength of this emotion washed away, and the focus of her consciousness moved on to the uncertainty of her future. Though it was impossible to predict what lay waiting for her beyond the mountains, she believed that it would be best to leave Pendon as quickly as she could. This would ensure she would not have time to change her mind or find out what Andrillo had in store for her.

She held a scrap of paper in her hand. On it, her father had quickly scrawled a list of what would be most useful during her time away. She would pack everything he had suggested, but little more. This was not just because there no was time to consider what to take: most of her clothes were useless for her journey. If other towns were as affected by the mist as her own, anything that was not drab and colourless would just be useless extra weight in her bag. Her own town had thrown out the traveller when the mist had been at its lightest. Who knew what men like Andrillo would do to rebellious foreigners in places where the ordinances had already become entrenched?

For a moment, she considered going down to the market to buy a grey cloak. The idea was disposed of quickly: it would feel too much like defeat. Still, she imagined the horrified look of the store-holder as Florence asked to purchase one of her pieces of stock.

"Too late my dear," Florence pictured the store-holder saying, "now you'll see what this town does to traitors."

The old crone said this while she gleefully stroked her crooked finger across the drooping skin of her neck. Florence tried to remove this picture of the grinning woman from her imagination as she collected items for the journey, but it would not go away. What had begun as a piece of fun was starting to disturb her. With concentrated effort, she focused intently on what she would need to take with her. Eventually, the image melted away

The rucksack she would take was the one her father had used it during his own apprenticeship journey. He had fashioned it himself out of darkly dyed canvas and cheaply acquired leather straps. It mainly consisted of two compartments that opened along the stretch of the bag which faced the wearer's back. The top section was for a tool-kit, while the larger, lower part was for everything else. After neatly packing the few dark coloured items she owned, Florence descended the stairs to collect her tool-kit. Before she reached the kitchen, she heard a loud rapping on the front door.

"Sergeant Tallow," she heard her father say, "this is an unexpected visit. What can I do for you?"

"Morning. Sorry to bother you," said the guard as he stepped into the shop. "I've come on an order from the council."

Florence looked around the still ajar kitchen door. Luckily, the sergeant, one of the leaders of the town guard, had his head down. He appeared disgruntled. Florence was not sure if it was due to the nature of his duty or because of his demeaning role as a messenger boy for Andrillo.

When he raised his head he saw Florence peeking at him. His face seemed to harden for a second before becoming entirely neutral. The man was probably used to dealing with difficult situations, so it was a necessity for him to be able to hide his own emotions. This thought perturbed Florence. It suggested he considered this could well turn out to be one of those troublesome episodes.

"The councillor Andrillo has summoned Florence to his office," stated the sergeant. "He has requested that she be taken there immediately."

When Florence's father turned and saw his daughter, he aged a year. The same thought ran through both their minds. Perhaps she had made her decision a day too late.

"Well Florence," the watchmaker said heavily, "I suppose you'd better go with the sergeant."

Florence did not hesitate. She paced through the workshop, passed the two men and went out into the alley. She might have to go and see a man she despised, but she was not going to be humiliated even further by being seen to be escorted there.

Florence's quick action succeeded. The sergeant was left behind. He had expected verbal or even physical resistance from an ordinance opposing girl in a brightly coloured cloak. He got over the surprise quickly, but by the time he stepped out into the alley Florence had already disappeared into the mist. He hoped that she was heading towards Andrillo. To find out, he hurried off in the direction of the council building.

\*\*\*

Florence lent on the cold light green stone of the council building while she waited for the sergeant to arrive. She had moved as quickly as she could through the market square as she was concerned to avoid the scorn she had come to expect from her fellow townspeople. However, she belatedly realised that she no longer attracted as much attention as she had over the last few weeks. Without her bright cloak to draw attention upon her, she remained anonymous. Most people kept their eyes fixed upon the cobbles of the square and saw no reason to pay any attention to her in the acceptable, if not recommended, black cloak she wore.

For the first time in some weeks, Florence found that she could relax in public. No one had thrown a cold stare her way before turning away in disgust. No petty whispered comments had been uttered behind her after she had walked by. As she could relax, she was able to notice how forlorn the square had become. Devoid of colour and much of its former hustle and bustle, the marketplace seemed as alien as anything Florence had ever encountered.

A figure started to form in the mist. It approached swiftly and as it drew closer, Florence could see its head scanning the stalls and the people milling around the market. She had no doubt that that it would soon come over to her. The indistinct figure transformed into the sergeant. After noticing her, Florence watched as the annoyance drained from his face. It was replaced by relief. He did not stop. He just nodded his head in the direction of the entrance to the council building. He did not look back to check if Florence had started to follow him. He did not need to worry.

\*\*\*

Andrillo was getting impatient. His first test as Pendon's emergency leader would soon arrive. He sat at his large oak desk and looked over his newly cleared office. Gone were the sheets of parchment that were usually strewn across the floor, interlaced with books he had borrowed or thought lost. He would have to present a certain image through this space. The cluttered mess of a busy life could not be part of it. If he was going to retain power for the good of the town, he needed to hide his weaknesses from those that would soon be coming through his door.

Andrillo had asked the other council members for a new office to help him deal with his newly acquired duties. They thought they had given him enough for the time being. Perhaps their refusal was also a reminder that the council still retained a certain amount of power and could take his new position away from him at any time. Andrillo would just have to make do with the office he already had.

A knock was heard on his door. Despite his previous concerns over time, Andrillo did not respond immediately. First, he got up from his chair and turned his back to the door so he could look out onto the white of the market square. He had mulled over how he could start off these meetings with an advantage and had decided that this was it. He looked over his grey cloak to check he was presentable and then finally asked whoever was waiting to come in.

"Florence Watchmaker is here to see you, sir," said the usher who Andrillo had now made sure knew to wait until he was told otherwise.

"Very good," said Andrillo "you may leave us."

Andrillo maintained his watch on the square until he heard the thud that signified the usher's exit. He swiftly pivoted around with the intention of taking Florence off guard. He had to hide his shock. She was wearing something that could only be described as acceptable. He paused for half a second and hoped that his indecisiveness was not too evident. After gaining his composure, his first thought was that he would never again use that method to open proceedings. His second was that he should say something.

"Please sit down."

The girl was staring straight at him with a fire in her dark brown eyes. He felt like she was attempting to read his very soul. He had to suppress a shudder. As she moved over to the green leather chair in front of his desk, she did not take her eyes off his for a second.

He could see how she had managed to avoid following the ordinances for so long despite the pressure put on her by the townsfolk. Her recent change of mind regarding the cloak did not fool him. Andrillo could see that her spirit had not given up. She was just as dangerous to the town as before.

"I'm sure you've heard about the council's last ruling," stated Andrillo, still standing by the window. Florence only reply was a curt nod of the head. "Then you understand that the council had given me the power to ensure that certain threats to Pendon are to be taken care of."

Florence widened her eyes slightly. But, she took hold of herself and her face became passive once more. Another short nod of ascent followed.

Andrillo drummed his fingers on the back of his chair. He had not expected this girl to be so quiet, so passive. He had not anticipated the black cloak either. He did not intend for her to gain any more points over him in this battle. He was displeased enough that her adoption of a black cloak took away one of his primary means of justification for removing this girl from the town's public spaces.

"I'm glad to see that you've changed your mind about flouting the ordinances" he said with a sarcastic smirk. "I've invited you here today to hear your side of the story. Why did you decide to keep on ignoring the ordinances when so many around you demonstrated that following them was the right thing to do?"

Silence descended. Florence could not just respond to this question with a nod of the head. For a while, it seemed as if there would be no answer at all. Time passed by. Andrillo repeated his question, but with the same result. He did not want to have to push the girl, not yet and not himself, but as she remained mute, frustration continued to build up within him. Then, just as he was about to demand a reply, she shocked him again.

"I'm leaving," Florence said quietly.

"Sorry?"

"I said, I'm leaving. As part of my apprenticeship, you see. It's necessary to visit a number of other masters to..."

"Yes, yes," interrupted Andrillo. "I understand all that, but why now?"

"I would think that a former merchant such as yourself would already know the reasons why, councillor. The new order of things has reduced the orders coming into my father, as it has for many of the craftsmen in the town. He believes it would be economically advantageous for me to complete my travelling now; until things settle down a little."

Andrillo held his rage down as best he could. Not only had the brat found a way to gain advantage on him again with this second surprise, she had also formulated a perfectly legitimate reason to escape from his clutches. His rage intensified and burned when the girl broke into a smile. He shattered the tension with a forced cough. Further spluttering followed as he attempted to disguise the reason for the blood rising to his face. He took a drink of mead and held up his hand in apology. His eyes were closed and he let his imagination run free to consider what he should do. The distraction did not work well on Florence, but it helped himself. The anger drained away as he poured the liquid down his throat.

Perhaps this was not such a terrible situation after all. He would be able to get rid of one of as the greatest threats within the town without having to take any action of his own. He would not lose favour with those who would see the detention of one of their fellow citizens as a step too far. Furthermore, in the time that Florence was elsewhere, Andrillo could bring in the changes that would prevent her from causing trouble when she returned. He finished his drink and put the glass down. A misshapen smile spread across his face.

"When do you intend to leave us?"

***

The watchmaker did not expect to see his daughter again so soon. His surprise turned to joy, and he hurried across the room to put his arms around his daughter.

"What happened?"

"I told him that I was going to leave. That I'm going to leave the town today."

"Today!" exclaimed her father stepping back. "But you've not even finished packing."

Florence was suddenly upset, not so much by her need to leave as by the pity she had for her father.

"I only need to pack my tools. Then I'm all set."

Florence tried to sound cheerful, as if she were looking forward to go. The response her father gave her made her lose the mastery of her voice. The end of her sentence was hollow.

Florence repressed her feelings. She did not have much time to spare. Andrillo could change his mind about her being able to leave at any time. She knew that those who favoured the ordinances were opposed to all but essential travel. This could lead him to question whether giving the most visible opposer of the ordinances a free pass to leave might negatively affect his public image, not to mention his position in the eyes of the council. It would not take much of a shift in public opinion to persuade the council to remove his new appointment from him.

With these notions in mind, Florence stepped out into the street and looked as far as she could into the mist. She wanted to check whether her former escort, or one of his colleagues, had decided to pay a repeat visit. She closed her eyes and listened out for the tell-tale sound of the guards' heavy stomp. All she could hear was the muted sound of quiet trade.

Having succumb to her paranoia, she informed her father of the reason she had given Andrillo for her imminent departure. She was ashamed of herself for asking him to lie on her behalf, but she more concerned about how it would look if his story did not corroborate with her own.

The rest of the preparations did not take too much time. Florence fetched her rucksack and brought it into the workshop to fasten her tool-case into the appropriate compartment. As she finished with the last holding strap, her father presented her with a folded piece of paper. In his neatest hand he had written a letter of introduction for Florence to the masters she would meet on her journey. She scanned the letter. He had asked them to treat her well and to make sure she worked hard. She expected nothing else. The letter was placed in a protective envelope before being stored away in her bag. Less than an hour had passed since she had arrived home. It was already time to leave.

"Take care of yourself," said the watchmaker.

"Are you not coming with me to the gate?"

"I would, but I'm worried that if I see you pass through the city gate, I'll run after you and not let you go."

She gave her father a hug, which was made awkward by the weight of the bag on her back.

"I've put a few items in the tool-case that should help you out there," said the watchmaker after they had parted.

Florence wondered what he might be referring to and then realised she had not checked her tool-kit in her haste to finish packing. This thought niggled at her. Had she packed everything? Her father misread the look of concern.

"You don't need to worry. I've completed the journey myself. It's safe enough. You might even be able to enjoy yourself on the road. I know you've always wanted an adventure."

They both smiled. Despite the fact that she was having to leave her father behind, Florence's mood started to lift for the first time in weeks.

\*\*\*

As Florence was walking down to the town gate, she noticed a number of grey cloaks up ahead. She knew that Andrillo could just have her picked up by the guard if he so desired. He had no need to send a group of lackeys to detain her from leaving. In spite of this, she did not want them to see her. She kept her head down, attempting to look as inconspicuous as she could.

As Florence drew closer, she could see that almost the entire group had turned to face her. Due to the combination of the mist and their hoods being up, she could not make out their faces. It was still possible that they had no interest in her, but she did not want to find out. She would leave the main road to the gathering and take the narrow walkway under the portico opposite them. She hoped they would let her be. But as soon as she altered her direction, a few of the hooded figures broke away from the group and walked over to the covered walkway. She was too close to them to turn around: it would look suspicious. She just kept on going.

The murmuring voices of the greys could now be heard by Florence, stirring up fear within her. The rest of the group crossed to join the others under the portico. Her way was still not blocked. If she just kept on going and they did not try and stop her, she would soon pass them by and be free to leave the town and many of her problems behind.

As she drew level with the group, their voices stopped dead. Florence almost stopped herself. She passed them by. She started to think that perhaps they would let her be until a large hand fall upon her shoulder. She tried to walk on, but the owner of the hand was too strong. He had gripped onto her tightly, digging his fingertips into her flesh and preventing her from taking another step. The hand forcefully turned her around and brought her face to face with the ugly visage of Butcher. The man was almost a head taller than Florence and twice as wide. As he brought Florence around, he laid his other hand on her free shoulder. His swollen hands wrapped around Florence with ease and tightened like a vice.

"We know who you are," said Butcher, bringing his face up to Florence's until their noses almost touched. "Trying to break another ordinance by skipping town are we? Trying to drag us all down with you?"

Florence attempted to wriggle free of the man's grip, but to no use. She stopped struggling and looked directly into the small dull blue eyes of her captor.

"Let me go, Butcher. I've cleared everything with Andrillo, you've no right to detain me here."

Butcher tilted his head slightly to assist him in his scrutinisation of the girl before him. This enabled the weak light behind him to light up the hairy and well picked growth on his nose for Florence. She curled her mouth in disgust.

"Your tricks won't work on me my dear..."

"Ask him yourself," said Florence. "I saw him this morning."

Florence did not want to mention the fact that she had been summoned to see Andrillo: giving Butcher this information would not help her cause. Butcher took his time to mull over what she had said. He did not trust the girl, but luckily for Florence his desire not to jeopardize his relationship with Andrillo was stronger. Butcher released his grip.

"Well, we'll see what truth lies behind this claim of yours. We are not unreasonable people."

Butcher started to turn, but quickly brought his face back into Florence's.

"Don't go anywhere!"

He moved back among the other murmuring grey cloaks. It was obvious to Florence that he was the leader of this particular band. Butcher cast his beady eyes on Florence once more before whispering something into the ear of the man standing next to him. The hood seemed to evidence the slight nod of the head inside it before taking the rest of the cloak with it down the street in the opposite direction from the town gate. Unsurprisingly, it seemed the group would not take Florence's word that she had Andrillo's blessing.

Florence took off her bag. It would be some time before the situation was resolved. The cloaks remained huddled together and did not conduct any further communication with her. The only way in which they acknowledged her presence was by flashing the occasional glance in her direction. Due to the poor light in the alley, she still found it difficult to pick out any of the faces assembled in the crowd. The only man she could discern was Butcher, who had taken down his hood to reveal the long greasy and curly red hair beneath.

Florence began to be concerned that as soon as Andrillo saw the reaction of this group to her being let go he would change his mind. She had no evidence that Andrillo had given her permission to leave: she was entirely in his power. Frustration grew within her, but she did not want to show any signs of weakness in front of the fools that had halted her progress. The day was passing by and she still had a long journey ahead of her. If she had to wait for too long, her trip would have to be delayed until tomorrow. Or worse, she would have to tackle the mountain pass alone by night.

"You can't expect me to wait here all day, Butcher. With the mist as it is, there's even less daylight to travel by."

The group turned to glare at her as one. She knew that by mentioning the mist she would get their attention. Butcher was incensed.

"And who has brought this mist upon us?" began Butcher in a shrill voice. He would have continued on with a rant if another member of the group had not let him know that Andrillo would soon be upon them.

"Now we shall see what's really going on," said Butcher with a grimace.

***

Andrillo approached the crowd, followed by two guards and Butcher's messenger. While Florence knew that it was Andrillo, she could not see him as he was on the other side of Butcher's little troop.

"This man here," said Andrillo, "tells me you've detained someone who was attempting to break an ordinance, and that I am somehow involved in the affair. Consequently, I came here directly myself. I would like to thank you all for your vigilance. If we all work together like this, we'll soon have the situation under control. Where is the culprit?"

The group parted in front of Florence. She steadied her nerve and suppressed an urge to run. It would be useless to try and escape: where could she run to? She was still unsure as to how Andrillo would react to the situation, especially now that he had made such a show in front of the crowd. She closed her eyes. All she could do was hope.

"Ah," said Andrillo. "Am I to understand that it is Miss Watchmaker that you have detained?"

"Yes, your honour" replied Butcher, acting as the voice of the group. "She had the audacity to claim that she had gained permission from you..."

Butcher suddenly fell silent. Florence opened her eyes to find that Andrillo had silenced the man by raising his hand.

"It seems that there might have been a slight misunderstanding. It is indeed true that Miss Watchmaker sought permission from me to leave the town this morning. Is it the case that you think she is breaking the ordinance that forbids all but essential travel?"

"You gave her permission, councillor?" asked Butcher in a blustering voice. He maintained a confused look upon his face while his lank hair fell down into his face "But why?"

"Would you question my judgement?" snapped Andrillo.

Butcher instantly curled up his broad shoulders and raised his hands in apology to Andrillo. Before he could verbalise the sentiment, Andrillo waived him off.

"I realise that you were acting for the good of the town here, and I repeat my thanks. However, as I've already said, I have given Miss Watchmaker my permission to leave. I'd be glad to elaborate on the details of my decision, but I don't think we should delay the young woman any longer."

Florence was taken aback. Andrillo's support had not been a given. But he had done more than that: he had humiliated the man who had led her detention.

"Sargent," said Andrillo "please escort Miss Watchmaker to the city gate."

At this, the guards stepped forwards through the body of the crowd. One picked up Florence's bag as if it contained nothing, the other put his hand behind Florence's back and started to push with some force. Florence responded with a short cry of shock, but the guard did not let up. She had to act quickly to prevent herself from being toppled forwards into the dirtied and broken cement that covered the floor. She had no time to protest. All she could do was to walk and do so quickly. Within a few moments, Florence and the guards had left Andrillo and the little troop behind.

She suddenly realised she was being forcibly expelled from her home. She was getting the same treatment the traveller had received before her. What was worse, it had been her idea to leave in the first place. The slight regard Florence had found for Andrillo that day melted away. She finally managed to match the quick pace set by the guards and looked up to see that the town gate would soon be upon them.

"Well," she thought, "at least my father will not have to watch his daughter being thrown out."

\*\*\*

As Florence was marched off by the two guards, Andrillo started to address Butcher's small gathering.

"My friends, you may be displeased with letting that girl go. I'm sure that like me you are not fooled by her sudden adoption of a black cloak."

A number of the group murmured or nodded in agreement. Florence had acted too late in the day to change their minds.

"However, you are missing the opportunity that this situation presents. There goes the last real public resistor of the ordinances and of her own free will. We still have hearts to win and fools to punish, but will the job not be easier now. And think of her too. Despite her poor choices, she is still one of our fellow citizens. She leaves here today to complete her apprenticeship travels. She'll visit towns nearby that are even more firmly under the sorcerer's grip than our own. Is there not a good chance that while away she'll learn the error of her ways?"

Most were placated by his arguments. Many of these were those who were more scared for themselves than anything else. It did not take much to convince these people to accept the idea of getting rid of the troublesome watchmaker's daughter from the town. Anything that led to the further protection of their own skins, especially when backed with Andrillo's authority, was a reasonable course of action. There were a couple in the group that obviously remained unswayed by Andrillo's explanation. Their hard stern faces vividly portrayed their displeasure in this trade off. They saw only an unacceptable breech of principle. Fortunately for Andrillo, they did not seem to want to air their opinions. In contrast to these two, Butcher congratulated Andrillo on his wit with such unctuous sentiment that the councillor had to hide a grimace. It was not too difficult to achieve. Andrillo only had to contemplate the meaning of the groups' reaction to engender a smile. No one had questioned his effective expulsion of Florence. "So," he thought to himself, "perhaps the town is ready for further measures."

\*\*\*

Florence was escorted at the same quick pace all the way to the gate. As on most days during daylight hours, the only practical entrance to Pendon was wide open and manned by a couple of guards. Guards whose main duty involved making sure the travelling merchants coming into the town paid the fare to enter. Their job had become particularly dull ever since the ordinances came into effect. Hardly anyone travelled unless they had to, and the only merchants that seemed to arrive were the few who peddled grey cloth.

The guards stationed on the gate were therefore roused from their uninterested state when they saw a girl in a black cloak being brought up to them by a couple of their fellows. They assumed they were about to witness the highlight of their week, especially when they realised that the girl was the troublemaking watchmaker's daughter. However, as soon as the small marching troop reached the bored pair, their pace slackened and the expected excitement did not come to pass. The disappointed guards watched as the girl thanked her escort for their assistance. The two escorts were mildly surprised themselves, though they did their best to not show it.

The guard who had carried Florence's bag helped her get it back on her shoulders. She thanked the men again and then turned to leave. Just before stepping over the threshold of the town, she looked over her shoulder and peered as far as she could down the mist soaked alley that led to her home. She did not know where she was going, but she knew it must be better than what waited for her if she remained here. She bid a kind farewell to the guards, returned her attention to the road and started to walk.

The men who had escorted the girl nodded to the gate guards and said they had to go. This left the two guards on the gate feeling quite disappointed. Hope that something exciting would happen remained until Florence disappeared into the mist.

# Chapter Five

Florence was pleased with the way she had handled the guards. She had not shouted or lashed out at them despite their needless manhandling of her. In a way, she even felt like she had achieved a small victory over Andrillo and all the other fools she had left behind. Though their treatment of her had been despicable, in her final moments in Pendon she had remained calm. She had forced herself to push down the anger and indignation they had induced within her. Through this, she had ensured that she would not suffer the humiliation of being forcibly ejected from her home. She had avoided the scene that had befallen the traveller. But perhaps the best thing that resulted from her self-control was that she had not had to leave with too much of bitter taste in her mouth.

Florence examined the lines of the undulating gravel path climbing steeply before her. The idea of the ascent up to the mountain pass and beyond was not one she relished. She could not even track her progress as the mist was all around her. Just like in Pendon, it was impossible to see beyond about thirty yards in any direction. Suddenly, she felt very alone. She had not left the town very often and this was the first time she had travelled without any company. This only emphasised her feeling of loneliness. Her pace slackened; her eyes dropped to watch the slow progress of her feet.

The barren space around her left her senses to focus on what little they could. Every loose stone of the uncared for road pressed into the bottom of her boots and could be felt in the soles of her feet. The sound of each piece of gravel that was scattered across the path as she scuffed its surface was magnified. For what seemed like an eternity, she kept on putting one foot in front of the other. It was no use trying to distract herself by looking around as the mist shrouded the beautiful scenery and just reminded Florence of why she was having to leave her home. She chased these notions out of her mind. As long as she could keep the road under her she would not lose her way. There was only one route through the mountain pass. Resignation to a long lonely dull walk was necessary. She carried on.

As she reached a level patch in the road, she heard the unfamiliar song of an unknown bird followed by the cawing of a crow. Her loneliness gave the sounds of the birds more significance: they lifted her heart. She looked up from the stony grey-green ground and noticed the bare armed trees that were dotted on either side of the path. At first, she could not see the birds, but it was not long before the spiky black shape of a crow entered her line of sight. She followed its course from a tree until it executed an expert landing on a patch grassy ground. In astonishment, she realised she was still able to see the crow even though it had flown some distance. She looked up and saw that the pale yellow winter sun was successfully breaking through the mist. Was it possible? Was she leaving just as the mist was starting to recede? She turned around so quickly she almost fell over.

As she looked back upon the space where she expected to see her town emerging from the grey, she saw only a path melting into nothing. She stood on the spot for quite a time waiting for the path to extend down the mountainside towards her home. Nothing changed. She turned back to the birds and trees expecting them to have fallen once again under the opaque veil of mist, thinking that the unfamiliar sounds and her isolation had made her see something she just wished was true. Instead, the crow was still visible to Florence. It was now even further away, waddling along the ground.

Florence rushed forwards. As she did so, she continued to notice the mist receding away from her. Finally, she got up to the pass. All around her the air was clear, she could see the high claustrophobic mountains that surrounded her town stretching to the sky; their snowy peaks clearly defined in the thin mountain air of a winters day. When she looked back upon Pendon, there was only a dull grey nothing where it should have been. Despite this, she felt a massive relief being lifted off her shoulders as she absorbed the beauty that defined the home she had lost some weeks before. It was all such a familiar sight, but something that had been hidden away from her for what seemed like such a long time.

Florence felt tears come to her eyes. A whirlwind of emotions seemed to be spinning within her. She let them burst forth and a sudden urge to return home emerged from nowhere. But another, stronger part of her no longer wanted to remain near the town. She had already taken her decision to leave: it would be foolish to go back. She would return one day as she feared what the sorcerer's influence and the power of Andrillo would do to her father. First, however, she had to find some answers and a way to overcome that which had destroyed the life she loved: one she had just taken for granted. She did not have many leads, but she did have one. She would seek out the traveller.

Michael Woods

# Part Two, Chapter One

By the time Florence found herself on the other side of the pass, evening was already closing in. Darkness would soon arrive, but for now there was still enough light for her to see that the mountains settled down as they rolled into the distance until the land eventually became flat and fertile. Her first destination was the city of Hesik and she looked off into the distance to see if she could see the town. But all that was visible was the gentle rolling hills and the distant fields.

Her father had informed her that all she needed to do was to follow the path she was now on. If she did this she would eventually reach an inn. From there she would be able to take a coach all the way to Hesik. Florence had to resolve herself to ignore an impulse to stop. Her tired legs wearied further at the idea that she still might have some distance to cover that day.

Just as her muscles were beginning to ache painfully, no matter how long a break she took, Florence noticed a small trail of smoke, coloured orange by the light of the setting sun. She pushed on, driven by a burst of energy granted by the notion that she was almost there. Soon enough she saw a building that had previously been hidden by the roll of a hill. As the dark was slowly descending, Florence was glad to see the end of her day's journey up ahead.

The inn was a wooden frame building, settled behind a courtyard for coaches. For the time being, Florence did not care about finding transport to Hesik. She was just looking forward to feeling the warm air of a cosy inn. Soon enough, she could even see the glowing yellow light emanating from the multitudes of cheap spun glass circles that made up the building's windows. Her pace quickened. She passed the courtyard and found a low wooden door, which once opened revealed a smoky atmosphere inside. She breathed a sigh of relief as soon as she crossed the threshold. The day had gone on for so long that she did not want to think any more about greys, the traveller or even if she would be able to get a room. However, if she wanted a bed, she had to endure a little more.

Florence dropped her bag onto the straw covered ground near the entrance. After its weight was removed from her shoulders, she felt for a moment as if she were rising up from the ground. In her lightened state, she approached a man she assumed worked at the inn: he was cleaning a glass. It turned out that he was the son of the landlord and ran the place. He must have already been in his forties and his rosy complexion suggested he had rather enjoyed the benefits his work provided. He told Florence that they did indeed have beds to spare, but she would have to share a room. Florence said she did not mind. She just needed somewhere to rest.

"New thing to us," said the innkeeper as he presented her with a key. "We've had a few thieves."

He lengthened the last syllable of the sentence and narrowed his left eye to scrutinize Florence. She was not sure what to make of the situation until the man let out a deep, full laugh.

"Don't mind me girl," he said to Florence's relief. "Your room's at the top of the stairs on the left."

Florence thanked the innkeeper and asked when she could get a coach to Hesik. He told her there was usually one every day in the early to mid-morning. He wished Florence a good night and headed over to the bar to fill up his now spotless glass. He then drank the beer himself.

Despite being tired from the long day, Florence was glad to have been able to talk to someone who still seemed to have a bit of cheer in their heart. She climbed the old wooden staircase that led to the first floor. The thing creaked and sang on every step, making Florence worry about her chance of getting any sleep: her room was next to the landing. The room was already occupied. An old woman dressed in an expensive charcoal cloak was sitting on one of two low beds while looking out of an opened window. In her own time, she closed the window and turned her attention to Florence.

"Have you got the right room dear?" asked the old woman with a heavy scrutinizing tone in her voice.

"I think so," replied Florence. "I'm sure the landlord meant this room. He said I would have to share."

"Typical innkeeper, cramming in as many people as he can. No matter, I ain't against sharing, just like to know about it first."

At this, the old woman returned her attention to the window. Florence tried to peek out as well without disturbing the woman, but she could only ascertain that it looked down upon the courtyard. Despite the window being open, the room was warm enough, and Florence decided that she should concern herself with her own business. She made her way over to the empty bed, gladly sat down, unstrapped her bag from herself and let it fall.

The skin where the bag had concentrated its weight ached. She pulled away the layers of cloth from her left shoulder to reveal a thick red line pressed into her by the friction of the strap over the day. She was sure the other shoulder was just the same. Though exhausted she wanted to check that everything was in order in the bag. A brief look into the compartments containing her clothes and tool-kit revealed that despite the hasty morning's packing everything needed was present. Indeed, it turned out there were even a couple of extra items. In the top of the tool-kit were two cloth covered bundles wrapped up with string. On each was a label in her father's hand. They stated: 'To Florence, to help you on your journey'.

Florence opened the first bundle with care and curiosity. In it were three ordinary watches and a small amount of money. It was not much, but enough to make Florence a little concerned about the thieves the innkeeper had mentioned, even if he had done so in jest.

The second bundle was smaller than the first. It posed Florence as a puzzle. Why would her father give her two rather than just one? She undid the cord slowly and pulled away the cloth to reveal an ornate watch-case upon which was the depiction of a city. Florence instantly recognised it as the one Andrillo had asked to be removed from his watch and then destroyed. She wondered what her father could have been thinking by not only saving the case, but giving it to her. If the first bundle had her a little worried about thieves, the second one made her seriously concerned. It was not only made of solid gold. The surface was also encrusted with a number of precious jewels which were used to mark out the high towers of the city. It was worth far more than the first bundle: more than everything else Florence owned. She quickly looked up at the old woman. To Florence's relief, her room-mate was still watching the courtyard. She hastily wrapped the case back in its cloth packaging and hid it away in her bag.

Florence knew the items in the first bundle could easily be traded to help her on her way, but she had no idea what to do with Andrillo's case. Would any trader believe that she, a foreigner in shabby cloak, had gained the case by legitimate means? There was even the possibility that they might recognize the thing. She did not know where it came from. Either way, she would have to explain how it had come in to her hands. Perhaps the best thing to do was to bury the thing in her bag and just forget about it.

As Florence settled down on her bed she realised two things. First, she was incredibly tired after the long day's walk. Second, she was desperately hungry. She was tempted to ignore the moaning of her stomach and go straight to sleep. But as she was not sure when her coach would leave in the morning, she did not know if she would get the chance to have breakfast. The idea of going hungry again the next day gave her just enough strength to get up once more.

Florence arrived at the bottom of the stairs just in time to see a small group of grey cloaked figures chastising the innkeeper. He looked rather uninterested in what they were saying to him, like he had heard it all before. He responded in an exasperated tone:

"That's all well and good my good sir, but do you want a room or not?"

"Well, what choice do we have?" replied the piqued pale faced grey. "There's not another coach station or even a town round here for miles, and it's already almost pitch black out there."

The innkeeper responded by presenting the man with a key. He told them that their room was at the back upstairs. He did so with a false smile, which remained on his face until the group had rounded the corner at the top of the landing. As soon as they were out of view, the smile dropped and was replaced by an expression of relief.

"Those greys think they own the place. Asking me why there ain't no ordinances up in the inn. They're getting worse if you ask me. Sorry my dear, no offence I hope. What can I do you for?"

Florence could see why the greys might be aggrieved by such a man. She responded with a smile. She happily informed him that she took no offence at all before asking if she could get something to eat. He directed her to a nearby table and soon came over with a plate of mushy vegetables and dark stew. Despite the unappetising appearance of the food, Florence devoured it. By the time she had finished, she was certain she had seldom tasted anything finer.

\*\*\*

With her stomach full, Florence had only one desire: to get to sleep. She wearily made her way back up the creaking staircase and entered her room. She noticed the old woman was no longer watching the courtyard. There was no longer any point. The angry grey had been right: it was almost pitch black outside. Instead, the old woman was going through her luggage. The contents of her bags were now spread all over her bed. All manner of fabrics were present in a wide variety of colours. Red silks lay on deep blue velvet; clusters of yellow satins were interlaced between unknown fabrics of green and purple. Florence was so surprised to see such an array of colour that she instantly woke up from her stupor.

"Ah, my dear, why do you look so shocked?" asked the old woman. "You're not one of those folk are you?"

Florence shook her head.

"Good, those fools practically bankrupted me once. I'm from Mullhaven, you see. It's a town well on the other side of Hesik. Been trading in and around the place all my life. Could get you anything you wanted or needed, within reason. For years, I kept up the same line, bringing in the best quality fabrics from lands you couldn't even start to imagine. But about a half decade back, maybe more, a number of idiots started getting all agitated by some talk of some distant saucy man. Next thing you know, the sales of my wares drop through the floor. Thought it was a fad at first. I just waited for it to pass. Over the next few months, I watched my customers and my reserves disappear. Just before I went under, I had a bright idea. I started travelling to the next town over. There I traded some of my best material for the cheap grey fabric I could sell in my home town. Since then, I've had to travel further and further each year to get a decent exchange. Most suppliers of anything but the grey stuff go bust in the end."

"Is your town under the mist as well?"

"Ha! Don't you know dear? Nearly all the towns are covered in mist these days. It's always the same. The greys start appearing then that mist follows. Next, you can't sell a decent piece of fabric for toffee. Nor buy a good book or get an interesting conversation. Seen it again and again on my travels. But you have to live and old legs can only go so far. On the way back after my last trip, got rid of as much of my stuff as I could. Here, you can take anything you fancy. I've no use for it anymore."

Florence looked over the piles of folded cloth, some of which must have been worth more than her father could earn in a year. She hesitated. What could she do with the cloth if she took it?

"You see my point dear, you can't even give it away. This stuff is going back into my cellar. Just hope I don't have to burn it. It'd be nice to keep some so I can remember the old days. No, I'm giving up travelling and I'm going to concentrate on the only thing that really sells: that ugly grey cloth they all wear. That's what I got out there, you see."

The merchant said this last sentence while throwing her thumb in the direction of the courtyard. Her keen observation of the outside world now made sense to Florence: she had been watching her stock.

"Got a big pile of that rubbish from a distant place for some decent cloth. They still know quality out there. But it's too far to go every day, and they know the demand for grey stuff."

"Could you not just move?"

"Family. Got a whole bunch of them back home. Too many mouths to move. I have no trouble getting away. Last time, I told the authorities I could get them enough grey cloth to cover the town hall. The rest of my clan can't even visit my poor old sister in Hesik. The only other member of my family I can get out is my son. He usually drives my cart. He'll be taking the thing on tomorrow. Can't drive the thing anymore myself. Hands freeze up; especially in this sort of weather."

"So you've travelled around the area quite a bit?"

"Oh yes, all over the place. Round here especially."

"Have you ever met a man, says that we have to work to stop the spread of the influence of the sorcerer. He's quite tall, I suppose, dark hair and eyes."

"Got your eye on one have we? Ha, don't worry, no need to blush. Sorry, can't help you. See a lot of people and nobody in my job."

Florence thanked the woman, but she was disappointed by what she had been told. If all the towns were as bad as her own, it suggested that a man like the traveller would be very difficult to find. Discovering answers as to what to do was probably going to be an even more arduous task than she had hoped. The universal coverage of the mist would mean she would have to keep her head down while travelling. It seemed this inn was an oasis in an otherwise grey desert.

The conversation soon died out after their discussion of the traveller. Florence was glad. Exhaustion had seeped back into her body. Her whole being was now demanding sleep. She got dressed for bed and hid herself under the covers. After watching the old woman pack her fabrics away, she began to worry that the noise of the creaking staircase would keep her awake. There was no need. As soon as closed her eyes, she fell into a deep sleep.

# Chapter Two

The next day started off well for Florence. The east facing window of the room let the sun stream in, and its pale yellow winter light brought a memory of the warmth of summer to Florence as she woke. It had been an age for her since she had seen the light of the rising sun. Disregarding the chill of the air, she moved over to the window to admire the light blue winter sky. She was displeased to see that a faint mist had formed around the inn during the night. Hope endeavoured to persuade her that it was only a work of nature.

Florence was distracted by someone shouting as well as a few dull wooden thumps. She thought she recognized the voice. She looked down into the courtyard to see her former room-mate ordering her son about on what must have been their cart. The old woman carefully climbed down and after a few more choice words watched her son drive off.

The chill on Florence's face was starting to become uncomfortable so she closed the window. She quickly strapped up her bag before going downstairs to seek out some breakfast. A low hum of chatter filled the ground floor of the inn. The prospect of getting something to eat seemed good as she also heard the occasional sharp note of a knife scraping across a plate. The landlord's son sprang from nowhere and asked if Florence would like some breakfast.

"We've got some good sausage."

Florence chuckled with the man and said that would be fine. The rest of the morning passed quickly for the watchmaker's daughter even thought all she had to do was wait. Around mid-morning, the carriage to Hesik arrived. Florence was not looking forward to the ride. She had been in a coach only once before: a treat from her father when she was a child. Her abiding memory was one of almost constant discomfort. She had avoided coaches ever since, but now she had little choice. The journey to Hesik was long and she did not want to make the journey by foot.

As she walked up to the coach from the inn, she received a pleasant surprise when the old merchant woman suddenly appeared beside her.

"Where've you been hiding?" asked the merchant in a merry tone. "It seems we'll be sharing a coach as well as a room."

A man took their bags and placed them in a large container at the back of the coach. Florence and her new friend got into the small dark space that would be their uncomfortable roost for the next many hours. They were not to be left alone. Just after Florence had settled into her seat, a middle aged couple joined them. The new travellers greeted Florence and the old merchant before leaning back into their seats. The cabin of the coach remained silent for the next quarter of an hour. The peace was broken when the grey who had complained to the innkeeper the day before appeared at the door with one of his followers. As the man got on, he swept his eyes across the occupants of the cabin before settling into his seat and closing his eyes. His companion asked if he could get him anything before they left. Without opening his eyes, the man replied with a slight shake of his head.

Florence took the opportunity to examine the face of the grey. He was a middle aged, hairless man with podgy red cheeks and a nose that seemed just a little too small for the rest of his face. There was nothing there to suggest the menace that emanated from him, but the mood of the cabin had certainly changed when he had joined them. Indeed, this sour mood was not felt by Florence alone; it was also painted across the old merchant's face.

These thoughts were soon cast from Florence's mind as the coach lurched forwards. While Florence was taken aback by the sudden movement, the couple and the old grey did not even open their eyes. "You know, I've been thinking," said the old merchant woman to Florence after they had watched the inn disappear from view. "This man you're looking for. A good place to start would be The Old Star: it's just about a hundred paces inside Hesik's main gatehouse. They get everyone in there. What's better, the crowd isn't too bad. Good landlord: keeps the order. Why did you say you were looking for this man again?"

Florence was horrified by the turn of the conversation. Her stomach sank even further when she looked over to the old grey. She found that she was looking straight into his pale blue eyes. His hard stare transfixed her and she let her mouth fall ajar. Her lack of a reply became increasingly emphasised by the sound of the moving coach. Eventually, the man broke his gaze and shut his eyes once more.

"What's got into you dear?"

After composing herself, Florence returned her attention to the merchant and said it was nothing. The old woman tried to push a little for an answer, but Florence remained silent on the issue. Eventually, the old woman lost interest and started to talk with the man sitting next to her. In contrast to his snoring wife, he was wide awake. Florence felt a pang of resentment grow within her towards the woman. She pushed the feeling down. She had created the problem for herself.

The rest of the journey was uneventful. The greys and the man's wife remained silent while the old woman and the man continued to talk about their business. They found out that they were both merchants who had fallen into the same problems and subsequent solutions. Florence kept herself to herself, glad to not be the focus of anyone's attention.

\*\*\*

Unlike Pendon, Hesik had long ago spilled out of its fortifications to cover the land lying around. Not that Florence could tell as her coach approached. Instead of a city, all she and her fellow travellers could see was a hazy grey mass. It was possible to pick out a number of lone buildings that lay on the extreme outskirts of the city, but everything else was covered.

"Been like that for a few years now," whispered the old merchant to Florence in a consoling tone. She had obviously noticed the concern on Florence's face. The girl sat back in her seat. The coach clattered on. By this time, Florence dearly wanted the day's journey to end. It had not only seemed interminably long, her legs had also become numb and stiff in the confined space of the cabin. Despite the previous days long walk, she had longed to stretch her legs for several hours. The coachman had given his passengers almost no occasion to walk off the effects of being cramped up in his carriage.

They soon arrived at a scattering of buildings that marked the outermost edge of Hesik. The place seemed dead to Florence, so to comfort herself she cast one more rueful glance back at the clear blue winter's day that they were leaving behind. As soon as the last of the blue faded away behind them, Florence felt like she was back in Pendon. The mist grew thicker with every roll of the wheel meaning the coach had to progressively slow down. They wound their way through the plain dark wooden buildings that made up the outskirts before reaching a coach station that stood just outside the main city gate. This was their destination.

The first to get off were the greys: a few of their fellows were waiting for them. Without a single word of goodbye to their fellow passengers, they soon disappeared. After Florence gladly got off the coach to stretch her legs, she thought about the merry innkeeper. The hustle and bustle of his inn now seemed like something from a dream: one where her own old town also resided. Once again her vision was full of slow moving, silent, drab figures. The majority of them were making their way in and out of the city gate in what seemed like a silent solemn procession. The old woman brought Florence out of her thoughts by tapping her on the shoulder. She pointed up to the space above the gate's arch and talked in a whisper.

"See that space there. There used to be a magnificent red and gold crest above that gate. Always reminded me I was on my way home. Been gone for a few years now."

The old woman sighed. In the unkind light of the mist she seemed to look much older than she had at the inn. Florence retrieved her bag and proceeded to bid farewell to the old merchant. She responded by giving Florence a warm hug and telling her to keep a good watch out for herself.

"Good luck finding your man," she added with a wink. She left Florence to disappear into the coach station.

# Chapter Three

Florence had been given an address of a fellow watchmaker by her father. She had no real idea of how to orientate herself in Hesik, but she had to start somewhere. She did know that the watchmaker lived in an alley somewhere near the main gatehouse on the outside of the city walls. Her father had also told her that the man kept a large battered clock-face above his door. After passing through the slow procession of people that were making their way through the city gate, she headed towards an alley that gently faded into nothing.

As Florence entered the alley, she noticed the wooden buildings of the area had been joined by a few constructed from stone. They demonstrated the area was prosperous, but they were just as plain as their wooden counterparts: unshapely rough grey blocks made up their façades.

The few sounds that came from the area near the main gate were soon submerged under the thick grey air. The alley all around Florence took on a deathly silence. As she made her way deeper into the unknown streets, taking note of the many blank spaces above the front doors of the houses she passed, Florence thought she saw something in the mist behind her. She just assumed that it was a local making their way back to the main gate and so, at first, she did not give the issue any more attention. But she could not completely suppress her unnerve and soon started to quicken her pace. The silence of the street, the chill of the air and the falling darkness engendered a familiar feeling within her. She told herself that she was being foolish. Even if there was someone there, they were not concerned with her. Despite this, she increased the speed of her step again. Florence tried to distract herself by concentrating on her search for the clock-face, but its continued absence only agitated her further.

Florence was determined not to look back again over her shoulder. This would just be a sign she was giving into her needless fears. But the desire to see what might be there grew. Part of her was convinced that there would be nothing. This meant there would be no harm in checking. Finally, this part of her overcame the others and she turned around. She saw two shapes emerging from the mist. She was suddenly gripped by a strangulating sense of fear as the memory of the undefined figure in her room leapt into her imagination. She stood on the spot without moving a muscle until relief swept over her when the swish of a grey cloak emerged from the clouded air.

Just after Florence recommenced her search for the watchmaker's, a niggling thought started to agitate her. Despite her speeding up, the people behind her had got closer to her. She increased her pace to a brisk walk. Though she did not look back, she listened out for the dull footfalls of her potential pursuers. Their rate increased. Her followers were gaining on her. She still could not be sure, but she wanted to know. She increased her speed again. Once more, their pace quickened. Florence could not take the chance that she was wrong. Despite the weight of her bag, she started to run.

Florence's legs ached and she had no idea where she was going. All she knew was that she needed to get away from whoever was behind her. After about fifty paces, she came across a crossroads. Without thinking, she turned right. Her breathing was becoming rapid and the different endurances of the last two days were making her body scream at her to stop. She kept on going.

Frantically, she searched the façades of the buildings around her with her eyes, but she still saw no sign of the clock face. The footfalls had reduced by half. "One of them must have taken another path," thought Florence. It did not matter. Her lone pursuer was getting close. Then, to her horror, she saw something starting to emerge from the mist in front of her. It was a meagre light atop what must have been one of the towers along the city wall. She hoped that her assumption was wrong, but deep down she knew she was running down a dead end. Her pursuer slowed down. He, she or it did not have to run any more: there was no way out.

Just as Florence was about to stop running, she saw it. On her left hand side, above one of the doors was the face of an old clock nailed into a wooden beam. She drew up the last of her strength and threw it all at the effort of moving as quickly as she could towards the watchmaker's.

Florence slammed the door shut behind her. She fell back against it as there was still a chance that the owner of the footsteps would try to get in. She was sure that they would not have been able to see her in the mist: they had slowed down too far back. Nevertheless, she did not want to run the risk.

Florence peered into the gloom of the room, but she saw no one. Suddenly, Florence heard a handle rattling as someone tried to get in. She used all her remaining strength to secure the door, but the effort was pointless. The noise had come from inside the house. Relief swept over her.

"Who's there? Coming in at this time of night. Is that you Windlow? Trying to scare me to death."

"I'm sorry to have startled you. I'm Florence, the daughter of Edward Watchmaker, from Pendon."

The old fellow held up his candle to frighten away the gloom around him. He was wearing a worn out brown jacket and his eyes were invisible behind the thick lenses of his glasses, which reflected the light.

"Well," began the old man, "this is unexpected. What the devil are you doing here, bursting through doors and disturbing people when they should rightfully be left to their sleep?"

Florence decided not to inform the man that it was only eight o'clock. She told him instead about how she was beginning her apprenticeship travels. The man responded with a look of incredulity. She took off her bag and rifled through it to find the letter her father given her.

"Well," the old man said after carefully reading through the letter, "I suppose you are who you claim to be. I assume your father did not tell you, but my name is Arthur Starling. He was bad with names even when he was an apprentice. You can call me Mr Starling."

After putting down his candle on an empty shelf, Starling left the room without another word. Florence was left alone, but expected he would return soon enough. In the meantime, she occupied herself with examining her surroundings. Unlike her father, Starling's workshop did adjoin the street. Instead, she seemed to be standing in some sort of shop. She believed this was the case due to the display cases that lined the walls. They were not only furniture in the room, there was also a battered brown leather couch and, sitting opposite, a matching armchair.

Florence wandered towards the light of the candle and discovered that the display cases were made of some unidentifiable dark wood. At first, their shelves seemed to be completely empty, but on closer inspection it became clear that here and there a small unwound pocket watch sat in isolation. More obvious than the watches themselves was the dust. Each shelf was coated in a thick layer. Instinctively, Florence drew a finger across the wood letting the dust ripple up before her fingertip.

A few minutes passed, but Starling did not reappear. Though Florence was a little worried that her host had forgotten about her and returned to bed, she did not have the courage to venture deeper into the house. She walked over to the leather armchair to take a seat, but before her back reached the leather of the chair, Starling finally made his reappearance. He was holding a bucket.

"I was just about to cook. But, I need more water. I'd fetch it myself, but you'll be much quicker. The well's at the crossroads. You'll have passed it on the way."

Florence took the pail reluctantly. It had not been that long a time since she had managed to escape from whoever her pursuers were. She did not relish the thought of going out again, but she also had no idea of how to explain the situation to Starling. She did not even know what position he had on the greys. If she told him that she had been chased to his shop, he might just turn her out.

"Could I unpack my bag first?"

"Oh, don't worry about that now. You can do that later," said Starling as he moved Florence over to the door. "Now, don't take too long."

\*\*\*

Florence found herself on the cobbles of Hesik. The door to the watchmaker's had been closed behind her before she had been able to utter a single word of protest. It was dark on the street, but she could just about make out her surroundings by the shrouded light that made its way through the mist from the watchtower.

With the handle of the pail tightly held in her hand, Florence started to walk back to what she assumed was the crossroads. She kept her eyes on her feet as they clopped on the cobbles. She ignored the plain fronts of the terraced houses around her: they were too heavily shrouded by a mix of mist and dark. Consequently, she did not see him. He noticed her. As soon as she had passed him by, he made to follow. As the street had been completely silent except for the sound of her own footfalls, Florence clearly heard the man's first steps. She did not care if it was her pursuer or not; without a moment's thought, she started to run. The idea that she did not have anywhere to go had just entered her head when she collided at full speed into someone standing in her way. Her bucket fell from her hand and rolled away as she thudded to the ground.

The man she had run into was obviously much stronger than she as the force of her speeding body had only managed to make him step back one pace. Florence looked up at the tall shape before her and feared for the worst. She was therefore surprised when the grey cloaked man apologised to her and offered to help her up.

As Florence got to her feet, the other man approached. He picked up her bucket and placed it back in her hands. Florence was still not sure what to make of her situation. She was certain that the two men were the ones who had been following her, but for the moment at least they were not posing her any harm. This only comforted her to an extent. Their motives were still unclear and Florence now faced the problem that it would be difficult to get away. Despite the thick mist, it would be impossible to once again disguise her escape to the watchmaker's shop and as she had left her bag behind she had nowhere else to go.

"May I extend my apology again for having to run into you in this unfortunate way," said the man she herself had crashed into. "Please let me introduce myself. I'm Baba Sewan. We're sorry if we frightened you, but I assure you it was not our intention."

As Sewan spoke, Florence took note of the man. He was more than a head taller than herself and despite the poor light she could see he retained a handsome face and a pair of green eyes.

"We've heard that you're trying to find a traveller, a man who has been known to speak out against the sorcerer."

The man's looks suddenly became unimportant to Florence and her suspicions tightened. She was still not sure what intention the two men had in talking to her. How could they be aware she was looking for the traveller? Perhaps they were trying to trick her into admitting something that she would regret.

"I see you're worried, but there's no need," continued Sewan. "We think that this traveller that you're looking for is our friend. You might be thinking we're trying to make you incriminate yourself, but we aren't going ask you any questions. Instead, we want to give you some information. We think you should pay a visit to the common green, just outside the east gate, mid-day tomorrow."

"We need to go," said the other man, whose continued silence up to that point had made Florence half forget he was even there.

Sewan nodded and they both started to walk away. Before they disappeared into the mist, Sewan shouted back:

"Goodbye. Remember, the east gate, tomorrow at noon."

In another moment both men could no longer be seen. Florence was left standing alone wondering what had just happened.

\*\*\*

Bewildered by Sewan and his strange request, Florence unthinkingly completed her task of collecting the water and returned the shop. Starling was waiting for her in the leather armchair.

"Where've you been all this time? The well is just down the street."

"I couldn't find it at first, I must've walked right passed it. I'm sorry if I took too long."

"No, no. No problem. You'll soon get used to the layout of the streets. At least there is only one way out here. If you go the wrong way, you'll soon know about it."

Florence laughed a little at the watchmaker's remark to humour the man, but the confused look she got in response made her realise he was being deadly serious. Perhaps he always was.

After having a dinner of some sort of stew with an assortment of boiled vegetables, Florence set up a camping bed that she had retrieved from the old man's basement. The thing had seen better days, but once she had given it a clean with the remaining water she had collected, it looked presentable enough. She had set the bed up in Starling's workshop, which like the watchmaker's bedroom was on the first floor.

She lay wide awake on the camping bed, listening to the thunderous snoring that exploded through the old man's bedroom door. As she could not sleep, her thoughts turned to Sewan. Why had he told her to visit the east gate? Florence was apprehensive about what she might discover there, but she was intent on going. "I have no choice," she confessed to herself. "What other leads do I have?"

# Chapter Four

Over breakfast the following morning, Florence asked Starling if she could spend the day exploring the city. She explained that as she had just arrived she could do with gaining her bearings. Starling was very taken by the idea. Florence suspected that his support stemmed from a desire to be home alone.

"But seems as you're going into town," continued Starling, "bring some supplies back with you. I don't have enough food for two people."

"What should I buy?"

"Oh, anything will do."

Soon after their discussion, Starling disappeared into his workshop. Florence was of the opinion that he would probably spend the rest of the day cooped up in there. His curt attitude and Spartan house strongly implied he was not really interested in anything apart from his work. This did not really concern Florence. It provided her with the opportunity to investigate the east gate. It also reminded Florence of her father and made her feel at home; the disappearing act Starling had just pulled strongly reminded her of her childhood. She was glad she had been able to get to know her father a little better since becoming his apprentice.

Despite her excuse for leaving the house, Florence had no intention of exploring Hesik. The city had already succumb to the grey ideology of reducing display, colour and noise to a minimum: there would be little to see. She was only interested in what waited for her at the east gate. However, as noon was still hours away, she had to wait. To help the time pass she spent the first half of the morning cleaning up Starling's shop and kitchen; both of which showed signs that they had been neglected for quite some time. Florence was not even sure if the old watchmaker would notice: his customers would.

Just after ten, Florence left the shop and retraced her steps to the gate she had seen the day before. She assumed it faced south, but due to the mist she could not see the sun to establish if she was correct. Despite her reservations, she had to ask one of the nearby guards which way was east. He was happy to have something to do and not only told her which way to go, but also asked if she wanted anything else.

Within the walls, there were no wooden buildings. Only stone structures lined the streets and had obviously jockeyed over the scarce space for generations. Finally, all the space on the ground had been taken, leaving the landlords only one choice, to build higher. Most of the crammed in structures were taller than anything back in Pendon. Florence was left feeling rather small.

The street that followed the inside of the wall was quiet and for the most part empty of people. Without much to distract her attention, Florence soon reached the east gate. It was quite a bit smaller than the south portal: only wide enough for one cart to pass through at a time. But the gate could have been smaller still: it just led onto an open green. Even the track that emanated from it only extended a few yards before turning into grass.

Florence checked one of the repaired pocket watches that her father had given her. She still had at least another half an hour to wait before noon. To waste time, she strolled over the green. It only took her a couple minutes to reach a steep bank that descended down to a narrow river. Two large charred beams marked the end of the level ground and suggested that once there had been a bridge. It had clearly burned down long ago, leaving the east gate with little reason to exist.

Florence sat down near the two beams and listened to the water running below. The sound of the gentle constant flow of the river was alien to Florence; she was soon lost in the noise. Her relaxed state enabled her to forget about her trip for a while, but the spell was broken by the light sound of her pocket watch chiming twelve times.

\*\*\*

Florence returned to the east gate to find that a small number of grey cloaked figures had appeared since she had left. Most were sitting on the grass. She glanced as briefly as she could across the faces that were present, but could not see the two men that she had met the day before. Nor did there seem to be anything of interest going on. She suddenly felt foolish.

Perhaps the men had just been playing a game. Not knowing what to do with herself, Florence wandered over to the bank once more and sat down. She took out the meagre meal of dried meat and cheese she had found for herself in Starling's kitchen. While she ate, she drifted off into her thoughts, guided by the ever transforming sound of the river. How could she have been so foolish to think her task would be so easy? It was ridiculous of her to have hoped that she could just bump into a couple of strangers and be led to the traveller. She waited by the bank for half an hour, finishing her lunch while mulling over what she should do with herself. She was brought out of her meditations by the distant sound of a bell chiming the twelve hours of noon. She checked her own watch again. It now read half past. She doubted that the watch which had been wound and set by her father could have lost so much time. Confused, Florence quickly headed back towards the east gate. Unknown to her, Hesik ran on a different time: it was always half an hour behind her home.

\*\*\*

As soon as Florence got back to the gate, she saw the two men emerge from beneath its arch. Almost all of the people who had been seated on the grass got up as soon the two men appeared. Florence was still not sure what she was about to witness and remained as far back as she could while still being able to see what was going on.

The man who had remained almost completely silent the night before was carrying a wooden crate usually used for bottles of wine. In another moment, he chucked it to the ground. Sewan stepped on top of it and raised his arms in welcome as the people around him gathered into a small crowd.

"I'm glad that so many of you have come. Unfortunately, all I have for you is more bad news. It has come to our attention that the hand of the sorcerer has now spread to Pendon. Like in so many other towns before it, the mist has become entrenched. There appears to be no halt in the march of this curse. I'm sure most of you gathered here know someone who..."

"Liar!" shouted one of the figures from the back of the crowd. "How can you bring yourself to fill these people's ears with such lies? You mean to lead us all to our deaths. Like my poor son, he listened to the likes of you and now, he's gone. Don't listen to this devil," said the woman turning to the crowd. "Any of you!"

Sewan stepped down and move towards the woman while she continued to berate him.

"Keep back!" she called out as he got close, but he kept on walking towards her.

She took a few paces back and raised her hands up before her face.

"Keep away from me," she cried in anguish. Sewan stopped. "You killed my boy."

A tear ran down the woman's cheek and she dropped her hands to her sides. Without looking at anyone she directed herself towards to gate and walked away in silence. Sewan did not look as if he had been startled by the event. He just appeared exhausted. Florence assumed this was not the first time such a thing had happened to him, but it affected him still. Indeed, the whole crowd seemed to have been perturbed by the woman's words. The energy that had started to build as Sewan started speaking had been shattered by the heckler. As Florence looked around at the people's faces, she thought they all seemed to share a common pain. Had they known the boy? Known others who had been lost? She was not sure if she wanted to know.

Sewan listed a few more pieces of news, but he ran through them quickly. He said another meeting would be arranged again soon and that contact would be made in the usual way. After Sewan had finished, the small crowd started to drain away. Only a couple of minutes had passed since the beginning of the meeting, but Florence felt like her world had changed. Although she had been affected by the woman's words, unlike most people in the crowd, she had also been encouraged by what she had seen. Though it was short, the meeting had introduced her to a whole group of people who thought just like her.

Noticing that Sewan and his companion would soon disappear from view under the gate, Florence made to follow. She set a quick pace to ensure that they would not get away. She laughed to herself as she realised that she was now pursuing them. She did not have to track their movements for long.

Just a few houses down from the gate, they entered a small pub called The Cooking Pot.

The entrance to the pub was so low that Florence had to bow her head to enter. She was not familiar with such haunts and felt self-conscious when she discovered that the cramped front room was inhabited by a couple of old soaks and a collection of unfamiliar stale smells. Thankfully, the two men did not stir from their glasses, leaving Florence free to advance further into the pub. She steeled herself and then made her way through to the passageway beyond the little room.

The corridor was a narrow straw lined space with once white walls that through time had been stained a drip covered yellow. A few doors led off the passage and Florence began to worry that she would not be able to find Sewan. A burst of laughter erupted from an unknown source and filled the air, making Florence feel even more alone.

"Ah, what are you doing here?"

Florence turned around and to her relief found Sewan holding a pewter tankard in his hand. She half mumbled a response. She was not sure what she was doing there herself.

"Did you make it to the meeting? It didn't really go according to plan, but things could have been worse. Sometimes it's enough that people come at all. We're in the room down the hall if you'd like to join us."

Sewan walk down the corridor without waiting for Florence's answer. She was still not sure if she could trust this man. Even if he was opposed to the sorcerer and his grey minions, she did not know who he was, or what he wanted with regard to her. She stood on the spot and watched him walk along the hall to the room he had indicated. She felt as if she had arrived at a crossroads in her life: following this man would lead her down one path, turning round and returning to Starling another. She reflected for a further second on what her life would be like if she just continued her apprenticeship travels before meekly returning to the mist soaked grey town she called home. She darted for Sewan's door.

# Chapter Five

The room was small. There were only two tables and the walls were lined with a light pine-wood panelling, unbroken by windows. The only light in the room emanated from an oil lamp that was placed in the middle of the one occupied table. After noticing her standing at the doorway, Sewan waved his hand at the free chair opposite him. As she took her seat, a paunchy man joined the group. With an affable attitude, the man asked if he could get them something to eat. The seated party all claimed they were hungry, and the man nodded approvingly before leaving.

After the landlord had left, a silence filled the air. Florence was glad she had come this far, but she was concerned not to affront the men sitting opposite her by saying something out of turn. Eventually, Sewan broke the silence.

"Allow me to introduce my brother, Fare. You'll have to excuse him, he doesn't say very much."

Florence gave a nod of greeting to the grey cloaked man sitting next to Sewan. He returned the gesture without a word and let his brother continue talking.

"In our haste yesterday, I do not think we asked for your name?"

"Florence."

"Well Florence, we're sorry about how our first meeting came about; we hope we did not scare you, too much. As I said yesterday, we heard from a reliable source that you were looking for our friend." Florence was struck by curiosity and wondered who the source could be. She had no time to ask as Sewan quickly moved the conversation on. "We were glad you could make it to the meeting though. Our numbers are steady, but small. It wouldn't take much to make our numbers plummet, even in a freer city like this. Did you enjoy the meeting?"

"I was..." started Florence, stumbling on her words as she was still trying to ascertain who the reliable source could be. "I was glad to hear people speak about the sorcerer in the same way that I think about him. Can I ask you, how did we all end up in this situation? I don't really know anything about this distant man. Why are people so afraid of him? What can we do to stop him?"

Sewan put his hand up to stop Florence from asking any further questions. His face was knotted and his eyes bored into her own. Florence was worried that she had overstepped some rule of conduct of which she was unaware. Sewan then confounded her by starting to talk about supplies of wheat. Her confusion was soon dispelled by the appearance of the landlord at her side. He placed a large cauldron of brown soup and a small pile of bowls in the middle of the table next to the lamp. He wished the group to have a good meal and left. After he had gone, Fare got up and looked into the hallway. He stood by the entrance for a further few moments as he watched the landlord make his way back to the kitchen. Satisfied that the landlord would not soon reappear, he closed the door before uttering some of his very few words to Florence.

"Think before you speak."

Florence was mortified. She had only been with the men a few moments and she had nearly compromised them. She suddenly felt completely out of place and wished she was at home with her father tinkering on some watch. Sewan gave his brother a light elbow in the ribs and a stare much worse than the one Fare was giving Florence.

"Don't mind my brother, he means well enough. It's just that some of these landlords don't like talk of the sorcerer in their establishments. They're always happy to chuck you out and then inform the authorities of what you've said. Especially if there is a reward."

Although she still felt guilty, Florence was somewhat appeased by Sewan. His charming nature seemed to instil a calm over the tension that had built up in the room. Nevertheless, she tried to take the advice of Fare to heart.

"Where do you come from? I assume that it's not from round here," Florence stumbled, trying to fill the lukewarm air with a topic that might fare better than her previous list of questions.

"That's a difficult topic for us," replied Sewan.

"Oh, I'm sorry."

"No need for you to be sorry. The topic is difficult because the reason we are here is due to what happened in our city. You're right about our origins, we come from a place that is some distance from here. It was a beautiful city, full of high towers, wealth, noise and so much life."

"You must miss it a lot?"

"Yes and no. I miss what once was, but not what we left. You might not be familiar with the term, but our city is in the lost territory. It may seem as if places such as Hesik are under the power of the sorcerer's curse, but they are nothing compared to towns and cities like our own."

Both brothers bowed their heads while they remembered what they had left behind. Florence watched as sorrow rose up within the two men. Despite having suffered Fare's ill temper, Florence could feel nothing but pity towards even him.

"What made you leave?"

"We left over a decade ago. It must be. If you've lived round these parts for the last few years you'll have seen what happens in the beginning. First, the speeches in the street, then the growing number of grey cloaks, then the loss of joy, of talk and colour. After this comes the time when those who have not given into the petty demands of the greys are deemed a threat to the security of everyone else. The greys claim a terrible punishment will wreaked by the sorcerer upon the whole town due to the deeds of a selfish few. Soon enough, most will deem those who shun the ordinances to be such a danger that the only recourse is for them to be removed."

Sewan paused at this point. While he gathered his thoughts, Florence reflected on Sewan's apparent openness. She thought that this attitude stood in stark contrast to the warning that Fare had given her only a few minutes before. Surly they did not have that much reason to trust her. Perhaps they were more desperate for supporters than she knew. Sewan continued.

"It was during the beginning stages of the descending of the mist that our younger brother, Anir, decided that all the drama that the sorcerer fearing classes had drummed up was ridiculous. He was young and he felt like he had to do something to fight against those who were ruining the city. He joined a small group who were speaking out against the demands that were being made on everyone to placate the sorcerer.

"Despite the action of my brother's group, the city was soon as grey as Hesik is today. It must be said that neither I nor my brother here took Anir or his friends seriously. Indeed, there was hardly anyone in the whole city, other than the members of the group, who gave them much thought. Everyone just believed that the continuing rise of the greys and their morality was inevitable. Soon enough the ordinances were enforced by the city Authority itself; no protests, no ill talk of the sorcerer, no this and that. But our brother. He was an obstinate little so and so. Every day he would go to the market square to rip down the ordinances that had been replaced in the morning. He would even challenge the leaders of the city Authority when he met them in the street. He got away with more than most and for quite some time. You see, our father was the deputy head of the city Authority.

"Our brother did not spare our father from the treatment he gave the other city officials. If they were ever in the same room together, Anir would always end up berating him, denouncing him as a coward and a fool. He demanded that our father stop what was happening to the city. Father always remained calm. I think he believed Anir was just going through a phase that would pass. He also tolerated him because he was proud: he was glad he'd brought up a son with the will to speak his mind.

"The mist grew thicker, more people started to wear the grey cloaks. I'm sorry to say that Fare followed the others. Soon, it was just our little brother and a small number of his friends who were left wearing the traditional blue cloak of the noble classes. A symbol of tradition became one of defiance against a new regime. They kept on demanding that we change, but we didn't listen to them. We just dismissed their protest as attention seeking, youthful rebellion.

"Anir kept on banging on about how wrong our father was and how terrible we, his brothers, were, but the situation started to change. While Anir was in a very privileged position, most of his friends were not: many were arrested. Some of them were put behind bars on some jumped up charges, others were exiled. As this did not deter our brother from his participation in the protest, our father took matters into his own hands: he forbid Anir from leaving the family compound. If his son had been arrested or exiled, it could have affected our great father's career.

"So, Anir was cut off from the outside world and more importantly the small number of his friends who remained at liberty. He tried to escape a couple of times, but the city guards would just bring him back. His spirit was not broken by any of this and remained strong until one evening when he stayed out in the compound garden. He had been cultivating habits to avoid the rest of the family for a while. While the rest of us gathered for dinner, he would make sure he was somewhere else. That was until the evening when he appeared in the dining room with a face as pale as the mist. Our father greeted him saying sarcastically that he was glad Anir could finally join us for dinner. Anir just nodded blankly.

"He was never the same after that night. The shock never really left his face; he started to lose weight; he stopped arguing with father. In fact, he hardly did anything at all. Instead, he would just stand by the doors that opened out onto the garden in one of the evening rooms. He would remain on the same spot for hours looking out into the mist. Our father believed the change had come on from him reflecting on what had happened to his friends: that his spirit had finally broken as he realised that he was now all alone. We just thought it was the result of what father had done to him.

"A few days after the night of his strange appearance at dinner, Anir stopped going into the garden. Less than a week later he had even confined himself to his room. Fare kept on trying to talk some sense into him, telling him that he had to get on with his life. Eventually, Anir told Fare why he was acting so strangely. He claimed that he had seen figures in the mist. He would not say what they were, but he claimed they instilled within him a sense of overwhelming fear. He was sure they had come to take him away. Fare concluded our brother had gone quite mad. His frustration at Anir's continued foolishness boiled over and he lambasted him, told him that he was mad, that he had driven himself crazy with all this nonsense about the sorcerer. He explained to our poor brother that if he did not curb his ridiculous behaviour the family would lose the little bit of remaining reputation which he had not already destroyed. Fare then stormed out of the room. The next day, our brother was gone."

"We didn't realise at first. He'd been acting so strangely over the days leading up to his disappearance that we were not surprised to miss him for breakfast and lunch. It only became clear later in the day that something was amiss. Fare went to Anir's room to talk about the previous night's conversation, but the door was locked. Much later, Fare told me how he repeatedly banged on the door and yelled out that Anir should not be so childish and stubborn as to hide in his room. The rest of the day went by and it was not until night had fallen that Fare started to think that something was wrong. He came to me and asked if I'd seen our brother in the course of the day or heard anything from father about him running away again. I told him that I had neither seen nor heard anything. I suggested that he was probably just sulking in his room, demonstrating his stubborn streak. Fare was not appeased by my idea. To humour him, I went with him to the still locked door.

"Once I got there, I commanded Anir to come out at once as the little game with Fare had gone far enough. There was no answer. I went to father. He came up himself and attempted what his two sons had tried before. He received the same lack of a response.

"We all attempted to force the door, but with no success. It was not that surprising: the house, which had been in our family for many generations, dated from a time when sturdy doors and walls were a necessity if you wanted to keep your family safe. Father had to order a couple of the servants to fetch a battering ram hastily made out of one of the trees from the garden.

"Father tried one more time to reason with our brother. He yelled: 'this is your last chance Anir. I don't know why you're playing this stupid game.' He waited for a few moments. There was still no reply. 'You leave us with no choice Anir,' he cried, 'if you're in there, stand well back from the door. We're coming in!'"

"It took quite a few swings of the battering ram to get through. Eventually, the frame gave way. Once we were in, we found that Anir was not there. Tellingly, his bed was unmade and his key was on the floor having fallen out of the battered door. Fare and I were stunned. There was no way out other than the way we had come in: unless you wanted to risk your life by jumping out the window. But neither of these possibilities could have been taken by Anir. Both his door and the window had been locked from the inside.

"Fare and I asked our father if we could leave to search the city for Anir. Oddly, since we entered the room, he'd turned pale and just bowed his head. Such negative expression from our father was very unusual. I had expected only anger and leadership. He mumbled to us in a resigned voice that we should do what we though was best. I assumed father was just overtaken by the realisation he'd driven his own son from his home.

"We first asked all the servants when they'd last seen Anir. It turned out the last person to see him was Fare. After we'd determined that no trace of him could be found in the house, we left. We went to the city guard's main building near the Authority hall to see if they had already caught our brother. They claimed they had not seen him, but said they would keep a look out for him now they knew he was missing. We left for the gate houses on the city walls. The guards on duty there hadn't seen him either. We resorted to stopping people on the street, even though such action was generally frowned upon under the new ordinances. Many of the people we stopped did not just inform us of the fact that they had not seen our brother, they also said they were glad that such a troublesome figure had finally disappeared from the city. For the first time since the mist had descended, I was outraged by people's attitudes towards those who opposed the sorcerer. Their disinterest in our brother's welfare and their joy in their own finally lifted a veil from my eyes. I saw, too late in many ways, that a great deal of the things that Anir had tried to tell me were true.

"We ran around the city for hours, but our efforts to find our brother were fruitless. We finally decided that we would not locate him that day and returned to the compound. In the very bottom of our hearts, we hoped that Anir had returned in our absence. It's easy to say now, but I feel that despite all of the mad running around and grief our brother's disappearance had caused us that day, nothing would have been better than to find him at home, laughing at us for running around like fools.

"Unfortunately, he was there. When we returned, we found our father was still in our brother's room. He'd sat down on the bed just after we left and hadn't moved from the spot all the time we were away. I told him that we'd failed to find Anir. He tuned to me with tear-reddened eyes and said something strange: 'I hoped this day would never come.'"

"When I asked him what he meant, he said he knew of other disappearances. Fare and I were shocked to the core. What could he have meant? He told us that a number of the other protesters had just vanished: they too had sometimes disappeared in mysterious circumstances. The Authority, in their wisdom, had determined it was best not to search for the missing after their first few attempts to do so turned out to be a waste of time. After the first few disappearances, they had ordered an extensive search of the city and its surrounds. They even harassed the family and friends of the missing. But, the missing were nowhere to be found and their loved ones were always as mystified as the guards by the disappearances. When it also became clear that it was only those opposed to the ordinances that seemed to be disappearing, the Authority concluded it must have been the sorcerer's doing. Who were they to counteract his will?'"

"We couldn't believe what our father had told us. He claimed that he had done all he could to save Anir; that he had kept him from leaving the house for this very reason. I was sickened by his excuses. Like all of his fellow members in the Authority, he had no idea what had happened to the missing, our fellow citizens, nor had he cared to find out. They just gave them up for lost, but what was worse was that none of them even attempted to inform those who were still vulnerable of what could happen to them. Father had not even told Anir what he knew. He begged me for forgiveness, but at that time I just could not give it. He got down on his knees and took hold of my coat. I turned, ripped the coat from his hands and let him fall. It pains me to say it, but that was the last time I saw the old man. It's one of my biggest regrets that I could not bring myself to forgive what he'd done. I now have nothing but pity for him. He lost all three of his sons that day.

"After gathering some necessities, I made to leave the house. As I got to the main gate, I noticed that Fare was following me. He was not sure what to do. The whole of his life had come crashing down in the space of a few hours. He stood on the path in silence just looking at me. I didn't ask anything of him. I let him make his decision in his own time; eventually he broke his silence: 'wait for me'.

"Neither of us knew what we were doing. I guess a lot of people end up in such situations these days. Luckily, we had enough money with us to last on the road for quite some time, but we had no real plan where to go. The only thing I was sure of at the time was that I didn't want to return to the house: I was still too angry at father. We descended on a local inn outside the city to think over what we should do.

"We took a room and closed ourselves off from the world. This was our first opportunity to reflect on what had happened. Fare realised that if it was true that the mysterious disappearances had taken place, then the odd tale Anir had told him about the figures in the mist could've been true. This obviously made him distraught. He had cast off his brothers fears as nothing but foolishness and a demand for attention.

"After Fare told me about figures, I came to the conclusion that perhaps my missing brother was right about the sorcerer. Without us even realising, the sorcerer had destroyed our family life from afar. It was stupid of us not to recognise this earlier, but our idea of the sorcerer had been entrenched.

"Anir had also been right about the Authority. They had taken it upon themselves to decide that the welfare of a number of their citizens were just not worth worrying about. Many like my brother had disappeared from their homes; others while they were under the care of the Authority in the prisons. In response, the Authority had done nothing but inform the worried families that it was not their responsibility to find out where the missing had gone.

"In the inn, after talking long into the night, Fare and I determined that as we could not find our brother, we would at least honour him. Our ideas of what we should do demonstrated what naïve boys we were. The next day we made our way to the main square. In imitation of our brother we tore down the ordinances that had been posted over a large column. Knowing who we were, but being uninformed about the rupture in our family, the guards just looked on. After we had left, they put them back up.

"Despite the fact that our petty vandalism was about as effective a protest as doing nothing, as well as being a good deal more dangerous, we both felt exhilarated by the experience. In fact, it was the only thing that made us feel good after our brother's disappearance. We did the same thing the following day and the next. Each night, after completing our deed, we would make our way back to the inn. On the third evening, while we were eating our dinner in the main room, we were joined by one of our brother's friends.

"The fellow was called Morum. After he'd sat down beside us without a single word of greeting, he asked us what we thought we were doing by pulling down the ordinances. His voice was quiet and firm. He halted our merry mood in an instant. Taken a back, I went on the defensive and informed him of what had happened to our brother, his friend. I called him a hypocrite. He had been one of the few protesters who still met up with my brother before father imprisoned him in the house.

"Morum told us that the story of our brother was more common than we might've thought. We said that we knew a number of people had gone missing from the city, but this was not what he had meant. He explained that the disappearances were not a phenomenon exclusive to our home. You could find tales of the missing anywhere that had fallen under the mist. Sometimes, though very rarely, they came back. He explained this was not a cause for hope. Those who returned were not the same. Before they disappeared they were often the most fervent opponents to the sorcerer, when they came back they were his greatest supporters.

"We asked Morum how he knew all this. He took his time to answer. Hesitantly, he divulged to us that a small network existed: one composed of those who were willing to admit to the dark nature of the sorcerer. They fought as best they could to curtail the misery that the mist brought by attempting to curb its spread. Before we could ask any questions, Morum went on to say that the movement had recently altered its tactics. It now gave up on towns when the mist became too dense. The movement was losing too many good people in places that would probably never see the blue sky again.

"In a way, I already knew what he was going to say next. He told us that our own city had just been deemed a hopeless cause, the latest member of the lost territory. He said if we really wanted to strike a blow against the sorcerer and fools such as those in the Authority, the best thing we could do was leave with him and work for his group. Still not knowing what to do with ourselves, but seeing an opportunity, we both agreed.

"Morum stayed with us in the inn that evening. Our plan was to leave the city together in the morning. After we retired to our room, Morum continued to tell us about the network he'd joined. The conversation drifted over to the topic of how he'd survived while so many others had disappeared. Fare saw this as an opportunity to ask Morum if he'd heard about the figures in the mist Anir had mentioned. Our brother's old friend stated those beasts had been seen by many who opposed the sorcerer, but unfortunately they had little information on them. There were a couple of reasons for this. Most people, even in the movement, found it very difficult to discuss the mysterious manifestations. Even when they didn't think they were going mad, they still wouldn't talk about what they'd seen for fear that others would think they were. On the other hand, those who were willing to say they'd seen these demons, or whatever they are, as anything more than just a grey shape soon disappeared. It's still the case, as far as I'm aware, that no one has seen one of these strange beasts full in the flesh and remained about long enough to tell others of their experience.

"Morum told us that in the early days of the movement many of the members disappeared in this way. They'd report they'd sighted one of the figures and then never be seen again. All manner of things were adopted to keep the beasts away from odorous potions to carrying swords. Nothing seemed to work. That was until it became plainly evident that one group within the network seemed to be hardly affected by the disappearances: the spies. The major difference between those who conducted espionage and the rest was that they had to adopt the manner of the greys to avoid suspicion. Other's started to do the same with great success. I can tell you from experience that this is a sound policy: it's kept my brother and me safe ever since we left that inn. As long as you follow this advice, even if you venture into the lost territory, you're much less likely to be taken."

# Chapter Six

Florence sat still and silent through the whole of Sewan's story. His words streamed out of his mouth at an incredible pace. After he finished, the room filled up with a silence that still seemed to ring with his voice. Florence could hardly believe what he had told her. Through his tale, he had lifted another weight off her shoulders. She was not the only person to have seen the strange figures in the mist after all. Though she had been almost completely sure she was not mad, that she had not just imagined something in her room that night, there has always been a lingering doubt.

"I've see them." whispered Florence. "I've seen those things in the mist. They were never fully... formed, but I just knew they were there."

"Yes, it does not surprise me" replied Sewan. "Their appearance is all too common. But as I said, nobody has seen them up close, fully formed as you might say, and managed to remain around to say anything more about them."

"Why do you trust me?" inquired Florence out of the blue.

"Well, there are a few reasons why I don't consider you a threat. First, I was informed by my source that you were petrified by the mere mention of our travelling friend. It was clear you had something to hide. Second, it was you who sought us out. We told you about the meeting, but you didn't have to come. Third, you're wearing a black cloak. No self-respecting grey would be seen in such an item, even if their mother's life depended on it. There's also the point that it's safer to speak out in cities such as this than you might think: as long as you avoid real greys and reward hunters. Most people, even here, are uninterested in what others have to say. They don't want to know for fear of getting themselves in trouble. The only problem is this same self-interest often leads people to become dedicated followers of the sorcerer.

"If I add all these things together, I safely conclude that I can trust you. In fact, let me tell you a little more. I'm the leader of the movement against the sorcerer for the area around Hesik, from Pendon to the Pear hills in the east. We're quite a small band. This is one of the reasons why the work of the sorcerer's influence has always been one step ahead of ours, but it's not the only one. No leader has ever reported a reduction in the sorcerer's power. His mist has been spreading for long as I've been part of this resistance, despite all our efforts."

Florence was not too surprised about the difficulty the group had had. Despite Sewan's reasons, she thought it did not bode well for an underground organisation when its leaders were so readily willing to take in a stranger like herself. It suggested either a high degree of carelessness or, equally troubling, desperation. However, when Florence reflected on her situation, on her father and the home she had lost, she knew she had to join. She could not return before the mist had risen from her town. Despite Sewan's honest statement that he and the resistance he was part of had achieved nothing, Florence knew she had to do something, even if she was destined to fail. She may not have known anyone who had been taken, but she had been forced out of her home, her family and her entire way of life. Florence was resolute, she would join the cause so that perhaps one day she could return to Pendon.

"I want to join," said Florence just as Sewan was about to stuff a torn off tuft of soupy bread into his mouth. "I need to join. I don't care if the situation is hopeless, I still need to try."

"Great," stated Sewan dropping his bread back into the soup and astonishing Florence by being as quick to accept her into the group as to trust her. "We hoped you would, as we've something we'd like you to do."

\*\*\*

"You're the perfect person for the mission" said Sewan. "In a way, you started it before we even met. You see, I need you to track down our common friend. You can't comprehend how extremely fortuitous your appearance has been. My problem is I don't have anyone to spare for the job. On the other hand, it's absolutely essential that I communicate with our missing man. Yes, yes, it's just perfect. You even already have a cover story for your travels."

Sewan went on to describe how the traveller was a member of his troop and had left to find out if information they had received in a letter was true. The message had claimed that a journey to a distant destination could provide a new and powerful weapon for their cause. Sewan had released the traveller from his other duties so he could carry out the mission. Another operative had been set up as an intermediary, but Sewan now knew this man had been lost, severing the line of communication to the traveller.

Sewan also explained that it was key to the mission that she would be able to recognise the missing man. This was not just because the traveller would be suspicious of anyone looking for him, but because it would be impossible to ask after the man in the towns and villages he was known to have passed through. As soon as Sewan mentioned this point, Florence reconsidered her assessment of his trust of her. Perhaps it was not such a surprise that he had been so quick to recruit her. His position would not even be compromised if she was a spy for the greys. In her travels, she would see nothing of the operations of his troop.

"There's just one more thing you need to know," said Sewan.

"How I'm supposed to go about finding him?"

"You're sharp enough, that's good."

Sewan did not tell her anything more straight away, he just looked at his brother in silence. His hesitancy made Florence wonder if he was still deciding if he should trust her. Eventually, he continued:

"He was heading for a town in the lost territory. It won't be as difficult to follow his trail as you might think. If you keep your eyes open there'll be plenty of signs to lead you on your way. In terms of making a start, well, there's only one main road to the lost territory from here. You just need to head towards Wellbridge. I suggest you start your journey by making your way there."

Florence was dumbfounded. If what Sewan had said about the lost territory was true, she was about to walk into a place more dangerous than her own town had ever been. What was worse, unlike the sheltered life she had spent with her father at home, on the road she would be out in the open alone.

"Don't worry too much about heading out there. You won't be doing anything to compromise yourself and your cover story will protect you from the suspicious. The people who went missing while working for the movement were nearly always those who drew attention to themselves. They were anti-sorcerer preachers and disruptors of everyday grey life. Your job will just be to pass through. Most of the time, you won't even be in the towns, you'll be in the clear air of the open road. In a way, I envy you. No, there is no real reason to fret. Stick to the ordinances and you'll be fine. So will you do it?"

"You're sure it's safe?"

"It's not risk free. I won't deny that. On the other hand, if you want to help fight against the sorcerer, this is your chance. To be honest, I won't have much use for you otherwise at the moment. An untrained operative in the field can be a serious hazard to themselves and the mission. And as I said, my people are busy. I won't be able to train you for at least a few months. This mission requires none of that, but could seriously make a difference."

Another two paths opened up before Florence. A future of safe regret at Starling's followed by a miserable return to Pendon, or one where she really made a difference.

"I'll do it."

The two men left Florence not long after she accepted the mission, but they did not depart before giving her something to remember them by. Fare handed her a small turquoise stone badly carved into the shape of an ugly dog's head. A string ran through a small hole at the back of the trinket. Sewan told her to keep it hidden under her cloak at all times. They claimed the little head would help her on her journey, but did not explain how. Instead, they just told Florence to keep a low profile.

Fare pointed Florence in the direction of one of the grey cloak merchants as the trio made to part outside the dark façade of the public house. Both brothers wished Florence good luck for the journey ahead and, like the old woman had done before, surprised Florence by saying goodbye with an embrace.

\*\*\*

Florence found herself sprawled across her uncomfortable bed with her new grey cloak rubbing itchily against any flesh to which it was exposed whenever she moved. It was late, the watchmaker had retired to bed long before she had even got back. Her physical form ached for home, comfort and sleep, but she knew what she had to do. She had to leave as soon as she could. Things would get more difficult for her than they had ever been before on the road, but her resolution to carry on was not shaken. The chance of being able to do something to return one day to her father in a grey free town made the effort more than worthwhile. As these thoughts drifted though her head, though she was still in her grey cloak, she drifted off into a deep sleep.

# Chapter Seven

The watchmaker's face was quite pale. There was no mistaking it. As soon as Florence had walked into his kitchen, still dressed in her new garb, the watchmaker had lost a good deal of the colour from his face. The moment was awkward for Florence as she wanted immediately to broach the subject of leaving, but she was taken aback by the old man's response to her new grey cloak. Silence weighed heavy in the air and Florence had to dig deep to muster the confidence to clear her throat. She repeated the act once more, slightly louder. Now the silence had been broken, she felt she could talk.

"I..." she started with a dry and croaking morning voice that for a moment made her pause. "I've decided to move on."

The old man looked down into his breakfast, unconsciously turning a spoon in his hand.

"Oh," he responded quietly.

"I have to thank you for your hospitality. I've already gathered my things together. I plan on leaving today if that would be possible. I know it's only been a couple of days since my arrival, but I if I want to seize the opportunity to the visit the wider world, I must move much further on."

Florence continued to talk; now that she had started she found it difficult to stop. She waffled out further reasons for leaving, every one of which seemed as hollow as the last. Finally, she mentioned the idea that she could return to his store after she had travelled further afield.

Starling responded with a non-committal noise that was close to a grunt. He did not quibble or question any of her brittle arguments for leaving, but nor did he say anything else. Florence decided after a few minutes that she would just have to take this response as an acceptance of her proposal: otherwise she would not get anywhere. She collected her bag and returned to the kitchen to find Starling still sitting at his breakfast table where she had left him. She thanked him again and made her way to the kitchen door. She turned and told herself not to look back for fear of changing her mind, or worse, capitulating and telling the old man the real reason why she had to leave. As she got to the front door, she head the scrape of his stool against the stone tiles of the kitchen floor. She did not turn around, but she heard his voice.

"Take care."

\*\*\*

Florence made her way into the misty streets of Hesik. The coach station that gave passage to the lost territory was on the other side of the walled centre of the city. As she had time on her hands, she decided to walk through the walled enclosure. As she meandered through the streets she let her mind wander. It was not until she found herself within the central market square that she started to notice the signs of a lost opulence in the buildings around her. Chiselled blocks of stone hung from the corners of buildings, the last remnants of lost gargoyles; empty alcoves evidenced removed statues and patches of light colour still played out the faint lines of scenes that clung to the few scraped walls that had not yet been whitewashed. No one else paid attention to the signs of destruction. All the heads around her were either cloaked or hunched down, their eyes set upon the horse fouled cobbles at their feet. But, it was not just the architecture of the square that had been affected, even commerce seemed to have declined. There were signs that the square once paid host to a busy market: worn white lines marked out the plots for hundreds of different stalls. Less than a quarter of the plots were now occupied.

While she contemplated what had been lost, a full bearded man dressed in a dirty and ragged cloak approached Florence. He was pulling a small boy along with him. Florence did not notice them until the man opened his mouth.

"Please, please, young lady, if you have anything to spare. Have pity, my son must eat."

Florence was not accustomed to strangers asking her for anything. Her heart welled up with pity for the pair. The boy held out his hand in supplication, and Florence started to reach for her bag without another seconds thought. Before she produced anything from within her sack, a man appeared from behind her.

"What are you doing?" said the indignant figure. "Guards!"

Unsure of what was going on, Florence soon found herself in the centre of a small group of townspeople that was almost immediately joined by three guards.

"Sargent, this man was begging for food, here in the town square. I've seen him before: he knows full well that it's prohibited."

"Of course councillor, we know what to do with him."

One of the larger guards took a hold of the man's ragged cloak and pulled forcefully, tearing a piece of cloth away. He dropped the torn fabric to the ground and took a hold of the man's scraggy neck before dragging him away to an unknown fate. Before he vanished the beggar managed to turn his head so he could look back at the boy. Slowly, he then raised pleading eyes up to Florence. The moment between them was soon over, ended by a forceful shove on the man's head by his captor.

The crowd dispersed as quickly as it had gathered, leaving Florence alone with the councillor and the now crying boy. The boy, after wiping the tears from his face, turned with a disgruntled face towards Florence as if she had done something wrong.

"Be more careful next time, tourist!" stated the councillor. Florence looked up into his eyes. He glared at her until she had to turn away. His work done, he calmly walked away.

Florence stood stock still on the spot not knowing what to do. Her hands found their way into her pockets of their own accord; one of them found a coin. Florence knelt down to console the still crying boy. Quickly and surreptitiously she pressed the coin into the boy's hand. His tears continued to flow as he ran away. The coin was gripped tightly in his fist.

\*\*\*

The coach station Florence found looked similar to the one on the other side of the town. Like its counterpart, it was situated just outside one of the main town's gates, probably to avoid certain taxes. It had a large three story inn to service the coach passengers and drivers alike. But unlike other coach station inns, customers did not have to contend for space. Indeed, not only was the inn sparsely populated, but the whole area around was practically deserted. At the time Florence was glad to be away from Hesik's crowds. She needed a little time to recompose herself after having partaken in the distressing scene on the market square.

Florence made her way into the wattle and daub fronted inn to seek someone who could tell her which coach to take. She found a middle aged barmaid in the humid low ceilinged bar who informed her that there were several coaches that could take her. The barmaid wafted her arm in the general direction of a number of life worn men clustered in a corner and said that one of them would probably take the next coach.

Florence had been given the name of one town, Wellbridge, to start her on her way. Sewan had not told her that it was almost the only crossing point over a major river that still largely separated the lands he considered to be free from those that were lost. Florence approached the coach drivers with this single name in mind and hoped that it would be enough to take her further on.

Most of the coach drivers seemed to be either fast asleep or so drunk as to be virtually oblivious as to what was going on around them. Florence came up to one, carefully turning his drink in a clockwise motion, sitting at the end of a bench. Florence asked him if he knew who was going to take the next coach to Wellbridge. He responded by nodding a bald red head towards one of the comatose members of the group. Although her driver seemed to be fast asleep on the table before him, he was still clutching a glass in his hand.

"Don't worry love, he'll get yer there, though he don't look it."

This started a small chuckle amongst those live enough to join in.

"Just make your way to black coach five. He'll be there right enough in half'n hour."

Not wanting to linger around the smell of stale beer and ancient smoke, Florence left the group and walked directly to the coach despite the chill of the air outside. She found to her surprise that the glass turner was right. Soon enough the man who had been dead to the world appeared near the coach as an awake and alert as any of the other people present. He even helped Florence attach her back to the roof of the coach with surprising agility. A moment later she had started her journey to Wellbridge.

# Chapter Eight

Florence travelled through a number of towns, most as grey as Hesik, some a little worse. Their general similarity started Florence thinking about how she would know when she had entered the lost territory. The name implied that there would be a notable difference, but she could not think how the towns could get any worse. All the time she was travelling to Wellbridge, she avoided thinking about the traveller. She knew full well that she had no idea how she was going to track down the man once she arrived at her destination. Instead, when such thoughts emerged, Florence distracted herself with various techniques such as noting how the ordinances in the towns passing by seemed to differ from one another. The ordinances were easy enough to notice as they were often displayed on large signs in the coach stations that acted as stops and rest spots along the way. She did not think about what the differences meant too much. Rather, each town's list of rules just acted as a passing reminder of the trouble citizens from her own town had gone through as they struggled to formulate their own set of rules. Soon enough, she would push these thoughts from her mind: they just made her think of her father, her home and how much she wished she was back in Pendon.

After a few days of travel, Florence finally found herself on the coach that would take her to Wellbridge. There was only one more village to pass through before she arrived at her destination. In this village, Florence observed that perhaps for the first time since she had left Hesik there was a noticeable difference in the mist. It was not so much in what she could see, but in the affect the mist had on the movement of the coach itself. Due to the poor visibility in the village, the driver was not only forced to slowly edge forwards through the dense opaque air, but also to stop frequently. After what seemed like an eternity, the coach made a planned stop near the village's centre. Here, they picked up two further travellers who were dressed in the finest grey cloaks Florence had ever seen. Soon after the men had found their seats, the coach resumed its fragmented progression.

Only a mile or so on from the mist sodden village, a river appeared alongside the road. Florence looked out on the great expanse of water before her. She had never seen anything like it. Flat and slow moving, it captured her full attention. She continued to stare out at the water until one of her fellow travellers made her jump. Since she left Hesik, the silences that had held sway over the occupants of the cabins of the coaches seemed unbreakable. Hours passed without a murmur, the only vocal sound being the occasional stifled cough. So, when one of the two men who had joined the group in the previous village started to speak, Florence could not have been more taken aback if the coach driver had suddenly veered off course and plunged them all into the swirling turquoise water of the river.

"Ah, my friends, we'll soon be in Wellbridge."

A further cause for disbelief followed as none of the other travellers criticised the man in any way. Nor did they just apathetically ignore the breech of the peace. Instead, each man responded to him with a solemn nod.

The speaker was quite right. As they rounded a bend in the road, the grey mass that covered Wellbridge hoved into view. The city was obviously of a fair size, probably bigger than anything Florence had seen before. The coach moved at a fairly steady pace until they came up to two huge billboards, one on either side of the road, firmly stating the city's ordinances to anyone who approached. Just after they passed the signs, they entered the mist. The resulting effect was as if someone had aged the light of the sun, leaving only a weak grey yellow illumination.

As they crawled along the road, further through the mid-day gloom of Wellbridge, the speaker turned to Florence.

"I think I recognise everyone here. Everyone except you. May I inquire what your business is here in Wellbridge?"

Florence felt the eyes of her fellow travellers fall upon her. She was worried that they would peer through her and see her real intentions as in that moment they burst forwards to the front of her mind. She wanted to respond to the man by telling him to respect the quiet as his attempts at needless conversation went against the ordinances of the sorcerer. Something made her hesitate. There had to be a reason why none of the other travellers had quietened the man. Also, she was intrigued by his suggestion that he knew all the other people present, even though four of the six passengers had got on long before him.

"I'm an apprentice, sir," said Florence, trying her best to mask her concern with formality. "I know that it is not acceptable for people to travel for the most part, but unfortunately my career demands it. It does at least enable me to see the work of the sorcerer."

"Ah, all is good and proper then. I'm sure our guards won't give you any trouble, will they," said the speaker, tapping his finger on the knee of the man sitting next to him. "My name is Jacob Orohund. I'm the city Protector here in Wellbridge and I'd like to extend my warmest welcome to…"

"Florence Watchmaker."

Orohund extended his hand out to Florence. She hesitated a moment when she noticed it was badly scarred. If he had seen her hesitation he did not show it. Florence caught a hold of herself and took his hand in her own.

"Do you think you'll be staying in our fair town long?"

"I was planning on making a short stop."

"Splendid, I'm sure you'll have a good and productive time in Wellbridge. Which craft did you say?"

"Watchmaker."

"Oh yes, of course. Good. I've a fine time piece myself. Unfortunately for you it's in good order, so I'm afraid you won't get any business from me."

A forced chuckle broke from the other sitters in the coach in response to Orohund's light joke. He looked around at his fellow traveller's to assure himself that the joke had gone down well.

"Perhaps you'd like to know a little about our city," resumed the Protector, giving Florence no time to express her true feelings which were firmly in the negative. "Since the great mist descended our city has improved no end. I believe we have one of the most comprehensive lists of ordinances anywhere in the sorcerer's lands. Not only that, I think you'd be hard pressed to find another city that has distributed its ordinances as well as

Wellbridge. Our production of ordinance posters and signs has been improved year on year. Almost every home now has a copy, for the good of each citizen and of the whole city. Is that not so, my friends?"

His question was answered with nods and murmurs of approval all round. It seemed odd to Florence that this obviously powerful man needed such reassurance and it worried her. She feared that it might not be pleasant to be in the man's company if he felt he had been rejected. Moreover, she did not even want to think what might happen if she were the one to reject him. Florence thought this same fear was also present in her fellow travellers, causing them to humour Orohund no matter what he happened to say. Such considerations led Florence to attempt to adopt an approving and interested attitude towards the Protector. She did not want to have to see his other side.

"I've also had most of the decadently ornate buildings from the time before the mist pulled down or refurbished. I'm sure you are happy to hear that, my dear. Such decadence is a threat to us all. I have also seen to it that all music education has been stopped, buskers removed from the town and needless chatter virtually eliminated. The solemn silence that now fills our streets is not only beautiful, it also enables our citizens to contemplate the good the sorcerer has brought them. But, that is not the entire story..."

Orohund continued to list his and the towns achievements in complying with the will of the sorcerer. Though Florence maintained a face which implied she was listening, her mind started to wander off elsewhere. She started to notice the deep contrast between the inside of the coach and the city surrounding them. While the noise of the glorious Protector continued to fill the cabin, almost no sound came in from the world outside. Though it was true that the thick mist muffled distant sounds, Florence perceived there to be only a hint of a whisper of noise even when they travelled right through the middle of the market square. It was not even as if the square was empty: it was crammed with stalls and hundreds of shadowy figures were visible from the cabin window. The punters and stall holders alike seemed to conduct their business in silence: not a word of bargaining or chatter was to be heard.

Soon after the final stalls passed by, the coach stopped. As the other passengers alighted, Florence waited patiently in her seat so she could get off last. All she wanted to do was disappear into the city and find somewhere to stay. She was therefore disappointed to see Orohund was still standing near the coach when she finally stepped out onto the cobbles of Wellbridge. He continued to wait while her luggage and her father's letter approving her travel were fleetingly checked by the city guards. His presence would not have disturbed Florence too much if any of the other passengers had waited as well, but they had all gone. As soon as the guards had finished with her, the situation only seemed to get worse as Orohund approached.

"I'm glad to see that all has worked out for you, my dear. I must admit that you are somewhat of a novelty in these times. It would be interesting to hear more of your journey. Indeed, I hope you'll not think ill of me for asking, but I wonder if you'd like to stay up at the Protector's residence while you're here. I could make your visit all the more pleasant."

"You are very kind," replied Florence, "but the rules of my apprenticeship demand that I remain in the home of the master I'm visiting."

"Of course, of course. Yes, what was the craft again? Mending watches. Yes, I think I've heard that rule before. Well then, if you cannot stay, you must at least do me the honour of coming to dinner. Tonight? Eight? I assume there are no rules against having a good meal after a long distance travelled."

"No, I..."

"Good, then we shall resume our conversation very soon. The guards'll help you find the way to a watch masters house."

With a wave of the Protector's hand, Florence once again found herself being guided along by city guards. This time they were not removing her, but taking her to the city's heart. Soon enough, they arrived at their destination. The guards burst into the house of the watchmaker without even a knock on her door. The woman did not seem to be too troubled by the intrusion, or at least she did not show it. Nor did she lose her composure after being told she would play host to a girl who had just been escorted to her home by the city guard. Florence introduced herself briefly to the watchmaker, but her host did not get a chance to reciprocate. As soon as Florence's bag had left her shoulders, she was whisked away.

Florence was led back to the main square of the city, which despite its grand size was made to feel claustrophobic due to the poor visibility. It was also so quiet that Florence felt she could have been in the middle of the mountains if it had not been for the cobbles underneath her feet. She was brought up to a large doorway which rose up to about fifteen feet in height. One of the four guards guiding her moved ahead of the others to strike the thick metal hilt of his swords against the wood of the door. He stepped back to join the rest of the group as soon as the weighty doors started to move. The entranceway opened so slowly that Florence was left with sufficient time to notice there were a number of crude portraits on the walls either side. Under each of the portraits was a notice: 'Wanted by the city for questioning.' There was also the amount an informant could receive as a reward. Curiosity rose within Florence and moved her forwards to examine the posters further. But after only taking a couple of steps, the guards overtook her as the large doors had opened wide enough for them to enter. Florence glanced ruefully at the posters, but did not get a good look at any of them before one of the guards turned back with a hard stare that pulled her away.

As Florence moved beyond the threshold into the relative darkness behind, she was greeted by a long corridor. There was little light, but enough to see the undulating shapes of the rough stones that made up the walls. Florence caught up with the soldiers who were standing patiently several yards into the corridor. She looked back to the entrance to see four men straining to close the large doors behind her, a pair for each one. Each pair then moved over to one of two large wheels attached to the walls. After the men grasped hold of the long poles that protruded from the wheels, a wedge was kicked away from beneath. Straining once more, the men slowly turned the wheels to lower a massive beam to barricade the door. Florence was left wondering what they were trying to keep out; the meek and quiet inhabitants did not seem to pose a threat.

One of the soldiers moved into Florence's line of sight and pointed to the corridor behind her. After she turned around the soldier led her to through the gloomy space until they reached another grand entrance. Unlike its counterpart on the outside wall, this entry had a small door cut into it. As the soldier pushed the wicket door open, blinding light streamed in. Florence's eyes took a moment to adjust, but as they did the sight of a courtyard garden radiant in its plurality of colour came into view. The sight of such an array of colour brought forth a burst of emotion in Florence's chest. She felt as if she were transported away from the gloom of her journey and the miserable city around her. Tears welled up in her eyes. She looked up to the guard who was trying to persuade her to go through into the garden. His face portrayed a strong nothing compared to hers, he had seen the garden and reactions like Florence's many times before. His cold countenance steadied Florence and brought her back to her situation.

The guard led Florence along a gravel path to a small stone fountain that marked the centre of the courtyard. Behind the fountain, the Protector was waiting for them, now dressed in a purple cloak. He greeted Florence cordially and asked if she what she saw.

"I haven't seen so many colours, since...," started Florence. "I've never seen anything like it."

"Yes, it's quite something. Sargent," he said turning to the soldier at Florence's side, "you may wait for us in the corridor."

Florence heard the creak of the small door closing behind her. She was now all alone with Orohund.

"You see, my dear, a Protector is allowed certain privileges. Indeed, you must see some of the more sumptuous rooms of my home one night. I am sure you will find them most agreeable."

Orohund took a few steps closer to Florence.

"But, unfortunately, we'll have to wait. There are a number of city matters that I need to attend to. We'll even have to detain our meal."

"Oh, how unfortunate," said Florence.

"Yes, it is. But, I believe I'll be free tomorrow? I'll have my guards pick you up, of course. So," continued the Protector as he laid a hand on Florence's lower back, "until tomorrow night."

***

Before Florence had even got back to the watchmakers, she was trying to formulate a plan that would enable her to leave Wellbridge as quickly as possible. At least she did not have to pack; her bag was still unopened on the watchmaker's shop floor.

Florence waited for the soldiers to leave before properly introducing herself to the watchmaker. She then apologised and said she needed to move on. The watchmaker did not seem surprised.

"If we're quick, we still might be able to get you on the last coach out of town."

"The last coach. You mean I can leave tonight?"

"Yes, but we'll have to hurry."

"What about the guards? Will they let me go?"

"They don't usually stop outsiders leaving. With a bit of luck, and as long as you don't draw any unnecessary attention to yourself, I think they'll let you through."

Florence felt a wave of relief flow over her. There was still a way out. She indicated to the watchmaker that she wanted to leave straight away. In less than ten minutes, they had traversed the city and found that the last coach had still not departed.

"Take care, my dear. The road doesn't get any easier from here," said the old watchmaker as Florence stepped into the empty cabin.

"I'm sorry that I'm leaving so soon. Thank you for helping me."

"Think nothing of it, my dear. I understand why you have to go. I know what our Protector is."

***

Florence tried to stay awake on the coach, but her travels and the day's events had drained most of her energy. Despite the sound of rattling wheels and her uncomfortable seat, she slunk down into a deep sleep before the glowing grey cloud of Wellbridge disappeared from her window.

As she slept, she dreamed she could hear her father. His voice was distant and unclear. She was in Pendon, the streets were colourful and, along with his voice, music was drawing her towards the town square. She started to run down street after street, but she could not get any closer to the sirenic sounds. If anything, they were becoming fainter. She sprinted round another corner and saw a glimpse of a figure disappearing down a narrow alley. She knew it was the traveller. She ran as fast as she could to catch up with the man. Bland grey smudges of streets flew by as she ran on, but she was just too slow to catch up. Then, all of a sudden, there he was, facing the town square with his back to Florence. Finally, she had found him; her journey was over. With relief, she walked over to the man. He turned around and caught hold of her.

"Got you," said the laughing figure of Orohund.

Florence woke up and attempted to stand. In doing so, she hit her head on the wooden ceiling and then fell to the floor. The coach drew to a stop and the driver leapt down from his post to look into the cabin. Florence looked up at the man, who was little more than a silhouette before the first yellow light of the morning.

"What is it, my dear? Why are you on the floor?"

"I'm fine. I just woke from a dream and bumped my head," grumbled Florence as she rubbed a surprisingly large lump.

"Well, be more careful with your dreams please. You could've had a hole in my roof there with that. That'd be all I need."

"Sorry, I didn't mean to."

"Well, all right, but no more of that."

The driver made his way back up to his perch, mumbling all the way.

"Bloody travellers ruining my coach. It's all I need, a rain hole. Difficult to get travellers these days as it is."

The driver continued to speak to himself, but as the coach pulled away the rattling of the wheels drowned him out and Florence could no longer make out what he said.

# Chapter Nine

Florence went through the next town without even attempting to find out if there was a local watchmaker. She stayed at the drab, cold and empty inn on the edge of the town for one night before moving on. In her mind, she had the image of the posters she had seen in Wellbridge. She worried that posters depicting her own likeness would soon be spread around all the nearby towns as soon as it became clear that she would not be coming for dinner at the Protector's residence. She assumed that she would have to keep a low profile for some time, avoiding town centres and other public spaces as best she could. If anyone recognized her, the mission would be over. That was not all. If she were caught, it seemed entirely possible to her that she would be returned to Orohund.

Florence left the inn by taking a morning coach to another unknown town. It had the same thick blanket of mist as Wellbridge, and was just as quiet and unwelcoming. She had at least avoided meeting any eager men of power. Florence alighted in the outskirts and walked around for a couple hours before finding a watchmaker's. She could have asked for directions, but she did not want to arouse suspicion; she just hoped that the mist had shrouded her face from the potentially wary citizens.

The watchmaker's she had stumbled upon was run by a middle aged couple, both of them masters of their craft. They were happy to take her into their home. In the days that followed Florence found the pair to be quiet, kind and happy to give her a list of chores to fill her time. Florence was glad of the work. As she kept herself busy completing thought numbing tasks such as cleaning the store and helping mend pieces, she almost forgot about the mission, the mist and the sorcerer. Only at the end of long days, as she lay sleepless in bed, would these thoughts return and light the fire of a burning irrepressible guilt in her gut.

\*\*\*

Though the days were long and filled with work, Florence soon found that a month had passed. Since arriving in the town, she had not ventured out from the house. Fortunately, Sandra, one of the watchmakers, liked to collect all of the necessities they needed at the market each week. This meant there was no real need for Florence to go out at all.

Florence was still concerned that if she went into town she might find a picture of herself waiting for her. She feared that someone would recognise her staring at her own portrait. They would notify the guards; soon enough Florence would find herself bound for Wellbridge and another rendezvous with Orohund. This meant she had no desire to venture into the town. On the other hand, her work, as it was becoming familiar and routine, was slowly losing its power to keep thoughts of her mission and home from her consciousness. Eventually, the veil over real life that it provided completely fell away, and the meaning of the dull grey mist outside started to plague her every waking moment.

Sandra could see that something was troubling her visiting apprentice. Indeed, she knew something had been wrong since Florence arrived. At first, she did not say anything, thinking that Florence might either move on from her problems or at least confide in her; especially after she had let the silence that ruled the streets outside fall away. Neither of these possibilities had come to pass and things had progressively worsened. When she first arrived, Florence's work had been exemplary. Not a spot of dirt had been left in the shop and her repairs were almost always beyond reproach. But as time progressed, dust was left to sit and gather and Florence's orders had to be tended to by Sandra's husband.

"Florence, perhaps you should take the day off. We've been working you very hard."

"I'm fine Sandra, it's nothing, just..."

"Home playing on the mind? I know those thoughts. I remember when I went on my apprenticeship travels. David and me were already engaged; we'd planned to travel together. But when my master said I should go, his said that he wasn't to leave for another few months. I had no choice but to depart without him. My only journey abroad and all I could think of was home. Did you leave someone behind?"

"It's nothing like that really. Although, I do miss my father."

"Well," continued Sandra, "I still think you should take the day off. It'll do you good. Why don't you write a letter to your father to let him know how you're getting along?"

Although Florence did not feel a letter would help her, it would probably do her father the world of good to hear how she was doing. She decided to act on Sandra's advice. She wrote to her father about the different masters she had stayed with and how she had moved on from Hesik. Although, on the latter point, she did not explain why.

Florence took the completed letter to Sandra. After placing it on her desk, Florence asked if she would take it to be delivered the next time she went into town.

"Why don't you go?" said Sandra with a little chuckle. "It'll give you a chance to get out of the shop and clear your head. Why, you've hardly left the place since you arrived."

Florence mumbled that she would rather not, but Sandra ignored her and retrieved Florence's cloak as well as a pair of fur-gloves and threw them over Florence's arms.

"Just go to the market square and find a man called Nathan Longfellow. He's a courier. If he's in town, he'll be standing by the main notice board with his horse. He'll take your letter onto Wellbridge."

Sandra finished by pushing a few coins into Florence's hands, which were still outstretched due to the cloak and gloves resting on her arms. Without waiting for Florence to put her things on, Sandra hurried Florence onto the street, placed the letter on top of the cloak and, with a smile, closed the shop door.

Florence hesitated for a moment on the front step. The idea she would be seen by an unknown bounty hunter in the mist passed through her mind. She saw before her a scene where she was captured, bound and taken back to Wellbridge. She shook her head. She had to cast these thoughts from her mind. She could no longer remain in her self-imposed isolation. Otherwise, she would just stay in this town and never leave the shop behind her; never complete her mission or return home.

Florence found Longfellow soon enough. He was easy to find despite the fact that like many in his profession he was a small man. He was standing next to his horse beside a pillar covered in notices, just as Sandra had said. He accepted the money and the letter without a word. This left Florence in the middle of the town with nothing else to do but walk home.

As Longfellow walked over to his horse to place her letter in his satchel, he revealed the reward posters that had been hidden behind him. And there, to her great surprise was a face she recognised. Shocked and without thinking she drew close to the poster. It stated the person was wanted for questioning and the reward was quite substantial: much more than her father could earn in a year. It also noted that the subject of the portrait had had been seen in the area.

Florence could not believe her luck, she had found her lead. The image was unmistakably that of the traveller. It had to be him. What was more, she could see that the poster was fairly recent. Compared to a number of the other pictures that were haphazardly strewn across the surface of the pillar, it was still a relatively fresh cream colour. The traveller's picture was also amongst the top layer of postings which covered the faces of those unfortunates who had been hunted in the past. She stood, glaring at the image with her mouth ajar trying to think what it meant when a guard came up beside her.

"Have you seen this man, miss?"

The guard's words, emphasised by the otherwise silent marketplace, brought her out of her trance. Florence turned to the man slowly. The joy of her discovery drained away and was replaced by fear. It would be impossible for her to deny she had seen the traveller. This fact was plainly painted on her face.

"Yes, officer."

"Where? This is very important, young lady," continued the guard who towered above Florence in his grey cloak. "The city is very keen to find him. Indeed, he is reputed to be one of the worst mist spreaders still at large."

A couple of passers-by stopped to check out the unusual commotion. They distracted the attention of guard for a moment, but with an authoritative wave of his hand he dispelled their curiosity, and they quickly moved on.

He returned his gaze to Florence and repeated his question.

"Yes, I've seen him," said Florence, "but it was quite some time ago. Maybe half a year. I was just so shocked to see him again. Many people in my town believe he brought the mist there too."

"You town? You mean you've not seen him here?"

"No, I come from a town on the other side of Wellbridge."

"Then what are you doing here?"

"I'm an apprentice. Unfortunately, a part of my training required me to travel far from home," said Florence with a confidence that surprised herself.

"I see," replied the guard, attempting to hide his annoyance with a transparent smile. "Well, keep a good look out for him. But, don't go near him, he's very dangerous. If you see him again, report his presence to the town guard immediately."

Without a word of farewell, the disappointed guard walked off into the mist.

\*\*\*

Florence was overjoyed. Not only had she faced a town guard, who would have arrested her if she was wanted by the authorities, but the road had been opened up once more. This was because the poster had not just carried an image of the traveller, it had also listed the name of the town where he had last been seen: Besketh. She had her lead. Once again she could leave the quiet heavy streets of a depressed grey town for the open horizons of the road.

Florence hurried back to the watchmakers' shop. Her heart was burning with the desire to get away as soon as possible. However, she could not leave without a word of goodbye to her hosts, and she still needed information. Florence first asked Sandra where Besketh was and how she could get there. The watchmaker claimed she was not sure and told Florence to ask her husband.

Florence was not keen on asking David, Sandra's husband. Unlike his wife, who had opened up to Florence, David was never keen to talk. Indeed, Florence had met hardly anyone who tried to maintain the ordinances as obstinately and completely as David. Either at work or table, his large pale bald head was usually bowed, only rising to cast meaningful glances at his wife and lodger whenever a conversation started to flow.

Florence approached David apprehensively as he sat eating a hard crust of bread in the dining room behind the shop. The man slowed his mastication while Florence drew herself up to the opposite side of the table at which he was sitting. He looked up momentarily to send a glance that contemptuously asked the question what do you want.

"Sorry, David," started Florence with a quaver in her voice. "Could you tell me how I can get to Besketh?"

David responded with a cynical curl of his mouth that begged the question why Florence would want to go to another town. But he kept his question to himself as the ordinances prohibited unnecessary speech.

"There are no watchmaker's in Besketh," came the hoarse reply from David.

Florence repeated her question. Despite pausing for some time and making his feelings clear with a hard stare, David eventually responded.

"Main road, south. Mid-afternoon."

The giving of the answer almost seemed to pain the man, but Florence had her information; she now knew where to get her coach.

As it was still morning, Florence resolved to leave the same day. After leaving David to continue his slow breakfast, she informed Sandra of her resolution. Sandra was visibly upset at the thought of Florence's leaving, but said she could understand. Florence felt a pang of guilt for being disingenuous about her motives for going and for leaving Sandra to the quiet world David would create in their home. But Florence had to move on. She quickly collected her few belongings together and soon had her father's bag strapped to her back. David did not appear at the door to wish Florence farewell, but Sandra made up for the void left by her husband by mothering Florence, providing her with food and trying to remind her of things she might have forgotten. After Florence's shadow dissolved into the mist, Sandra released a rueful sigh.

\*\*\*

David might not have been the most graceful host, but he was at least accurate when it came to timetables. Florence found she did not have long to wait on the South road before a horse drawn carriage made its way over a small hillock and into her line of sight. She asked the driver if he was going as far as Besketh. His reply disappointed her.

"No coach from here goes all the way over to that place any more. Been some time now since things have been like that. Still, if you want to get there, best thing you can do is to come with me. I'll get you to Ramskirk. You'll still have to pass through the mountains from there. Won't be easy. You'll also have to stay over in 'Kirk, and I tell you what, it's not a place worth visiting."

"Is there no quicker way?" asked Florence who despite hiding in Sandra's house for so long now felt a need for haste.

"Not that I know of, my dear. In fact, it'll be a bit of trouble finding anyone to take you through the pass. And don't even bother trying to get there by boat, the 'Kirk lads think Besketh is cursed. Yep, the thing is, anyway you go, you'll have to dangle some good money in front of someone's nose. 'Nough of this, you in or not?"

Despite what the driver had said, Florence had to get closer to the town. She was following the only lead she had: one that would only become weaker with the passage of time. After only a slight hesitation, she agreed to take the coach. The driver jumped down and helped Florence into the empty cabin before pushing her bag in after her.

"You can lie down and sleep in here if you need. Doubt we'll have to stop before we get to Ramskirk."

# Chapter Ten

The early dark of winter's night had already fallen by the time the little coach pulled up to an inn within the walls of Ramskirk. Florence had taken the advice of the driver; she was still asleep inside the cabin of the coach when the driver looked through the open window to check on his passenger. As he was standing on the iron step in front of the cabin door, he stamped his foot to let out a loud rap.

"Good to see you're awake," whispered the driver with a smile after Florence had been lurched out of her sleep. "We've arrived."

"Why are you whispering?" asked Florence with a croaky, drowsy voice.

"Have a look out here and you'll see."

Florence fought against the demand of her body to go back to sleep and clumsily hauled herself up so she could see out of the window. It took a moment for her weary mind to take in what was before her. It was a decidedly odd site. In the gloomy mist of this new town, Florence could see hundreds of people walking past the carriage; many of them holding torches; all of them wearing grey cloaks.

The scene was made all the stranger by the haunting silence that hung over the slow moving body of walkers. Not a voice was heard, even from the numerous children that walked along with their families. The only sound that made its way over to Florence was the rustling of material and the dull thud of wet leather souls on the cobbles of the street.

Florence found she was holding her breath. She released the air trapped in her lungs before turning to the driver. She was about to ask what was going on, but he quickly brought his finger to his smiling lips. Florence returned her gaze to the scene, but the driver did not want his passenger to gawp out of his carriage for the rest of the night. To prevent Florence from falling into a daydream, he nudged her shoulder with a knuckle. When Florence looked back at him, the driver threw his thumb in the direction of the dilapidated building to the side of the carriage.

Florence followed the driver to the unwelcoming local inn. The driver lifted up his lamp to discover a heavy iron rod stretched over the door. Lifting the lamp a little higher, he revealed a poster. It informed visitors that the inn had been closed by, 'An order of Mr Stone, Protector of Ramskirk'. Florence looked at the face of the old driver, lit by the golden light of his lamp, and noticed he had lost his smile. She had the feeling that this was the only inn around and it was no longer open.

Florence turned to the street behind her. Large numbers of people were still passing by in droves. She wondered what event could attract so many. If it was permitted by the local greys, maybe it was best not to find out. When she looked back to driver, he was still studiously reading the notice as if hard concentration on the letters would change their form and provide a solution to their problem.

As the man continued to read, Florence saw for the first time how short the man was, much more so than she. He must have been in his fifties, though working outdoors for a living had aged the man beyond those years. The clothes he was wearing did not seem to be sufficient to protect him from the chill in the air; he was only covered by a few layers topped by a thin and well-worn grey cloak with several obvious holes. But if the man was cold or uncomfortable, he did not show it. Florence was struck by a pang of pity for him. She also felt guilty for keeping him in such a strange town.

"Thank you for bringing me here," she whispered. "I'm sure I can find my way on from here."

The driver replied by first mumbling something to himself. He finally took his eyes away from the notice and turned to Florence

"I think you'll struggle to find a driver and there's nowhere to stay. If I'd known that even the inn had closed, I wouldn't have brought you here."

Florence's heart was warmed by the old man. He could have left without a word of goodbye or any regret and still taken her money. In contrast, he really seemed concerned. He looked up and his smile returned.

"I tell you what, I'll take you. As I said, you'll have to wave some good money in front of someone to drive you there. Why not me?"

Florence laughed a little too loudly, mainly from seeing the cheer return to the old man. The two glanced over to the passing walkers and found a few were glaring at them, checking the pair's newly found good humour.

"Perhaps we should get a move on," whispered the driver.

"Yes, I think you're right. Thank you for agreeing to take me to Besketh, Mr...?"

"Foss, but call me Charlie if you must."

"Thank you, Charlie. I'm Florence."

After shaking hands on their deal, Foss informed Florence that he needed to feed his horses. He knew a place where he could take them, but he would be gone for a couple of hours. Florence's first thought was to go with him to avoid any trouble in the town. But she found that now her transportation was settled her curiosity grew. She had been cooped up in the watchmaker's for quite some time and was as ready for some excitement as she had been many months before back in Pendon. Foss did not even have to ask if Florence wanted to go with him, he could see the interest in her eyes. They agreed to meet up again at the inn around seven. Foss assured Florence that this would give them plenty of time to get to Besketh, especially as the sky promised to be clear and there would be a waxing gibbous moon that night. Foss nodded a farewell and returned alone to his coach.

\*\*\*

The silent procession of torch bearers had noticeably reduced in size by the time Florence joined their number. This suggested that most of the people attending the unknown event up ahead had already passed Florence by and that whatever was going to happen would soon begin. Florence picked up her pace.

The procession led Florence down the narrow and cobbled streets of Ramskirk, which were lined by the dark red terraced brick buildings that made up the majority of the city. As she continued to walk alongside the grim townspeople, Florence started to feel a little trapped. The mist shrouded everything before and behind her. Either side, all she could see were the seemingly endless walls of the three story houses. Though she was being funnelled along to an unknown fate, her curiosity would not let her turn back.

Florence sighed with relief when the dual lines of terrace houses finally ended. But the claustrophobic atmosphere of the street behind her was just replaced by the equally uncomfortable cramped conditions of a crowd. Florence had arrived at the edge of Ramskirk's town square where almost all of the city's citizens had gathered. Florence was just about to try and make her way forwards through the throng of people when she suddenly heard what she thought was the surging sound of heavy rain. The noise burst out again, but did not completely fade away. Florence assumed that she was about to get soaking wet, but no rain came. She stretched her left hand out as far as she could in the closing space of the crowd, but it remained dry. She was flummoxed. As no one else seemed to be reacting to the noise, to avoid drawing attention to herself, she tried to ignore her disquiet. Unknown to Florence, the square was situated near Ramskirk's harbour. All she was hearing was the breaking waves of the sea against the harbour's protective unseen stone arm. It created a calm pool where the city's boats hid from the capricious open water. This was the city's economic heart and the sound was as common to the people around her as Pendon's towering mountains were to her.

The sound of the breaking waves was occasionally joined by another: one that was much more disturbing. When the wind blew towards her from the sea, a voice could be heard: the lone voice of a man in distress. The people around Florence seemed as unaffected by this dismembered voice as by the sounds of the waves. She did not even know if they were disconnected.

"Perhaps I have finally stumbled across a demonstration of the power of the sorcerer," thought Florence. She had to take a hold of herself to keep calm. Appearing out of place could be dangerous. Nevertheless, she was still curious and was pulled forwards by the unknown. The voice grew louder. Words soon became clear. Though Florence could not make out all of what was being said, it seemed that the speaker was pleading for mercy.

Florence soon found herself immersed within a large crowd full of people happy to go no further. She squeezed through shoulders and inched her way forwards until the shape of a raised wooden platform, lit by four large flaming torches, emerged before her. The outlines of two people were also discernible. As they were not clear, Florence moved closer still. When the glowing outlines formed into the solid shapes of two men, it was plain that one of them was source of the pleading voice. The man stood, as far as Florence could tell, unbound and under no threat from the other man who looked as ancient as the mountains of Pendon. The old man broke his silence.

"I will be brief," he announced with a booming voice, "which is right for us all. You all know this man had been found to have breached the ordinances which protect us. Thus, we say he is no longer fit to wear the grey cloak that marks our common bond under the good care of the sorcerer. Markus Dranford, remove your cloak."

From the platform floor beneath him the old man picked up a red cloak, much like the one Florence had worn in protest in Pendon. Dranford did not follow the old man's order, he just sank to his knees and wept into his hands. With the cloak still tightly held within his outstretched hand, the old man looked down on the kneeling figure with obvious contempt.

As Florence continued to watch the weeping figure, wondering why so many people would want to watch this man's humiliation, she did not notice the two large hooded men climbing onto the platform. Their form became apparent only when they lifted the weeping Dranford off the boards of its floor. The man swung his body in the air and repeatedly choked out a cry for them to stop. The two men responded by throwing him to the floor. The thud of the man's body against the wooden platform brought a short cry from Florence, one of very few people to respond in the crowd. Florence desperately glanced at the people around her, but they had not stirred.

When she returned her attention to the platform, she saw one of the two hooded men place his thick hands on Dranford and drag him to his feet. The hooded figure then proceeded to curl his broad arms under those of the pleading man. However, the latter had not given in and started to swing his heels into his captors' shins; the grip did not loosen. The other hood stood in front of the twisting form of Dranford and used his strength to rend the condemned man's grey cloak and tear it away with force. Once the cloak had been removed, the struggle ceased. Dranford's captor released his arms, and the form he had held slunk slowly to the ground without a noise. Only the waves could be heard.

The two hooded figures slowly moved to the back of the platform, one still holding the shards of torn fabric in his hands. The old man made his way over to the crumpled form of Dranford. He dropped the red cloak.

\*\*\*

Florence had walked back among a silent crowd to the inn. She still had plenty of time to wait for Foss when she arrived, and so she sat down on the cold stone slab that used to function as inn's front step. Many people passed by, their heads down, returning to their homes. It was not long before only a few individual shadows were making their way through the mist. Soon enough, they disappeared too. The darkness of the winter night seemed to close in without the light from the passing walkers' torches, and time started to slow its pace.

One more torch appeared in the gloom. Florence looked up to see the terrified figure who had been the centre of attention in the square, dressed in his new red cloak. He moved cautiously under the light of his torch, throwing wild glances into the space around him. As he drew close to Florence, he saw her sitting on the step. He flinched and lifted his torch over his shoulder, draining the light from his face. He muttered something to himself, too quietly for Florence to hear, before quickly moving away.

# Chapter Eleven

Florence was glad to see the coach driver return. He apologised for being a little late, but Florence was just happy that she would be able to leave. As Florence's bag was already in the cabin, she just jumped in, and in another moment coach pulled off. Before they could get out of the city, they had to pass through a brick gatehouse. Florence was worried that they would be stuck within the city for another night after the guard informed them it was too late in the day to leave; curfew had already passed. Fortunately, Foss soon settled the situation.

"Barney, it's me. Got a pay-day inside my cabin. I'll be back from Besketh soon enough. You know I always pay my debts."

Barney greeted Foss's suggested bribe with laughter that suggested he agreed to the proposal. Foss drove the horses forwards. Florence was a little shocked to hear the sound of mirth so soon after the scene she had seen by the harbour, but she was glad that Foss had got her through the town gate.

As they travelled south, the mist melted away, and the large mountains that prevented an easy passing to Besketh appeared. The mountains dominated the horizon until they abruptly ended as craggy high cliffs that plunged down into the churning waves of the sea. The road ran alongside a pebbled beach, and the bumpier than usual ride evidenced the many high tides that had covered the road surface with the detritus from the sea.

As they made their way along the road, a fainter version of the sound that had so perturbed Florence back in Ramskirk drew her attention. But now she could see the waves breaking over the pebbles on the beach and knew it was no trick of the sorcerer. She laughed a little at herself for being so foolish. She had heard tales of the sea from her father when she was a child. He had often told her stories of its constant battle with the land, its attacking waves and strange open horizons as well as the men who braved the water for trade and food. There was no doubt in her mind that she was at that moment looking out onto a body of water the likes of which she had never seen before. The river that led to Wellbridge seemed like a mere trickle in comparison.

A sharp turn in the road led the coach away from the sea and up a slow climb. After several bends along a winding road they arrived at the entrance to the pass. Florence looked up at the tall dark shapes under the moon lit sky and was transported home. The romantic vision before her took some of her stresses away and she decided to give in to her tired body. Despite the jarring road, she drifted off into a dreamless sleep.

***

Florence woke. She was still drowsy and felt as if she had only fallen asleep for a second. But as she looked out the window, she realised she must have been out for some time. It was almost pitch black outside, and the coach had slowed to a crawl.

"What's going on?" called Florence.

"Snow's come in. Don't worry through; I know this road better than my wife's bread. Though, we would've been stuck back there if we'd set off any later. We were lucky. We'll be there soon."

Florence put her hand out of the window and felt a small number of flakes settle and melt upon her skin. The coach continued to trundle along the pass at a snail's pace, but the driver was as good as his word as they reached the other side of the pass soon enough.

The snow clouds broke up in the sky ahead of them, leaving the moon free to light their mist covered destination. Florence leaned out the window and looked back on the path they had taken, but could only see darkness. She wondered how Foss had managed to bring them through.

***

Besketh, like Ramskirk, was on the coast. The open sea was visible up head as a dark flat mass below the light of the moon. The town itself was invisible. Through a small place, and to Florence's disappointment, it was covered in as thick a mist as Florence had ever seen. She had no good reason to be disappointed as every town she had seen since leaving home had been covered. Nevertheless, deep down she had hoped this town would at least be somewhat clearer than the last. If this had been the case, she could have believed that the man she pursued really was up ahead and had managed to find something. This would also have meant that her long journey really was coming to an end. But the mist was just as it had been in Ramskirk. The town's streets started soon after the pass finished. As the coach continued on into the mist, the sight of the black sea melted away.

Unlike the red brick buildings of Ramskirk, the structures that emerged in the mist were constructed from large grey stones. Most also were topped with thick grey slate slab roofs, though not all. Many of the houses had been deserted. Uncared for and unprotected, the roofs had either fallen in or had had their slates stolen, causing further decay. These gutted and weather worn houses were often clustered together, leaving stretches of road to resemble rows of monstrous rotten teeth.

Foss stopped the coach in a small square and got down from his seat. Florence alighted as well. She could see her driver was not pleased to be where he was. She attempted to placate the man by saying she would be happy to pay for his board while he waited for the snowy pass to be cleared. He slowly regarded the empty grey square and half-heartedly thanked Florence for her offer, wishing he could refuse to stay at all.

The driver had once again lost his cheer. It was obvious to Florence that he was regretting his decision to take her through the pass. He told Florence that he thought he knew an inn where they could stay, but he was unsure if it was still open. Florence said that it was at least worth trying.

The coach stopped in front of The Fisherman's Rest. Fortunately for the pair, the inn still seemed to be in business and they went in. The front room was a cold, grey, small affair that smelled strongly of fish. It also looked as if the place had fallen upon hard times as dull stains on the creamy yellow walls indicated spaces were pictures and wall ornaments had once hung. The two traveller's knew it was just as likely the inn was just conforming to the demands of the local Protector.

Behind a table, at the back of the room, sat a middle aged women with short auburn hair. She was embroidering what on closer inspection turned out to be a set of ordinances. As Florence admired the fine quality of the work, she wondered if the woman had found a way to put something attractive on her walls by protecting it with the very words that forbid almost everything else.

The woman's concentration was enveloped by her work, and she neither reacted to the arrival of the two travellers or their first attempts to gain her attention. Finally, Foss cleared his throat so loudly that Florence thought he would have rattled the picture frames of the room if they had not already been taken down.

The woman looked up slowly, but still said nothing. Florence was not sure how to handle the situation and found herself leaving any explanation to Foss. He, in turn, wanted to leave it to her. After a long pause, Foss finally took the initiative and removed his cap.

"Two rooms please."

Without a word, the woman placed her work on the dark wood of the table and disappeared behind a grey curtain that hung across the middle of the back wall. Florence looked over to Foss for reassurance, but all he could provide was a shrug. In time, the woman returned with a sour expression and two keys.

"Top floor," she said to Florence as she handed over one of the keys. "Back," to Foss. Her duties completed the landlady once again sat down and recommenced her task of stitching words together. The two travellers passed under the curtain and found a tiny passage hidden behind. The low door of Foss's room was directly before them. A narrow, steep wooden staircase rose up on the left hand side of the passage and led to the next floor. Florence assumed that her room could be found somewhere upstairs, but she remembered that her bag was still in the coach. She told Foss she wanted to retrieve it before she went up to her room.

"Be careful round here," he replied.

Florence was not sure what he meant. She attempted to be careful in every town she visited and saw no reason why Besketh should require any greater degree of caution. Foss was not to know this, so she just nodded to him and left him to his room.

\*\*\*

Florence unpacked her bag in the tiny attic space that was to be her room. She wanted to check that everything was still in order, especially after having knocked the thing against almost every square inch of wall beside the steep wooden staircase that led up her room.

Even though she did not have much, it seemed that her belongings could still fill the tiny attic. The space was indeed small, tucked in under the steeply slanting roof. When she first entered the room, she had been entranced by the faint silver moonlight that illuminated the space and had hoped that its proportions would make it feel cosy. But the spell was soon broken by the sound of wind rattling a pain of glass in its ill-fitting frame, the creaking of the house below her and the chill of the air as it set into her bones.

There was not much furniture in the attic, but a small bed had been pushed into one of the nooks beneath the sloping grey tiles and wooden beams. Florence tried to memorize the location of the bed, fearing she would soon have a bruise on her temple if she were to forget. This was not the only potential hazard; a good portion of the floor was taken up by a steep set of stairs that fell away to the room below.

So she could see what she was doing, Florence lit a candle before she unpacked and placed it on a short plank of unvarnished wood that functioned as her bedside table. After spreading out her belongings, she sat on the rough woollen bedding provided and was glad to see that everything was in order. Just after she finished, a knock came from the door at the bottom of the stairs.

"It's open."

No reply came from below. She assumed it was the mistress of the house trying to gain her attention. Cautiously, she descended the stairs, hoping she would not fall like she was doing repeatedly in her imagination. She opened the door to no one and was mystified until she heard the voice of Foss.

"She's gone down below. I think she was calling you to tea."

Florence looked round the open door to see the driver already sat at the table with a fish and root vegetables on his plate.

"It's not bad, no seasoning though," chuckled the driver, regaining some of his warmth from the meal. "I think yours is on the counter there."

Florence creaked over the floorboards to the sideboard beside the table. A steaming pile of vegetables and another fish was waiting for her on an earthenware dish. She joined Foss at the table and hungrily tucked into her meal. The driver got up from his seat and walked as silently as he could over to the steep stairwell that led to the ground floor. He looked down and after making sure that there was nobody at the base of the stairs, he crept back to his seat. He picked up his nearly empty plate and moved it closer to Florence's.

"Here, you know what I said before, 'bout this place," he whispered. "There's good reason for it. As I said, I know the road in that pass. I used to drive people here. Before things changed."

The man paused and while taking a moment to think, plopped a chunk of turnip in his mouth. Before quite finishing the vegetable, he continued.

"Don't know if you've noticed already, but this town has a ton of empty houses. When I used to come here, regular, it wasn't like that at all. There was always a lot going on, even though it's a small place. Main thing was fishing of course. Bet you don't realise how fresh that fish of yours is.

"Anyway, thing is, when I first came here there wasn't a mist at all. It was a busy place, full of life," continued the driver looking up and smiling, before remembering he did not know where Florence stood on issues such as the sorcerer. He cleared his throat and took on a sombre face. "That all started to change after word spread about the mist falling in 'Kirk. A man here started to talk, like they all do about oncoming disaster and such. He's called Johnson or Jameson, or something like that. Like in all places, after that the mist was soon here. Thing was though, while Johnson, or what's-his-name, made the people who stayed in the town believe every word he said, takin' up those grey cloaks and all, the fishermen who came home every so often thought he was talking rubbish. Problem was the fishermen here use small boats and crews, though they can still stay out long enough. Never stay home long either, most of them live on the sea, poor beggars.

"Anyway, I'm getting off the point. This meant that when the fishermen came home, they were always in little groups. Ones that could only watch their town fall into Johnson's pocket and do nothing about it. Most didn't like the changes, but they didn't do anything until it was too late. After a while, most of 'em started to complain about the ordinances that Johnson put up, but the land folk, wives and so on, were already set in the new ways. Before most of the fishermen thought of doing anything to stop it, there was a thick grey mist over the town. It did not matter, the stubborn fools live on as before, making merry whenever they came back from the sea. They sang; drank and took no notice of Johnson, their wives or the ordinances.

"Johnson started up a big deal against the fishermen, used his words carefully in the land folks' ears. Started saying that if the fishermen carried on their tomfoolery they would get the town destroyed by the sorcerer. Soon every babe that died in its mother's arms from freezing cold to fever was blamed on the actions of the fishermen. They were seen as selfish fools, unable to change their ways to save the children of the town. It wasn't long before everyone in the town was at each other's throats. Luckily, I didn't see too much of that.

"In a way, I was like the fishermen. I only saw the place now and again, when I was here with the coach from Wellbridge. That came to an end soon enough too. Johnson banned the folk here from all but essential travel. This meant pretty much no one took my coach. It wasn't long before my boss said I was wasting my time coming here, wasting a few of his pennies more like, and he shortened the set track to Ramskirk.

"I did make a few more trips here, like with yourself. One time I arrived, after about half a year or more of never seeing the place, to find things had completely changed. The town wasn't fighting itself any longer. I don't know what happened; people here don't talk. But the changes were plain to see. You no longer saw any merry fishermen down near the dock or here at the Rest. And I don't just mean they'd changed their ways, I mean they were gone. I can tell you what the wives thought, the sorcerer had shown his hand and taken them. And you know what they felt? For their husbands and brothers who were nowhere to be seen? For the folk they would've cried their eyes out for if lost at sea only a few years before? Relief!"

Though he kept his voice low, Foss had steadily lost his temper as he got to the end of his speech. He had even stood up from his chair and his face had started to go a worrying purple from lack of breath. Florence had raised her hand out to the man to try and calm him down. She was concerned he would die on the spot or, at the very least, the landlady would be disturbed by his shrieked whispers and lead both of them to the door. But the cathartic release of his opinion on the townsfolk of Besketh was over. He crumpled down into his chair and soon return to his normal unhealthy red.

"That was quite a few years ago," continued Foss in a croak. "People in 'Kirk say this place was cursed by the sorcerer; that's why they've lost more people than anywhere else. They won't come near the place. Maybe they're right. Besketh's as empty as an old bird's nest in winter."

It was plain that Foss was quite affected by what had happened in Besketh, though Florence was not sure why. After finishing the remains of his dinner, he soon made his excuses to go to bed.

# Chapter Twelve

Florence found the morning in Besketh as welcoming as the night. In this odd little empty town, the sorcerer's mist mixed with the freezing fog that drifted in from the sea. Whirls of water vapour could be seen twisting in the wind amongst the steady grey mist she knew from so many other towns. This only seemed to exacerbate the cold, giving it a stronger bite and forcing Florence to cling to herself tightly as she ventured outside.

The road that led on from the pass through the mountains continued down through the town until it reached a little harbour by the sea. Behind the harbour, looking out over the blue grey water, was a building that functioned both as harbour house and residence of the man Foss called Johnson. The building stood three stories high and was constructed from the same rough grey stones as the rest of the town. It was by far the largest building around.

Florence braved the cold of the morning to visit the building in the hope that she could find further information on the traveller. She did not want to have to ask any of the taciturn locals about his whereabouts for fear that her curiosity might be welcomed with a less than helpful response. It was possible that there would be more posters of her quarry in the town as it was stated to be the last in which he had been seen. However, as she walked around the building with the wind buffeting against her, she could find no sign of the usual collection of portraits.

After circling the entire building, she ended up in front of the main entrance of the harbour building. She pulled the hood of her cloak tightly around her face to keep out the worst of the freezing wind and wondered if it was worth risking another meeting with a Protector to see if the posters were inside.

Despite the cold growing on her skin, her instinct was to stay outside. But as the alternative was to turn around and go back to the inn with nothing but the need to return once more, she willed herself to enter.

It was not a great deal warmer inside the lobby of the building, but at least the wind remained beyond its walls. A cold grey stone staircase led up to a reception desk. Behind the desk sat a young man curling himself towards a small, faintly glowing fireplace situated under a list of the town's ordinances. Florence ascended the staircase slowly. As the blustery world had been left outside, the comparative quiet of the empty lobby made each of her footfalls sound like a clap of thunder; every step drained her confidence. But the effort was worth it. As she reached the landing, she saw the image she sought. She forgot herself for a moment and hurried over to the picture. To her disappointment the poster just listed the same information she had seen before.

"Can I help you?"

Florence turned round, ashen-faced. Concerned what the man would think, she blurted out the first thing that came into her head.

"I've seen this man before," she said, before regretting it completely.

"Yes, many of us have. That's beside the point. What are you doing here?"

Florence was taken aback by the frank response of the receptionist. He had seen the traveller before and freely admitted it as if it was an everyday occurrence. She wanted to ask where he had seen the man, but his deep set eyes burrowed into her and dampened her curiosity.

"I'm on my apprenticeship travels," she stuttered, her default response to such questions. As she finished her line, it seemed to her that in this dreary and remote place it lacked the necessary defence it usually provided.

"I have..." she continued as the receptionist continued to glare at her coldly. "I have heard that there is no watchmaker here."

"Correct," said the young man, looking confused by Florence's line of reasoning.

"Well," continued Florence trying to think of something fast, "I thought it might be a good idea to come here as there was undoubtedly a fair amount of work to do. Also, I've already worked for a number of masters and I'd like to know what it's like to work on my own; to improve my knowledge in the other areas of my profession."

The receptionist did not reply immediately, making Florence worry that she had said something wrong. Unbeknownst to her, his slow response was mainly due to not hearing so many words from a visitor to his office for as long as he could remember.

"Well," he managed eventually, "you'd better talk to Mr Jesson."

Florence was unsure as to whom the receptionist referred until she remembered the difficulty Foss had had remembering the Protector's name. She tried to formulate an excuse to defer the meeting, indefinitely if possible, but her mind was blank.

\*\*\*

Florence was sat in a large leather chair. She had been there for the best part of an hour. It turned out that Mr Jesson was not free to talk straight away. Indeed, he had not even been in the building when Florence had first talked to Wolf, the receptionist. Wolf had only informed her of the whereabouts of the town Protector after he had set Florence down in Jesson's office. Before Florence had a chance to say she would return on another date rather than wait, Wolf had disappeared.

In front of her was a large and imposing oak desk. But, apart from that, there was little in the room to demonstrate that she was in the office of the most powerful man in the town. Unlike Orohund, it seemed the Protector in Besketh had foregone any of the other material privileges his position could provide. Still, the idea that Jesson might adhere to the ordinances himself did not enable Florence to relax. He could still be a very dangerous man.

Ideas of what would soon befall her wound round and round in Florence's mind until she heard the creak of hinges behind her. She could not turn around for fear of facing her unknown future. Instead, she froze and did not see Jesson until he walked into her line of sight himself. Jesson turned out to be a man of no real features. Like everyone else, he wore the grey cloak, but it was not just that. His hair was short, brown and indistinct. His face was reminiscent of a number of people Florence could not quite remember. It was not until the man spoke that he seemed to have any character at all. As Jesson greeted Florence, he did so in a gentle whisper.

So faint was the voice that Florence unconsciously lent forwards despite the quiet of the office.

"You're a watchmaker and repairer, I believe?"

"Yes, I would..."

"I have talked to Mr Mackenzie," interrupted Jesson. Florence was not sure who he was talking about, but as her confusion was plain to see, Jesson came to her assistance. "Our friend Mr Wolf. I think it is an acceptable proposal. You have my permission."

His work with Florence done, Jesson sat down at his large desk and started to move around some paper. Florence did not know if the meeting had begun or finished and found herself watching the forgettable form of Jesson carry on as if she were not in the room. She took his continued silence as a signal that he had given her permission to leave. She stood and a contorted and near voiceless 'thank you' stumbled across her lips. She walked to the door in near perfect silence, the only noise the faint scribble of Jesson's pen and the occasional distant howl of wind outside the thick stone walls. She really was thankful. Thankful that the ordeal of the meeting was over.

# Chapter Thirteen

Florence set herself up to work in the Fisherman's Rest. A number of locals started to appear in the empty downstairs room after hearing about her new business. It seemed that news spread fast even though the people in Besketh hardly talked. Although she had only said that she wanted to work on the spur of the moment, she was glad she had initiated the scheme. There was nothing to do or see in the town except visit the abandoned houses of the missing fishermen or watch the sea. Florence was glad that she could pass her days in concentrated work and again avoid having to think about what she should do next.

After a week had passed, the snow blocking the mountain road finally melted meaning Foss could leave. He had usually managed to manufacture a little good cheer when he and Florence ate their meals together, but it was obvious to Florence that his ability to do so was on the wane. While they were apart, he had increasingly spent his time brooding in his room. Florence was therefore very glad to be able to let Foss go. This was not just because she was paying for his room, but because she felt guilty for bringing him to that desolate place. When he left, it was clear a darkness had departed from within him. They parted on the best of terms.

A day after Foss had left, another man arrived in town from over the pass. As there was nowhere else to stay, he took up Foss's small room in the Fisherman's Rest. Florence was not sure what to make of the man. He did not appear to be any sort of merchant as he had not brought anything to trade with him. Not only that, once he had arrived, he hardly ever left the inn and no one ever came to visit.

Meals were still served at the same time each day. This meant Florence had to share her table with the new arrival; she did so in complete silence. She decided it was best to avoid making conversation as the man was an unknown quantity. She just focused on her food. Occasionally, she would look up from her plate to find the man looking straight at her with a blank expression. He would not turn away when she caught him staring. He kept his eyes fixed upon her until he chose to return to his mean in his own good time. Florence usually looked away first. When she bumped into the man at any other time of the day, he would focus his gaze upon her and not let up unless she left the room. After a couple of days, she thought it best to try and avoid the man as much as she could.

Time soon started to pass. Days merged into one another as weeks went by. Florence started to lose track of how much time she had spent in Besketh; all she was sure of was that it felt like an eternity. Florence found the grey town, the grey sea and the grey silent people unbearable; this made her work all the harder. Soon she started to pile up a little sum of money, earned from mending the ancient salt ridden time pieces that the locals continually dug up from who knew where. She kept note of all her earnings in a little notebook she bought from the innkeeper. After what she guessed to be two months, she decided to return to the Protector's building to declare what she had earned not knowing if she was supposed to be paying any tax.

Florence returned to the harbour house and ascended the stairs to find Wolf was once again trying to protect himself from the cold by standing as close as he could to the minute fireplace behind his desk. After giving the man a moment to tear himself away from the precious warmth, Florence held out her notebook to Wolf. He looked perplexed at first, leading Florence to curtly inform him that she wanted to know how much money she owed the town. His perplexity only deepened. He said he would have to seek help to find out.

Wolf was reluctant to take the book as his task required him to leave the warm glowing embers of his fire behind. Nevertheless, he did accept it and vanished down a passageway on the opposite side of the hallway. Florence was left alone with the many faces of the wanted. She recalled the throw away comment Wolf had made when she was last in the building. She walked over to the crudely drawn portrait of the traveller and wondered if she would ever get any closer to finding him.

\*\*\*

If you wanted something in Besketh, you had to wait. Wolf was absent so long that the cold started to break Florence's patience. She paced up and down, but the chill on her skin only seemed to spread further. She was only distracted from her fight against the biting cold when an old woman appeared at the main door. The woman clung to the banister carved into the stone and carefully ascended the staircase. It was only when the woman got to the landing that she saw Florence. She pursed lips and performed a disgruntled gulp to indicate her displeasure at seeing the unknown girl before her. She turned and started the slow descent back to the outside world. As she opened the door, a lick of cold air forced its way into the building and made its way up to Florence. This last rush of cold finally broke Florence's composure and she rushed behind the reception desk to crouch beside the barley living fire. She reached her hands down towards the small glowing pile and was happy to find it produced enough heat to sting her hands. As the warmth brought feeling back into her hands, she looked up to find the ordinances of the town in front of her. As there was no other entertainment to distract her during her wait, except the terrible faces on the posters behind her, she started to read.

She ran through the list of ordinances, both unsurprised and unhappy to learn that they were much the same as those she had seen in every town since her own. That was until she reached the final point on the list, a regulation that she had never seen before.

Wolf reappeared, his perplexity cured. He approached with something akin to a smile on his face and handed Florence her notebook. She flicked through to find that someone, possibly Wolf himself, had written a sum on the front page in a firm neat hand. It stated that a payment was to be made each month. As far as Wolf was concerned their business was complete. He returned to his station by the fire.

"What's this?" asked Florence.

Wolf responded with a heavy sigh. He followed Florence's finger and furrowed his brow. She was pointing to the final ordinance on the list. It struck Florence as odd as it claimed: "No citizen should associate in any way or form with the other village." Wolf was obviously unsure as to what to say in response. He first looked over to the passageway down which he had vanished before. Slowly though, he gaze returned to his small fire. After another deep breath, he talked.

"You've been here a while. Suppose you should know. There's a village down the shoreline. It's a lost place. People there wanted to destroy our home. Wouldn't follow the ordinances. To save the town, Jesson said they could go if they didn't return. Many took the offer. Couldn't see what was right for themselves."

It suddenly became clear to Florence that the town had not been as badly struck by disappearances as outsiders were usually led to believe. It was also apparent what she had to do next.

\*\*\*

Florence knew that the traveller could still be in Besketh. He could also be almost anywhere else. But the fact that there was an ordinance in Besketh that prohibited the townsfolk from visiting the village down the coast suggested the possibility that something was there. It might not be the traveller, but it could at least be a lead. As Florence packed up her things in her tiny room, she wondered about the contents of the letter that induced the traveller to journey so far; it must have been something special. But then she thought again, remembering how easy it had been for Sewan to convince her to come to this forgotten town.

Florence managed to finish fixing the last timepieces she had taken on. She worried a little about the quality of her final jobs. As time progressed she found it increasingly difficult to maintain the appropriate degree of care and concentration the work required. The pull of wanting to move on continually grew.

Florence returned to the harbour house once more. She strode in as confidently as she could to declare that she would leave the town and cease to do business, meaning she had to pay her monthly fee. She hoped that the payments would make Jesson happy enough to let her go without a fuss. Unfortunately for Florence, Wolf was so unsure as to what to make of Florence's announcement that he had to go and ask for advice. It was not too long before she was in Jesson's office once again.

"We'll be very unhappy to see you go," whispered the Protector.

"I'm sorry to go to," lied Florence, "but the supply of broken timepieces is drying up; the town is not so large. I'm very grateful, though, for the opportunity you provided me here; to work on my own. But, unfortunately, I have to move on."

Jesson tried to persuade Florence that she should stay. His motive was unclear to Florence until she thought about all the people who had left the town before. Was it possible that the man was racked with guilt and regret whenever people asked to leave the ghost-town he had created? Florence was not sure, but the Protector did seem sincerely unhappy to see her go. She left with a half promise to return once she had finished her apprenticeship travels, mollifying Jesson's concerns sufficiently to receive a wish for a speedy end to her journey.

Florence left the town leader with the impression that he was at least a good man. Nevertheless, his character did not overturn the negative impact he had had on his town. He was still the man who had introduced and enforced Besketh's ordinances. He had even created his own ordinances to maintain the sway of the sorcerer's hand in the town. He was convinced he was doing the right thing, though Florence could not understand how. In what way could he think it right to exile people from their homes and prevent those who remained from seeing those who left; their brothers, friends and children.

# Chapter Fourteen

Florence paid off her bill to the landlady in silence. She was glad to be able to leave the inn whose cold atmosphere had never thawed. She also bought some food for a journey whose length she did not know. The landlady did not bid her farewell. Once their transaction was over, she just returned to her embroidery. Florence took one last look around the front room of the inn. It still looked as if someone had just moved out. She was glad she was going and happy that her fellow tenant was nowhere to be seen.

Besketh abruptly ended a few streets away from the harbour and broke into a narrow beach of light brown sand. Florence stepped out onto the beach expecting her leather boots to sink into soft ground. She was therefore pleased to find that the ground was firm under her feet. As she walked on, the mountains started to drift away from the sea, leaving first sand dunes, then pine forests in their wake. The beach became broader and Florence clung to the sand dunes to avoid the unknown tide and swell of the sea. For the first time in as long as she could remember, an unforced smile crept across her face. The weather was even beginning to be mild.

As the land around was fairly flat, Besketh was still visible behind Florence. It sat as a distant grey smudge beneath the tall mountains that dominated the horizon. She looked back to the grey of Besketh several times, happy that she had escaped. But as the light of the day started to fade, part of her felt sorry that the nearest bed she knew of was so far away. After the sun had sunk into the sea, a blanket of unbroken cloud spread over the twilight sky. The bright moon that had greeted her into Besketh would be nowhere to be seen that night. This meant Florence had to quickly find somewhere to sleep while the grey yellow light of the end of the day still lingered on the horizon.

Florence stepped up through the avalanching grains of sand to climb one of the dunes and proceeded to run down the other side. She found herself in a sparse pine forest. Before the last of the natural light faded away, she gathered as much dry wood as she could find and started a fire. Though the night air was cold, the fire provided enough heat for her to get a few hours of broken sleep on the uneven sandy soil.

***

Florence woke abruptly from a terrible dream. The lodger from Besketh had been standing next to her, glaring down at her on the ground. She had been looking up at the man towering above her, but she had been unable to move, to speak or to scream. She collected herself together, telling herself that her dream was just that and nothing more. She breakfasted on a fish pie she had bought from the innkeeper, but she did not finish the meal. Instead, she left much of it to a nosy seagull that seemed to be much more interested in the meal than herself.

Unlike the day before, Florence walked along the tops of the dunes. She thought that being a little higher up might help her to spot the village up ahead. She struggled along for a short distance, but soon found that the soft sand of the dunes was much harder going than the harder ground of the beach below. She persevered for a time, but eventually her exhausted legs demanded a rest and she sat down, letting the weight of her bag sink into the sand. She looked along the beach and, in the distance, spotted a wooden fence. Florence did not consider it too interesting in itself as there was no mist. The meant the village had to be further on, but at least there were some signs of life.

As Florence got closer, she could see that the fence was constructed from tall unworked pine logs. The sand dunes petered out not too far from where she was standing, and the beach narrowed considerably. This left the fence free to extend from the still standing pines of the nearby forest to the lapping waves of the sea. Easy progress along the beach was blocked. Florence started wondering how long it would take to walk around the fence when she noticed a man was standing at its top.

As soon as Florence saw the man, she knew she had found the village. Not only that, but she could now see why the traveller would have journeyed so far to get here. Though Florence was still some distance away, she could see that the man was wearing a fabric top split diagonally from left shoulder to right hip. One side of the top was blue, the other yellow. It seemed such an odd sight to Florence that she stopped walking. Just as she halted her progress, the man who had so distracted her noticed her on the beach and started to shout.

At first, the wind coming off the sea made the calls of the man incomprehensible. Florence responded by moving closer. That was until the tail end of a broken sentence, blown over by the turning wind, stopped her dead in her tracks.

"...I will shoot!"

Florence had not previously noticed the crossbow held by the man; now it became the centre of her attention. Fear told her to run, but she had come too far to do that. She quickly put her hands in the air, with her cold fingers spread apart, and called out that she meant no harm. No bolt was let off, but the crossbow remained aimed directly at her.

Concerned that the man might shoot even if she withdrew, Florence decided that she had to act on the spot. She lowered her hands slowly and cautiously brought her bag down from her shoulders. She sought through it as quickly as she could looking for anything that might help her get out of her situation. She found no clothing or cloth that could make it clear that she was one of them and ruefully remembered the expensive material the old woman had offered her near Hesik. She searched a moment longer, but found nothing. She looked up to the guard who was still standing watch. Florence started to feel foolish. She had come all this way and was going to fail when she was sure her final destination was right before her. The guard drew the sight of his crossbow up to his eye. She threw her hands up once more and closed her eyes.

"I mean no harm," she shouted in desperation as loudly as she could.

To her great relief, the guard did not let off a shot. She opened her right eye, then her left, and to her great relief he had finally lowered his bow. Florence grabbed her bag and swiftly made her way up to the fence. As she got close, the guard raised the weapon once more.

"Who are you? What do you want here?"

Now she was closer, she could see that the guard was only a boy, not even fourteen. She could hear a half-hidden quaver in his voice. She worried about lying, calling herself a merchant or something else, for fear that the boy would just turn her away. She knew he would not give her a second chance. His question hung in the air, heaping pressure on Florence to think of something quickly. Unconsciously, her hand passed to her chest. She felt the almost forgotten trinket she had been given by Sewan long ago and in a flash pulled it from around her neck and threw it up to the guard.

"I've come to find someone."

The boy instinctively caught the ugly little blue dog's head while almost dropping his crossbow. He took a moment to compose himself, pushed down his fear and attempted to play the role of the diligent guard once more. He took a few moments to examine the piece until he was satisfied.

"The gate you need is in the forest," said the boy with as calm a voice as he could muster and with his eye still on the trinket. He looked up. "We'll be keeping a close watch on you though, seems as you've come in one of those cloaks."

\*\*\*

"Don't mind our Geoffrey," said Tom. "He's still young, see, and you can understand how outsiders would make him nervous, I'm sure."

Tom, another guard, had greeted Florence at the gate. Geoffrey, the boy with the crossbow, turned out to be the man's son. Florence wondered what good a boy and a portly man like Tom could really do for the defence of the village. She supposed that perhaps there was not a great deal of people to choose from in such a small place, meaning there was little choice. Tom guided Florence into the village. He explained how it had originally been a collection of disused fishermen's huts that had been out of use for years before the current occupants arrived. Tom talked with pride about how the newcomers had quickly built the pine fence to keep out the other folk and extended the village to suit their needs. Due to the man's good cheer and the seeming unreality of her surroundings, Florence unthinkingly nodded in response to whatever Tom said.

Although the village was a small simple place, it still astonished Florence. As Tom continued to talk and walk, they past a number of small brightly coloured huts including a makeshift school which resonated with the uneven singing of children. As people passed by, they briefly paused their chatty conversations to happily greet Tom. This was just normal life for the villages. Florence felt like she had wandered into a dream, and nothing made this feeling more apparent than the fact that above her head was a clear blue sky.

The villagers greeted Florence as well, but they did so coldly. She had not felt so unwelcome since she had worn red back in Pendon. She wished that she still had her mother's cloak to show that she was just like the villagers who were now grimly regarding her as an unwanted visitor. As the cloak had been left at home, she responded to their glares by shrinking into herself more and more. That was until Tom brought them both to a sudden stop.

"Well, here we are," said Tom as he opened the door to a bright yellow hut.

"We're here?" asked Florence, now worried what she had got herself into.

"Why, at your friends place, of course."

"My friend?"

"Yes, isn't he your friend," continued Tom, his face losing its smile for the first time. "You had the dog."

"You mean he's actually here?"

"Of course, he's been expecting you for a long time. Let's not keep him waiting."

How could the traveller have known she was coming? She did not remember Sewan saying anything about her being expected by the lost man. It was her impression that it was precisely because the traveller had fallen off the known world that she had had to try and find him. Tom gave a knock on the low open wooden door. A grunt of a reply came from within. Tom ducked under the low frame and entered into the darkness of the room beyond. Florence stayed rooted to the spot, reluctant to find out if this really was the end of her journey.

"Coming in?" said Tom, poking his head back out.

After taking a long breath, Florence nodded.

\*\*\*

In contrast to the colourful world outside, the small living space within the hut was drab and sparsely furnished. Florence hardly noticed as she was distracted by the warmth of the room; the first pleasant heat she had experienced in weeks. The warmth was emanating from a pile of hot stones that had been placed in a pool of sand in the middle of the room. Beyond the stones was a man. He sat behind a table illuminated by the light that fell from several small openings in the hut's roof.

As she looked through the beams of light, glistening with small flecks of slowly moving dust, Florence recognised him. The man had not yet seen her as he was bent over his low unvarnished and crooked table writing a letter. Florence and Tom might have intruded on his space, but the man did not let them interrupt his work. Tom looked over to Florence and gave a short grimace, making Florence feel a little better by letting her know she was not the only one who felt a little awkward.

When the two turned back to the traveller, they found he had finally looked up. He sternly regarded both of them. To Florence, now she could see his face properly, he looked much older even though it had not been that long a time since she had last seen him. As they examined each other, a heavy silence filled the hut. Its pressure built, weighing down on Florence who had not expected this reception at all. That was until the grim expression on the traveller's face melted into a smile.

"So, you've finally arrived," he said. "Please sit down. I suppose we have a lot to talk about."

The traveller wafted his hand towards a wide wooden bench covered in an assortment of blankets on the opposite side of the room. Florence examined the patchwork of colours that made up the top quilt and thought how much more colourful it would be if it was cleaned. Not wanting to insult her host, Florence willed herself to sit down, perching herself on the very edge of the makeshift bed.

As she sat down, the traveller asked if he could have the little dog's head back. Florence nodded to Tom who produced the little token from his pocket.

"It's all I have left from a place I lost. It's good to see it again," said the traveller as he pocketed the trinket.

Tom, still standing near the low entry to the hut, asked if it would be possible for him to leave; he was keen to get back to his post. Florence was glad that he had finally plucked up the courage to speak as he obviously wanted to go. He had even started to wring his hands and dance on the spot.

"Of course," replied the traveller. The guard made a little display of thanks and departed.

"Did Sewan send any message?" said the traveller as soon as Tom had gone.

"No," stumbled Florence while wondering if the man before her remembered her at all.

"Did he tell you why I came here?"

"Not exactly. He said that you received a message, I cannot remember if he said from who. It stated that there was some valuable information to be found out in the lost territory. Information that could help the fight against the sorcerer. I can see from this place that there's some truth in what the letter said."

"Were you followed?"

Florence responded with a puzzled frown.

"Do you think someone followed you here? One of those grey Ministers?"

"I didn't see anyone," she replied.

"Well, it doesn't matter too much anyway. It's only a matter of time..." the traveller paused and briefly looked over his letter. "Have you seen the posters?"

Florence nodded and confirmed that she had seen him in almost every town since Wellbridge.

"I made the error of being recognised in Ramskirk. I had the unfortunate pleasure of bumping into a merchant who'd seen me speak in the Pear Hills. He followed me to Besketh and confronted me at the Fisherman's Rest. He asked if I still believed what I'd said when we last met. I tried to say that he'd mistaken me for someone else, but the man was adamant that he knew my face. He dragged me over to the town office they have over there. Fortunately, the Protector was elsewhere and that place can't function without him. I managed to escape and made my way here. That was some time ago. You might ask why I didn't try and return. I couldn't go back that way, not when they suspected what I was. Indeed, I soon heard about the posters after I arrived here; the links between the people of Besketh and this village are not entirely broken. So, I stayed here to collect as much information as I could to pass on to whomever came to find me. And now here you are."

The traveller stood up and moved out from behind his table so he could get closer to the pile of blisteringly hot stones. As he did so, he turned his back to Florence. It took a while for her to realise the implication of what he had said. If she was to take on the information he had gathered, what was to become of him? Before Florence could ask that very question, he continued.

"Have you seen them?"

At first, Florence did not take in what the traveller had said. She was still thinking about where he would go. He repeated the question. She knew what he was referring to.

"I think so. In my own town, but I can't say for sure."

"That's usually the way. Do you know what they do?" said the traveller as he turned round to face her and look directly into her eyes for the first time.

Florence did not reply. She did not even think about the question. She just looked into his dull tired eyes, ones she thought had been so full of life when she had seen him speak in Pendon.

"It's commonly believed that they take those who oppose the sorcerer," said the traveller answering his own question. "They take them from the street; sometimes from their homes. Rarely do those who are taken return; the few who do are never the same. The people here tell stories about those who vanished in Besketh. Such stories are common all over the lost territory, and beyond amongst those who've left. There are no stories about people disappearing from here though. Here in this odd little fishing village, in one dark corner of the lost territory, there are no figures looming in the mist. The people here believe the sorcerer to be some sort of daemon. They believe this because of the odd circumstance of their eviction from their home town. They brought a common conviction with them that makes them all oppose him. But why are they not taken? Obviously, because there is no mist. But why is there no mist? We're often told its spread is inevitable in those places that disregard the will of the sorcerer. Not here.

"This place is proof of what Sewan and I have believed for a long time. Disregarding the ordinances does not bring the mist, nor does public denunciation of the sorcerer, nor hatred of the man in your heart. This place proves that those who cry out against him do not spread the mist. That's just a myth. It is not them who bring the terror of those creatures. No," exclaimed the traveller raising his threadbare voice to a cry, "it's those who claim we must follow his ordinances or perish."

As the traveller finished, he fell back into his chair, breathing heavily. For a moment, the light Florence had seen in Pendon flickered in his eyes. She was still perched silently on the edge of the bed. Could the fight against the spread of the sorcerer's mist be so simple? It had been unstoppable, no matter what people like the traveller had done or said. But the evidence was before her eyes. This small village had no mist, no ordinances and apparently no tales of disappearances. The problem was, how could anyone inform the rest of the world about this little haven from the sorcerer's power? How could they convince those told never to travel to come to a place so far away? Florence looked up to the traveller to ask what had to be done, but was prevented when the sound of a large explosion broke through the air.

# Chapter Fifteen

As Florence and the traveller emerged from the little yellow hut they heard another explosion. It seemed to come from the direction of the main gate. Without a word, the traveller ran towards the source of the noise. Not wanting to be left behind, Florence went after him. Unlike before, the streets were silent. No one was chatting, no children were singing. The streets were not empty though. Many of the people who had been making their way around the village stood like statues commemorating the moment of the explosions. As he ran, the traveller turned to see Florence making her way after him. He stopped at once.

"What are you doing?" he exclaimed. "You must go back! You need to go back and get my letter. Take it to Sewan. Read it and destroy it. You're the only person with the power to help our cause now."

Florence did not move. She wanted to follow the man she had tracked for so long. She felt she was not ready to lose him again so soon. She could not understand why he wanted to leave her behind.

"I'm thankful that you got here before they came, but my waiting is over. I know it won't be easy to go on alone, but you must. Dig down to whatever helped you to get here and let it lead you on. I can't help you any further. Now go!"

The traveller ran on. Florence watched the man disappear. She tried to do what he said. She looked within herself and thought of her father. She made him tell her to turn, to go back to the letter. The pull of her curiosity was too strong; she was being drawn forwards.

Florence found herself near one of the houses behind the space which opened onto the village's main gate. Other villagers were gathered around trying to peer out from the safety the building provided. As Florence joined them to see what was going on herself, they recoiled and rapidly moved away. Fear was plainly evident in their staring eyes. Florence stumbled out a muted apology, but the villagers did not hear her.

As the corner of her building was cleared, Florence was free to look at the scene that had grasped the attention of those she had scared away. When she looked round the corner, she knew why the villagers had reacted in the way they had. She could see six men all dressed in grey, just like herself.

The men were standing in front of what had been the village gate with their hoods pulled up to obscure their faces. It was evident what had been the victim of the explosions. One side of the gate had been blasted off its hinges and lay smoking on the ground. Parts of the pine pillars nearest to the explosions had been fragmented into thousands of splinters, a number of which had been forcefully deposited into two still bodies that lay near the former gate.

As Florence's gaze returned from the bodies to the six men, she noticed that one of them had his foot on the head of a form dressed in yellow and blue; the heavily wounded, but still alive body of Geoffrey.

The boy coughed and spluttered. This raised a gasp from the villagers hidden behind the other buildings around. The man whose leather boot was on Geoffrey's head knelt down slowly, letting the weight of his body pass into the boy. Geoffrey cried out in pain. After his knee had touched the ground, the figure held his hand out into the air. Florence wondered what the man could be doing until one of the other five stepped forwards and placed a pistol into the waiting hand.

As one of man's hands tightened its grip around the pistol and lowered the barrel to the head of the boy, his other withdrew his hood. Florence instinctively shrank back from the edge of the hut. She could not believe that the staring eyes of the lodger from Besketh had tracked her down.

"We come here seeking a man," shouted the lodger with a phlegm filled voice. "A man who does not belong here. We do not want to have to kill you all," he said with a wide smile, "but we'll do what's necessary to gain our quarry."

A silence fell upon the scene. No reply came from the villagers gathered around.

"If you doubt the efficiency of our weapons, we can give a further demonstration."

The lodger pointed with his free hand, and one of the other five lowered a rifle and let off a shot, aiming at one of the huts. The lead it fired smashed through a window and buried itself into the clay brick wall inside. The destructive effect of the shot was as nothing compared to the noise and smoke. All around the villagers threw themselves back for protection, fearing more damage like that done to the gate. The rifleman reloaded his weapon.

Florence peeked around the corner of the hut once more. She noticed that all the men had rifles. She also saw that the crossbow that had threatened her only hours before was just out of reach of the injured boy. She wondered if the village had any more, or if its people were now left defenceless. She returned her attention to the lodger. His expression suddenly changed. At first, she worried he had seen her, but it was clear his gaze was elsewhere. She leaned out a little further and saw a man stood in the middle distance between the semi-circle of huts and the six men. Florence repressed a cry. The traveller had reappeared.

"I'll gladly come with you," said the traveller, "if you leave this place right now."

One of the five behind the lodger raised his rifle to the traveller, but the lodger called out for him to put down his weapon.

"Don't shoot him, you idiot. Do you want to carry him? It's much easier to walk. You two, kindly assist our new friend."

Two of the greys stepped forwards and seized the traveller's arms. The barrel of the lodger's pistol was slowly removed from the weeping boy's head. The lodger looked around the buildings of the village, seemingly unhappy that things had gone so smoothly; there was no need for mayhem. He threw his pistol to the man who had raised his gun and set off towards the remains of the gate, stepping on one of the lifeless bodies as he went.

The three free men of the crew scrambled after their leader. The two men holding the traveller followed, holding him tightly in their arms. Florence thought that their action was quite unnecessary as the man in their grip showed no signs of struggling.

As soon as the intruders had disappeared from view, the villagers poured forwards to see to the men lying on the ground. Many of them had tears streaming down their faces as they ran, ignoring the mass of shattered wood beneath their feet. Florence did not move. She could not breathe. The man she had come to find was gone. She had only seen him for a matter of minutes. As the bewildered villagers started to tend to the injured boy, he let out a scream of pain. Florence's mind was wrenched from its internal constraints, and she became conscious of her surroundings once more. She watched the villagers as they tried to comprehend what had just happened. Could she stay to help them rebuild their defences and their broken peace? No, it was impossible. There was a good chance some would say she was involved in the attack. She was still in a grey cloak. Even the generous villagers were likely to be suspicious of her. So soon after a group of greys had brought death to their quiet, happy home, the villagers would probably trust no one but their own.

Florence looked over to the space that once held the gate. It was impossible to leave that way. Not only would she have to pass most of the villagers, there was also the possibility she would walk straight into the men that had just taken the traveller. If she was captured, then there would no one to convey the traveller's message back to Sewan.

"The letter," whispered Florence.

She had forgotten the letter: it was still lying in the traveller's deserted hut. Florence ran back as fast as she could. She had to trust her instincts to guide her way through the passageways of the village. As she ran, she tried to think what she could do next, where she should go, but her blurry half formed thoughts refused to sharpen. Even when she found the hut, she still had no idea of what to do.

The hut's door was still open, inside it was still warm. Florence picked up the letter from the table. She looked at the paper, but was too unnerved to concentrate on the spidery handwriting. She hid it away in her bag.

Florence stood outside the hut with her bag strapped to her back not knowing where to go. Indecision weighed her down. Finally, she willed herself to move. As she thought there would still be a great deal of commotion near the main gate, she set off in the opposite direction. She just hoped there was another way out of the village.

As she made her way along a path of pounded earth that led to an unknown destination, Florence heard the sound of running water. She passed one further line of colourful houses to find the village stopped abruptly. There was no wall of pine on this side of the village, but the prospect before her seemed to bar her way almost as well. About ten feet below the bank on which she stood lay a narrow river. It created a natural defence against any intruder and created a prison out of the village for Florence. She watched a broken twig as it floated along the surface of the water. The current would eventually carry it out to sea, but it did not seem to be moving too fast. Though she could not really swim, she considered wading across. The thought of the cold water put her off. She made the right choice; the current was much stronger than she imagined.

Florence walked along the bank, following the river towards the forest. As she got closer, she could see the tall spikes of the pine tree fence up ahead. They barred her way out. Florence started to doubt there was another safe exit other than the main gate. What would the villagers do to her if she went back; an unknown girl, dressed in grey. Tom was aware of who she was, but a black thought engulfed the glimmer of light this idea brought. It was very likely that Tom was one of the two dead men. It was his intention to return to his post at the front gate. Apart from the seriously injured, potentially dead, Geoffrey, there was no one around who knew her as anything other than a dangerous intruder in their midst.

Waves of frustration and exhaustion crashed against her will, creating a current that dragged her down into despair. She stopped walking along the bank. She tried to regain her composure until tears formed in her eyes. She let herself cry in the hope that it would help her return to some sort of calm. Instead, while the weeping continued, she found she could only breathe with ever quickening sharp inhalations. As she tried in vain to gain control over her own body, another surge of emotional pain tightened in her gut. She let her legs buckle beneath her and fell heavily to her hands and knees. She muttered to herself between gasped breaths that she wanted it all to stop. She hated herself, she hated Sewan, the traveller, all of them. She forced out a pained cry, but it did nothing to lift the weight on her chest. She clenched her hands to squeeze the sandy earth between her fingers. So she remained, not knowing what to do. With no will to move she just remained motionless, staring at the ground, watching each tear fall. No one came, and nothing changed around her except the water of the river.

Time passed on until the grip of her despair slowly started to loosen. She sat back, letting the ground take the weight of her bag. As she did so, hope suddenly rose within her. She wiped her soil covered hands on the fabric of her cloak then tried to clear the water from her eyes. From her point of view on the ground, she could see that the last few towering pillars of the pine fence had been felled. She did not know if the explosions had made them fall; she did not care. What was important was that perhaps there was a way out.

# Chapter Sixteen

The two men held onto the traveller fast even though he had shown no resistance to their rough handling. He had no reason to resist; he knew what his fate would be, though he was still not sure how it would come about or when. As he was pulled along, he thought how fortunate he had been to have avoided men such as these for such a long time. It was lucky that help had arrived just before they had come.

Although the trip to Besketh only took a day if a quick pace could be maintained, the group would not reach the town that night. They first had to make a detour to retrieve the bags and gear they had hidden in the pine forest before their attack. As the light started to fade, Besketh was still some way off. The group made camp. Like Florence, the seven men retreated to the far side of the dunes, seeking shelter from the cold wind that blew in from the vast open space above the sea.

The seven sat in silence as they ate. A fire had been put together, and the troop sat huddled around as close to the warmth as they could. Though seated, the traveller was still flanked by his two escorts. They gave him no further grief as he ate, but this did not mean he was left in peace. Opposite him, on the other side of the fire, sat the youngest member of the group. Since the traveller had sat down, the young man had been staring at him. Whenever he looked up from his meal, he returned the gaze with a smile. He did this five or six times and then went a little further by saluting with his plate of barely edible beans.

All in one moment, the young grey sprang to his feet, threw his wooden plate to his side -- spilling beans over the man to his left -- and jumped over the fire to attack the traveller. Before he found his target, one of the two men beside the traveller shot up and grabbed the attacking youth. As the boy struggled in the large arms of his captor, the traveller returned his attention to his meal.

"Let go of me Fredrick or you'll regret it," screamed the boy. "That man needs to die! Why's he still alive? I know what his like does. They killed her. Let go of me, let go!"

The boy continued to struggle, but he could not break free. Eventually, his lurching died down. The lodger made his way over to the tangling pair and put his arm on the retrained boy's shoulder. He stopped struggling altogether and dropped his gaze to the ground. The lodger gave a curt nod to the captor, Fredrick, and the attacker was set free. The boy sheepishly moved away from the group and wandered into the darkness of the forest. He was embarrassed by his weakness.

"Look after him Fredrick," whispered the lodger.

The lodger sat down in the free spot left by Fredrick. The traveller ignored his new neighbour and looked around at the remaining men near the fire. It seemed the boy was not alone in his opinion. Another man now seemed to be staring at him with the same hate filled eyes.

"I don't think we've been properly introduced," said the lodger. "My name is Avitus. And you are?"

The traveller did not respond. He just continued to look into the eyes of the man trying to stare him down.

"You don't need to worry about my companions," said Avitus. "They almost always follow their orders. It's just that when strong feelings are stirred." The man finished his sentence by opening his hand in the air. "Our friend who wandered off into the woods, for instance: lost his mother just days after one of your fellow mist spreaders visited his town. She was the only member of family he had left. It's odd how common a story like his is. He's not even the only member of this little troop to have told such a tale.

"Yes, it's true that many of the people in bands such as ours act for monetary gain, some for pleasure," said Avitus with a laugh. He leaned closer to the traveller so he could whisper into his ear, "but a growing number act purely out of revenge. It's interesting, isn't it, the way so many think the mist is spread by people like you."

The traveller shot a glance at Avitus, losing his previous control. Avitus replied with a smile.

\*\*\*

Florence held her hands out to the warmth of her fire. It had taken her some time to gather the dry wood she had, but the small collection of flames suggested she had found enough. Now the village -- with its mist free sky -- had been left behind, it seemed to exist in some distant past. The events of the day seemed unreal. She had fulfilled her mission by finding the traveller, but she felt no closer to any end; no sense that she had achieved anything. Instead, she had been burdened with another task. Florence thought about the long road ahead, and how she would have to pass through territories where her face was already known. She pushed these notions away. She knew to some extent she was procrastinating: she was putting off reading the letter.

Florence fished around in her bag and quickly located the letter. She settled down near the flickering light of the fire before opening up the folded paper to reveal the unfinished text. Many of the words were still unreadable. However, Florence was better settled than when she was in the village and had more time. This meant she was able to make out most of the spidery calligraphy. As she scanned over the lines, a sense of disappointment grew within her. The text mainly consisted of information the traveller had already given Florence during their brief meeting. That was until a promising penultimate paragraph.

"As to the figures in the mist," ran the text, "I have come across a great deal of evidence that suggests they are not just savage beasts like some of us believed. I now hold the opinion that they are much more human and capable of a good deal more thought than we would like. This is partly evidenced by their connection to disappearances. For instance, in our mist free town of New Besketh alone, the people gave me dozens of stories describing how a person would see one of the figures in the days or hours leading up to their disappearance. Obviously, this is nothing new to us. What is new is that many of the people disappeared despite wearing grey cloaks and following the normal list of ordinances. These were individuals who had been publicly denounced by the town leader, as well as by other members of the community, for assisting those exiled from Besketh. This seems to suggest either the possibility that the town leaders are able to control the beasts or that the beasts can gather this information for themselves. Either way, this makes this foe of ours much more of a threat that we had previously supposed."

This description of the figures left the air around Florence feeling a little cooler. She gripped her cloak and attempted to pull it closer around herself even though she was warm enough near the fire. Despite the dark that dominated the forest about her, she was glad that she was not in one of the distant mist covered cities. She did not want to have to think about the prospect of meeting one of the figures just described.

The next paragraph started on a topic about which the traveller had touched upon during their conversation. He had noted that he: "fervently believed that the mist had something to do with the town leaders and the people of a town." To Florence's annoyance, the letter stopped abruptly at the end of this sentence; the point at which the traveller had stopped writing when she had disturbed him. She wished she had arrived a few minutes later. It could have made all the difference if she had just given the man enough time to finish that last paragraph. Florence read out the text four more times, trying to remember it as best she could. She placed the letter on the fire and watched the cream paper first brown, then disappear. She hoped that the thoughts it had contained had not been lost forever.

\*\*\*

"So you know that the mist is not spread by the sorcerer because of people like me," said the traveller, "or to protect citizens or any of that other nonsense that people often believe."

"I've had to live by my wits for long enough not to be fooled as easy as some," whispered Avitus.

"Why do you do this then, why do you hunt people down if you know it's for no good."

"I wouldn't necessarily say it's for no good," replied Avitus with a satisfied smile on his lips. "There are two reasons, you can call them good if you like. First, the money. I'm handsomely paid for what I do; as you will find out yourself. Second, I enjoy the opportunity to do what I like with those I capture. There are no requirements for me to hand over the hunted in perfect condition. Indeed, the opposite is often preferred by certain authorities."

Avitus leaned a little closer to the traveller and patted him on the thigh.

"I suggest you continue to be a good boy. We still have quite a distance to travel; Besketh wouldn't pay the bounty even if they could afford it. So, do what I say and you might just make it all the way to Wellbridge with your life and most of your body intact."

The traveller fixed Avitus with a stare for several moments before bursting into laughter. Avitus shot up from his seat. The traveller just kept on laughing. Fury grew within Avitus with a terrible speed. His limbs tingled with anger. He made himself feel the fury that resulted from the disrespect this dead man was showing him. He held on for a few more seconds and admired himself for showing so much will power in the face of the insult his prisoner was giving him.

The traveller did not see Avitus's foot, he just knew that he was now sprawled on his back while his blood trickled from the split skin of his skull to the sandy earth below. He slowly pushed himself back up into a sitting position and looked up at the towering figure of Avitus.

"You'll never get me to Wellbridge," he said, laughing again. "I've escaped those things before, but only just. They know who I am. They'll take me as soon as we enter the mist. You've done a lot of work and damage for nothing. You need a body for your bounty, but you'll be lucky to get me past a city gate. You could kill me now and take what remains. Oh, but I suppose I need to be alive for questioning."

"You better mind yourself," grunted Avitus. "There are men here who will gladly carry your half dead body if they get the chance to mete out some revenge. Just mind that you don't give me a reason to let them do it."

\*\*\*

The traveller and his new companions edged round Besketh as best they could to get to the mountain pass. No further harm came to the traveller as they made their way towards Ramskirk, but inside he was preparing himself for the end. His only consolation was in watching the horror of a human being in the form of Avitus contort his face in thought as to how to proceed. As the group emerged on the other side of the pass, letting the slopes of the rock pass by to reveal Ramskirk, Avitus ordered the group to stop.

"Perhaps we should change our plan. We'll go to Ramskirk for the bounty. I'm sure they'll administer justice with just as much care as they would in Wellbridge. We might not get as much in compensation for our efforts, but we can leave this one here and move on to the next hunt in the knowledge that the right thing has been done."

The traveller smiled. It seemed Avitus had not forgotten what he had said and had come to accept it would be too risky to take him through so much of the lost territory. The boy who had flown at the traveller back in the camp seemed pleased with Avitus's decision; a mixture of youthful impatience and a desire to see the traveller gone ensured this. He not only wanted revenge, but he believed that his outburst would be forgotten once the traveller had been left behind. Most of the others, though, were not pleased. They had a better idea of what a change in Avitus's mind meant, and they did not like the prospect of losing their money.

Avitus said they would turn over the traveller to the town's authorities without any delay. Night was moving in and so their time was short. He urged his troop to make their way down the rest of the pass as quickly as they could, even taking the steep short cut that veered off the main road Florence had taken several weeks earlier. Before the darkness of the oncoming night had truly sunk in, the troop arrived at a stumpy stone bridge that spanned a narrow stream. It was situated in the light mist of the edge of the city and greeted any traveller who had taken the short cut. Its rough grey stones contrasted with the red brown brick wall that surrounded the city and told a story of its age. On the other side of the bridge stood a two story high gatehouse manned by two figures. They watched the rounded light of the troop's torches emerge from the darkness of the pass and waited patiently until they thought the unknown and unexpected visitors had come close enough.

"Who goes there?" called out one of the tower guards.

No one in the troop replied. They just continued to come closer. The guard called out his demand again and extended his bow. This time, after stepping forwards in front of the rest of the group, Avitus responded.

"We've come to see the town Protector."

"At this time?" the guard called down. "Curfew has passed. Come back tomorrow, it's too late."

"I think your leader might be able to give us some time, once he knows who we've brought with us."

As he finished, Avitus signalled with a half wave, and the two bull necked men brought their prisoner forwards. While one of the strongmen continued to hold the arms of the traveller, the other held one of the torches up to the captive man's face. Though the light mist softened the features of the traveller, the guards recognised him.

"Perhaps it would be best for you to see Mr Stone," stated the guard. "John, open the door."

\*\*\*

Avitus entered the city with the boy, leaving the rest of the troop behind to look after the prisoner. The senses of both men were dimmed by the thick mist that greeted them on the other side of the wall. They never forgot the fact of the mist, but its reality was always something to contend with for those returning to it after any length of time. Following the instructions of the guard, the two struggled along in the dark empty streets to get to the unassuming house of the elderly Mr Stone.

"Could this be it?" asked the boy.

"Keep your voice down. Who knows what rules they have here," whispered Avitus. "This is the address the guard gave us, there's only one way to find out."

Avitus snapped the brass handle of the knocker against the door several times. The two were unsure if they were at the correct address; the place was a near identical copy of almost all the other terrace houses found in Ramskirk. No answer came from within. Avitus started to have second thoughts. He was not sure that a man who lived in such equality with his subjects would have the funds to pay the bounty, let alone hand it over.

"Maybe we should go on to the next town."

"I think someone is coming," said the boy in a shrill whisper.

The door was flung open revealing a woman holding a lamp at the height of her shoulder. She said nothing. As the pair on the doorstep were unsure of the situation, silence stood between the group for some time. Eventually, Avitus decided it was time for him to take control.

"We've come to see Mr Stone. Is he in?"

"Wait," was the curt reply from the woman. She promptly slammed the door.

"What do we do now?" said the boy stupidly, leaving Avitus to wish he had left him with the others.

"Make yourself useful. We may need to be efficient with our use of speech here. Go into the square over there. See if you can find a poster of our man and bring it back here."

The boy seemed pleased to have something to do and rushed off. Avitus hoped that the woman would return before the boy, but to his displeasure he was made to wait much longer than he expected. The boy was back long before the woman reappeared. When the woman finally reopened the door, she gave Avitus the briefest of glances before disappearing into a gloom that was only held back by the meagre light of her lamp.

"Ladies first," said Avitus pushing the boy ahead of himself.

The woman had made her way to the back room of the house, passing a narrow whitewashed staircase. The two men followed and found themselves in the presence of the white haired Mr Stone, who was seated behind an unvarnished wooden desk. Apart from Stone's desk and chair there was no other furniture in the room. Nevertheless, the room seemed crowded despite there being only four people present.

Stone was reading a book when Avitus and the boy entered; he did so by the light of a stubby candle clutched in his left hand. He continued to read despite the entrance of his visitors. Avitus was displeased, wishing that the man would forgo this unnecessary pretence so they could get down to work.

"Yes," said Stone without looking up from his book.

Losing his patience a little, Avitus grabbed the poster boy had retrieved from the square and slapped it down over the text Stone was pretending to read. The Protector looked up for the first time, but -- keeping his composure -- he did so slowly.

"You have this man?" said Stone almost indifferently.

"We do," said Avitus through quickened breath.

Stone placed his candle in its holder. He brought his elbows on to the desk before carefully placing the fingertips of one his hands against those of the other. He looked over to the woman with the lamp and gave an almost imperceptible nod. The woman exited, closing the door behind her. The three men were left in the light of a single candle.

"You can speak freely if you wish," said Stone, annoying Avitus further. As if he needed permission to speak.

"The issue is quite simple," replied Avitus, holding his scorn behind a smile. "We have this man and wish to collect the bounty."

"Very good. All you have to do is bring the man here. Once we have ascertained he is the right man and seen to it that..."

"I assure you, he is the right man. One glance is enough to see this is true. If you would just come and have a look, you'll be able to this for yourself."

"I'm afraid that will not happen. First, as you can see, I'm old. I don't intend to walk to the perimeter of our city on some unnecessary journey when young men like yourselves can just bring the prisoner here. Second, I don't have the time."

"But," replied Avitus while taking a few steps closer to the Protector's desk, "you must know that he might not make it to this house."

"Then justice will be done, and you should be glad to have played your part."

Avitus adjusted his shoulders to help him maintain his calm.

"Perhaps it would be best for my little troop to seek another town. We will have to bid you farewell Mr Stone. Thank you for your time."

"Oh no, I do not think so," replied Stone. "Now I know there is a man who could be a notorious fugitive on the edge of our city, you must realise that I cannot just let him leave. This man must be taken or tried; whatever comes to pass will be determined by the sorcerer. If you want your bounty, you must bring him here yourself. If he can be delivered and we find he is the man we seek, then our city will gladly pay your bounty. If you decide not to attempt the delivery of the accused, you must turn him over to our guards."

Avitus was furious. How dare this little man upset his plans. He brought his clenched fist down on the table and let out an unintelligible exclamation. The door swung open and the woman stepped back into the room. Stone was unmoved. He returned to his book after carefully placing the poster to one side.

"There you have it," said Stone without raising his head. "You may make your choice. Good day."

Avitus turned around with the intention to rush back to his troop. The face of the boy made him stop. The boy's gaze was fixed on the corridor, his face crestfallen. Behind the woman were a number of heavily armed guards.

\*\*\*

Florence was still sitting near the fire she had built the night before. The same forest was around her. She had managed to walk all the way over to Besketh in the day, but as she closed in on the grey mass of the town she slowed her pace before coming to a stop. She started walking in the opposite direction without letting a single thought form in her mind. By the time the evening blue sky set in, broken only by a few high pink clouds, she realised she had returned to where she had started in the morning. She crossed the dunes and soon found the pile of ash that marked her point of rest from the night before. She automatically collected more wood, lit another fire and settled down. She drank a little water from her emergency supply, refilled from a stream during the day, and tried to hide her hunger from herself.

She sat for some time in front of the light and welcome heat of the fire before laying down on the sandy soil of the forest. She did not care about her cloak getting covered in dirt or about the thick beach grass that needled through the coarse fabric. She tried to tell herself that she did not care about anything at all. Time passed and she blankly stared at the stars shining brightly between the pine needles above her.

"I know I have to get to Sewan," she said to no one, "but how? He's so far away. I only just made it to that village, how can I travel all the way back."

Florence turned onto her side to face the fire. As the short flames licked the blackened wood, she reluctantly recalled the moments in which she had last seen the traveller. She felt guilty for having let him fall so easily into the hands of his captors. She wished she could have done more to help him escape, to save him, to return him to Sewan instead of a few of his words. A grain of hope posited the idea that it was not too late. The rest of her mind knew she could do nothing to help him; she had no idea where the traveller had been taken. Even if she did, what could she do against a gang of men with guns?

\*\*\*

Avitus was approaching the town gate. The mask he usually wore to hide his true feelings had been cast off revealing his naked disgust. The boy trailed behind, avoiding him, staying close to the four soldiers that had been sent to ensure that the traveller was brought into the town no matter what Avitus decided.

As the gatehouse emerged in front Avitus from the thick mist, he found his troop and the prisoner on the inside of the already closed city gate.

"They will not pay," he announced as soon as he got close to the group. "They will not pay. But I won't gave up so easily. Their Guards are coming. Raise your weapons!"

The group, so used to following Avitus's orders, responded at once and got into line. This left the traveller free for the first time since his capture. He backed up to the gate. He could not run; the only way to go was further into the mist of the town.

Five figures appeared in the mist. Though their faces were not visible, their forms were clearly lit by their torches.

"Fire," screamed Avitus.

On hearing this cry, one of the approaching figures started to run, but it was too late. In another moment, the form crumpled to the ground with two others. The two men that still stood rushed forwards without realising what had happened to the men around them. Their bravery was rewarded with another round from the troop's guns.

From the gatehouse above him, the traveller heard a muted cry as the approaching guards fell dead before Avitus. An arrow appeared in the back of Fredrick's skull and he sank limply to the floor. Avitus turned, coolly removing a pistol from inside his cloak and shot the archer before he got off another arrow.

"We must go through the town," called the remaining bull necked man.

"We cannot," said Avitus.

"We don't have a choice," said one of the other men. "There is no other way."

Avitus looked back towards the gate and saw the traveller standing in front of a lowered portcullis.

"They dropped the thing just after we got inside," said the bull neck. "They also bolted the door to the inside of the gatehouse form the inside. We've got enough gunpowder for a few shots, but not to get through that door. If we stay here, we'll soon run out of ammo or gunpowder, then die. We need another way out."

Avitus struck himself in the head with his fist hard. He took a moment to settle himself.

"We'll split up," he said. "Sandson, you come with me and the prisoner. You two, meet us in the Crow inn outside Wellbridge. If you make it, you'll still be paid."

The traveller thought the other two looked relieved to be released of their fate and they disappeared into the mist.

Sandson, the remaining strongman, and Avitus approached the traveller.

"Do you really mean to pay them?" said Sandson as he took hold of the traveller's arm.

"No, but I don't think we'll see them in Wellbridge either."

"You'll never get me through the city," said the traveller.

Avitus turned pale and regarded the traveller coldly.

"You'll go where you're taken. I've had enough of people telling me what I can and cannot do today."

Together, the two men together were much stronger than the traveller. If they were going to force him to travel through the mist, he wanted to get to the other side of the city as quickly as he could. He did not to resist. Avitus and Sandson each took one of the traveller's arms and started to walk him into the town. After his first few steps, the traveller had to take a long stride to step over the dead body of the boy.

"I'm sure we'll make it," said Sandson. "We'll even get a bigger share of the cash."

Avitus did not respond, he just quickened his pace. By the light of the torch in Sandson's hand, the three men stumbled through the thick mist. They had no idea which direction to take to reach the other side of Ramskirk, so they just carried on down the long narrow road of terrace houses they found themselves on. Not a word passed between the men for some time. For a long while, the only noise they knew was the light crackle of the torch and the flop of their leather shoes on the cobbles beneath their feet.

"Stop," whispered Avitus.

The traveller felt the hands of the two men tighten around his arms. He listened attentively to discern why the three had paused in the middle of the town. He heard the faint sound of steps.

"Move," commanded Avitus under his breath.

The three headed off once more, but it was clear that their pursuers were gaining on them. Soon the light patter behind them became a discernible clatter of feet and weapons. Avitus looked back, but there was still nothing to be seen. His eyes scanned frantically around for a place to hide, but the walls of houses seemed to go on forever. Avitus moved his little band over to one of the walls of houses. He tried a number of doors as they continued on along the cobbles, but to no avail. The idea of breaking through a window crossed his mind. He immediately rejected the idea; it would be obvious where they had gone and the noise would alert the guards behind them. They just rushed on.

Just as the noise of their pursuers was becoming a deafening roar in the ears of the three runners, it stopped. They stopped to. An echo of the sound filled the alley of houses for a moment, then dissipated leaving the street in absolute silence. The trio turned to see a glow in the mist behind them. It was clear the pursuers had seen their own torch and halted without an order.

"We know you're there," said a voice from one of the glowing orbs of light. "Listen, if you hand over the fugitive, we'll let you go. The next gate is still some way ahead and it's heavily guarded. You only have one option. Give up the man and you might make it out of Ramskirk alive."

'Not after you find out what we did to your fellow guards' thought Avitus. He tightened his grip on the traveller's arm. At the same time, Sandson loosened his grasp and then let his hand fell away.

"Sorry boss," grumbled Sandson, "I ain't goner die here. If you make it, keep my share."

Before Avitus could say a word, Sandson threw his torch towards his leader, preventing him from reaching for his weapon. By the time Avitus had caught the torch, Sandson was deep into the mist. Avitus was now alone with the traveller. He was not strong enough to keep the traveller prisoner by himself. He let him go.

"Get out of here," whispered Avitus. "If you run, there's a dog's chance you might get away."

The traveller was perplexed and looked hard into the cold eyes of Avitus.

"And," continued Avitus with a smile, "if you escape, I have the chance to catch you again."

The traveller did not wait a second further, he ran.

"Hello there," called out Avitus. "I'm afraid I'm alone. My men deserted me when I told them there would be no money. Indeed, I think they might have taken their frustration out on a few of your fellow guards. But I mean no harm, I am your Protector's humble servant."

Avitus walked on with a smile and his head held high towards the flickering glow of Ramskirk's guards.

\*\*\*

The traveller ran as fast as he could along the line of mist ridden houses. The faint glow of Avitus's torch was now lost in the darkness far behind. He heard no footsteps, but his fear grew as he was now alone. He had no idea where he was headed, no idea how to escape. His only guide was the changing sound of the slap of his pounding footsteps on the cobbles as he came closer to the terrace houses either side of him.

Suddenly, he knew it was there. It was over. He continued to run, he even tried to speed up, but his pounding heart and quickened breath were at their limit. He was sure it knew him and would not let him be. He wished he could escape just one more time, but the reality of his situation descended. He felt arms gently wrap around his torso despite his continued pace. The dark world around him started to fade from his senses. In another moment, he was no longer running, he was no longer in the town.

# Chapter Seventeen

Florence felt like she had been walking along the pass for weeks. She had finally made her way past Besketh, though it had taken her another day to do it. Not that she had repeated her wasteful walk up and down the beach. Instead, she had spent the previous day hunting. Hunger had torn at her and after finding no berries or familiar plants to eat, she decided to search for something else. As it was impossible to return to Besketh or the village for food, she went further into the forest until she found a grove that was infested with rabbits. Florence was reticent about killing the animals as she had never done it before. However, she knew she had to act while she still had the strength and so hunger won the day. She chased the little beasts for some time without success. Finally, a chance presented itself. She managed to bring a large stone down upon one of the rabbit's small skulls, one of many methods she had tried. She found the skinning of the animal easier than she had anticipated and proceeded to overcook the meat, just to make sure. Despite her expectations, the meal turned out to be one of the best she had ever tasted. Her energy levels replenished, she decided to try and capture a few more rabbits. Her inexperienced approach to hunting was less than perfect, but as night started to fall she had nevertheless collected a few more meals for the journey ahead.

She set off early in the morning the next day. Darkness descended before she reached the other side of the mountain pass. As she had no torch, she had to slow her pace to a crawl, fearful she would trip on stones hidden by the night. At times, she wished she could climb to the top of the mountain above her, to see how much of the road lay ahead, but the pass was cut deep into the rock of the mountain. Perhaps a stream had once flown through a weakness in the rock and worn it away over many thousands of years until it was wide enough for man to place the level road she walked on at its base. All Florence knew was that the mountain rose far above her, leaving only a letter box view of the stars above.

She continued to shuffle along, occasionally taking a bite on her now less than appetizing rabbit, until she heard a faint rattling noise behind her. Florence easily identified the sound of a coach after travelling on so many. The noise did not unnerve her at first. She was curious to know who would be travelling on the road in the middle of the night. However, as the noise became louder her growing fear told her it would be best not to find out. She let her hands run along the stone at the side of the path as she walked on. She hoped they would find a place to hide, but the rough flat surface presented nothing before the light of the coach was upon her.

No words passed between Florence and the three figures that emerged from the coach. One just walked forwards and took her bag before stowing it away on the roof. Florence was too exhausted to muster up any resistance against them. In no time at all, she found herself sitting in the silence of the cabin as the coach continued to rattle down the pass.

Florence was in two minds over her new situation. On the one hand she no longer had to brave the elements or walk any further along the seemingly endless pass. On the other, she was in a coach with a number of serious looking grey clad figures who had not even given her the opportunity to choose if she wanted to join them in the relative comfort of their coach. They had not even asked her where she was going.

As Florence pondered over the latter point, a grain of panic grew within her. Exhaustion dominated her mind, but slowly she realised she did not know what sort of position she was in; perhaps she was in danger. The grain of panic rooted and spread around her body until it started to overcome her heavy tiredness. She looked into the eyes of the man sitting opposite her, the first communication she had had with anyone since talking to the traveller. She opened her mouth to ask where they were going. His stony face, illuminated by the dim blue light of the coach's side lamps outside, killed her nerve and her voice died in her throat. She would not attempt to ask any more questions. She laid back in her seat and closed her eyes. She hoped she could fall asleep and forget where she was, but panic had already taken over. She did not know who these people were, where she was being taken and, as terrible thoughts fought for consciousness at the back of her mind, perhaps she did not want to know.

\*\*\*

Florence woke up. She was still in the coach, but the other seats were empty. Her first attempt to get up was stifled by the stiffness in her back and legs. Her aching body suggested they had travelled some distance even though Florence felt she had only just fallen asleep. Weak grey light illuminated the cabin telling Florence that outside it was daytime in a mist ridden town.

She looked out of the coach window to see the familiar red brick of a Ramskirk terrace. Faint voices came from an unidentifiable somewhere. She turned her attention to the other side of the coach. In the mist outside the other window, she observed several shifting shapes conducting a conversation. The conference did not continue long before a shape transformed into one the three men she had travelled with the night before. Florence sat back just before he reached the coach.

"We'll stay here tonight," he said in a monotone voice and without even looking to see if Florence was awake.

The three men then left without any further communication with Florence. She waited for several minutes, but no one else came. Time seemed to stand still in the coach. There was nothing to see out the windows now but a wall and an expanse of grey. Eventually, Florence's patience crumbled. As her feet touched the ground, Florence wondered if the men had just meant to bring her to Ramskirk in their own quiet way. Hope raised its head and she went to the rear of the vehicle to retrieve her bag. Perhaps she could just stroll out of Ramskirk without anyone noticing.

Her hope melted away as she found a guard waiting for her at the back of the coach. He already had her bag in his hands. He indicated to his right, away from the coach. Florence started to walk, capitulating to the other's will now that her last ounce of hope had been lost.

The two walked in silence along the cobbles until they reached one of the many houses. Florence wondered how the people of Ramskirk knew which building was their own as they all seemed much the same to her. The guard returned Florence's bag to her before opening his door. She stood on the spot looking meekly at the man until he directed her to go in.

A thin, dark passageway with plain white walls greeted Florence inside. The only thing that approached decoration in the space was a narrow thin carpet which climbed up the staircase. Florence walked down the hall without taking much notice of what was around her until the hand of the guard fell upon her shoulder. She stopped still. The hand was lifted and the guard disappeared into the front room, closing the door behind him. Muted voices occasionally made their way into the hall. Florence ignored what they said.

The man re-emerged from the front-room and indicated that Florence should go upstairs by taking her bag away from her and ascending to the first floor. Florence followed him and found her bag already on the floor of a room at the back of the house that would be her own for the night. The guard did not pay any attention to her as she entered. He just walked straight passed her and then left the house without even another word to whoever was downstairs.

The room was Spartan, its only furniture a poorly constructed cupboard and a narrow bed covered with an ugly brown blanket. Florence sat on the bed and found it was even harder than it looked; the only softness provided by the coarse blanket. The woman who had just been a voice to Florence downstairs appeared at the doorway. Florence looked into her eyes but did not get up. She was young with long dark brown hair which cascaded down from her head over the back of her plain dress. Slowly, the woman shut the door, keeping her fearful wide eyes fixed on Florence until the gap was closed. A gentle click of the lock followed leaving Florence imprisoned and alone.

\*\*\*

The day became a half-dream. Florence lay on the bed and fell in and out of sleep. She could have taken something out of her bag to provide some distraction, but she just lay sprawled out on top of the blanket waiting for time to pass. At an unknown hour, the woman returned to leave some food before once again locking the door. After one of many of her short slumbers, Florence woke to find the light of the day had faded away. She still did not get up.

As night set in, Florence heard the woman retire to her room. Soon afterwards, someone came through the front door. Florence wondered if it was someone coming to collect her, but their footsteps passed her by. More time passed before Florence was woken from another dreamless sleep by the hard grunt of a loud snore. Florence was left wide awake. For the first time in hours, she led her feet to the floor. The window admitted no light and Florence had to fumble her way across the room to find the door. Though she knew it was locked, Florence tried the handle. It was to no avail.

She searched the floor with her hands until she came across her bag. She rummaged inside her watch repairing kit to retrieve a thin screwdriver and as large a polishing cloth as she could find. She pushed the expanded cloth under the half-inch gap at the bottom of the door. With great care, she pushed the small screwdriver into the lock. No sooner had she made contact with the key than it fell to the waiting cloth beneath. Due to the silence of the house, the clatter that followed sounded out like thunder. Florence paused a moment to see if her actions had roused her sleeping hosts, but the snoring continued. Proudly, she pulled the cloth back under the gap.

Florence returned to her bag. She had decided not take it with her. Despite its connection to her father, it would slow her down. She decided to take a couple of items just in case she had to bribe a guard if she was caught. She removed one of the cloth bags and slipped her fingertips inside. A forgotten city rose up before her mind's eye. This one would do. She stowed the case away inside her cloak and made to leave.

\*\*\*

The man did not seem at all surprised to hear of Florence's attempted escape. If anything, he seemed almost pleased. It turned out the guard Florence had heard walking up to his bed was almost always awake due to the persistent snoring of his wife. As Florence had opened the door, she had been greeted by the strike of a match and the lighting of a candle. The guard had acted as if he had been through the routine before. Without a moment's hesitation, he had brought Florence straight to the house where the three travelling men were spending the night. He had woken one of their number by knocking on the front door. It was plain that the man had not been pleased to be roused from his sleep, but his mood seemed to change when he heard of Florence's thwarted flight.

"Take her to the coach. Make sure she does not escape."

The man followed the order of Florence's captor as if he were the captain of the guard. This worried Florence. She had no real idea as to whom the three mysterious men were, but as they were moving her on from the town she assumed they did not come from Ramskirk. Nevertheless, the local guards seemed to follow their every whim. This not only suggested that the men were important, but that Florence was in deep trouble.

Florence was seated in the coach long enough for the chill of the morning to make her pine for the hard wooden bed she had left behind. In a way though, she was lucky as she did not have to wait too long for the pale grey light of the morning to overcome the dull flicker of the guard's torch. The emergence of morning soon brought the three men back to their coach. Now that Florence was sure she was in a perilous situation, she would drop all pretence of being a good grey. As soon as the men reached the coach, she started asking questions.

"Who are you? Why did you pick me up from the road? Where are you taking me?"

At first, the men were slightly taken aback, but they soon recovered their composure. They settled themselves and proceeded not to respond to any of Florence's questions. Instead, after listening attentively, the man who had sat himself next to Florence took a bottle of clear liquid from a compartment beneath his seat and tipped a small quantity of its contents into a cloth. He then quickly placed the cloth over Florence's mouth with one hand while holding the back of her head with the other. Taken by surprise, Florence breathed in deeply. Before even a murmur of protest could escape her lips, she lost consciousness.

# Chapter Eighteen

Florence found herself lying on a wooden board in a humid stone cell. Groggily, she pushed her torso up with the help of her arms and slipped her aching legs over the edge of the board. She rubbed her face causing shards of memories to fly into her mind. She saw the three men of the coach, images of towns she did not know and whispered voices. She also saw the spirit soaked cloth, repeatedly reapplied to her face just before any memory started sharpen into something clear.

She struggled to her feet. For a moment, it seemed as if her legs had forgotten how to walk. With effort she made them remember. Looking back at her bench, she found it was covered in a number of half-finished carvings including names, depictions of animals and detailed patterns. After running her fingers across a number of the names, she turned her attention to the rest of the room. It consisted of four walls of damp blue grey stone sporadically covered in moss. The only light came from a small high barred opening above a solid looking and handless door.

Florence slowly paced around the room. After getting the feeling back in her body, she attempted to look out the opening above the door. She tried to grasp the bars and pull herself up, but they were coated in a layer of slimy algae and were too slippery to grasp. She fell to the ground twice before giving up. On her final attempt, she did manage to catch a glimpse of the world outside: it consisted of the usual grey white mass.

An hour or two passed by and still no one came to her door. She got up off the hard bed once more and started to pace the edge of the room, gently sweeping her fingertips across the stones as she went. She noted the differences between the stones, some dry, some so damp they were even covered with moss. More time passed and she returned to the bench. Unthinkingly, she started to trace the lines of the carved names of past prisoners in the wood with her fingernails.

As the light started to fade, she attempted her own carving in the soft, damp wood. She found a space all of her own at the edge of the bench and got as far as the 'o' in her name before the door was flung open. Two guards were revealed. Without a word to Florence, they approached, took an arm of hers each and practically dragged her to the exit.

To her surprise, the cell had not been within a building at all. It sat at the bottom of a slope topped by an unfamiliar town wall constructed of the same blue stone as the cell. The wall and slope soon faded into the mist as the guards pulled Florence forwards.

She was taken across an open green. A long, two story stone building fronted by a protruding Romanesque stone porch emerged from the mist. The two guards led Florence under the porch and stopped in front of the door it concealed from the elements. One of the guards, using the base of his torch, knocked on a dented metal plate fastened to the door. As the guards waited for a response, Florence looked around and noticed the porch contained a number of empty stone alcoves; pick-marks were deeply notched into their bases.

As soon as another guard opened up the entrance, Florence was pushed forwards by one of the guards behind her. She did not want to find out what would happen to her if she resisted, and so she quickly moved over the threshold. The hall she encountered inside was well lit, floored with yellow stone slabs and backed by a large open fireplace. The only furniture in the hall consisted of one dark wooden table and chair, dwarfed by their relative size to the expanse of the space within which they resided. Upon the chair sat an elderly man dressed in a charcoal coloured cloak.

"Come forwards," said the man.

Florence made her way across the yellow slabs. She was nervous, but did not want to show it. Little by little she increased the pace and confidence of her step. That was until she heard the jangle of the weapons of the guards behind her. Her will started to buckle. It did not matter, she was brought to an abrupt halt by the words of the old man.

"Stop," he called. He paused a moment and looked down to read from a large leather bound book that was open on the table. After silently mouthing a number of words to himself, he returned his gaze to Florence.

"How do you plead?" asked the man.

"Sorry?" replied Florence.

"The court repeats, how do you plead?"

"I'm sorry," said Florence confused. "I don't understand what's going on. I don't even know where I am. I was just walking through a pass on my way to..."

"Enough!" cried the man, his voice reverberating through the empty cavern of the hall. He took a moment to let himself calm down and continued in a more gentle tone "You find yourself in front of a body a good citizen would have no reason to know of, so perhaps your ignorance is possible. As you well know, you were brought here by three Ministers. They have passed you over to this court for trial. They believe you were in breach of the sorcerer's ordinances by being outside of a city's jurisdiction without justification. They provided me with the information that this took place between Wellbridge and Besketh. So, I repeat, how do you plead? Are you guilty or innocent of the charge?"

"I am innocent," replied Florence in haste. She regretted the statement immediately; she still did not fully understand the charge. The judge grumbled to himself and made a mark in his book. He adjusted himself before returning the gaze of his sunken green eyes to the accused.

"What were you doing in the pass between Ramskirk and Besketh?"

"I was walking back to Ramskirk."

"And where had you been before you left for your destination?"

"I had been to Besketh to practice my craft."

"Yes, indeed. I have a letter here from the office of the Protector of Besketh, a Mr Jesson. He tells me that you had finished practising your craft, as you call it, some days before you were found in the pass. What did you do in the time intervening?"

"I..." Florence's mind floundered. She was still groggy and tired from her ordeals. She had to think quickly. It made no sense to tell this little old man the truth as she knew this would lead her into trouble.

"I had walked along the coast," she said. "I was in the woods for a few days."

"Hmm," remarked the judge making another note in the book. "A little odd for a young lady to take an unplanned trip into the middle of the forest on her own at this time of year. No matter, perhaps we should move on to another point. Why did you decide not to help the Ministers in their inquiries?"

"I'm sorry, your honour, but I don't know what you mean. All I remember these Ministers doing is detaining me and..."

"Ah," interrupted the judge, "and why did they seek recourse to the necessity of restraint? I have been informed that you attempted to escape while you were under investigation?"

"What investigation? They did not ask a single question of me."

"Did you or did you not attempt to escape?"

"I attempted to continue on my journey, I'm not sure I would call that an attempt to escape. None of those men told that I was the subject of any inquiry, the only thing they said to me was that we would be leaving Ramskirk."

"So you admit to knowing that you were in the ministers' care. Hmm, not too good, not too good." The old man let his voice fade away until there was silence in the hall. He made another note in his book.

"Now," continued the judge, "we move on to the final question. What were you doing in the area of Ramskirk and Besketh in the first place? I am assured by the authorities of each that you originate from neither. Unauthorised travel, as I am sure you know, is a serious breach of the standard of ordinances, as defined by the Treaty of Wellbridge. So what were you doing so far from home?"

"I'm a watchmaker's apprentice. I've been on my apprenticeship travels for some time. I've passed through a number of master watchmaker's workshops over the past few months."

"And yet you ended up in Besketh, which has no watchmaker at all. A little odd don't you think?"

The judge looked down into his book, ran his fingers along the brief notes he had made during the short interview and pursed his lips. Suddenly, he rose from his seat.

"The court has reached its decision. On behalf of the Protectors and citizens of the cities who have signed the Treaty of Wellbridge, this court finds that the defendant does not have sufficient evidence against her to order the removal of the protections of the sorcerer from her person. However, questions remain over the conduct of the defendant, which she has been unable to sufficiently clarify in the judgement of this court. Therefore, the court determines that the defendant must prove her asserted innocence before the eyes of the sorcerer himself. She will now be taken from this place to the Common, where she must remain for the period of one night. If the defendant is found to have been judged innocent by the sorcerer by first light tomorrow morning, her freedom will be returned."

As soon as the judge finished speaking, the two guards standing behind Florence moved forwards to take hold of her arms. Without letting her turn, they marched her back towards the exit. The old man looked at her with a steady gaze as she was taken away. When she reached the door, he closed his book. His job was done.

Florence said nothing as she was led back over the green away from the court. The way was lit by a third guard until they came to the small cell where Florence had woken many hours before. He placed his torch in a holder on the outside wall of the cell before picking up a chain from the ground. Clanking as it snaked across the grass, the chain was brought over to Florence.

"Don't struggle," said the guard as he opened the fetter at the chain's end.

For a second, Florence tried her strength against the two guards that were holding her. Her effort had almost no effect on them at all. She could not escape, she was too weak. As resistance was pointless she just stood stock still.

The guard with the chain knelt down in front of Florence. With a wrench like tool he fastened the two pieces of iron which formed the fetter around

Florence's left ankle. As he let go of the bond, it fell on Florence's foot with a surprising amount of force. The guard, still kneeling, tried the bolt he had fastened and moved the fetter around, causing Florence some pain in the process. Pleased with his work, he looked up to the other two guards and gave a curt nod. As the kneeling guard got up, the other two released their grip and disappeared into the mist. After collecting his torch, the remaining guard returned to Florence. He came unnervingly close and hunched down until his face was almost touching to her own. He looked her straight in the eye for the briefest of moments, then quickly retreated into the mist.

As the faint orange glow grew smaller in the dark before her, Florence felt her composure melt away. When the darkness became complete, she plunged into a state of absolute terror. She was frozen to the spot; not a single clink of metal came from her chain; the rate of her breath trebled. With no images to disturb her mind's eye, no sound to distract her from the darkness around her, she could not help but recall only those things which flung her further down the spiral of fear.

Into her mind came the sight of the man crying out for his freedom in Ramskirk. The white mask of fear he had worn on his face as he stumbled through the streets was almost visible. She thought of the stories from Sewan, the missing, the lost that no one looked for. She had become one of these people. Only her father would care now that she was gone, and she had left him far behind.

Her fear mixed with the guilt of leaving him. He had been left alone and would never even know what had become of her. Her fear and then her guilt ebbed away as the image of her father emerged from the darkness before her. Her imagination had provided a trace of comfort. It did not last long. The image vanished as a familiar but different feeling started to creep through the layers of her skin. A fear she had felt before when she was alone in her room so many miles away. She knew now she would never get any message back to Sewan or his people. She would never be able to lie to her father about what she had done. The freedom of the traveller and the lives of the guards in the mist free village had been lost for nothing. She felt the heat of a silent body behind her in the dark. She did not call out as she knew what was there. She did not even flinch as it wrapped its arms around her.

# Part Three, Chapter One

In her exhausted state, it took Florence some time to realise she was not in the same little cell she had been in before her ridiculous court case. She could not say for sure how long she had been awake, or how she had ended up where she was. However, as she started to take in her surroundings, it became clear that the walls around her were not composed of moss covered bluish stones. Instead, it looked as if the room had been carved out of solid rock. The walls, the floor and the ceiling were the composed of the same solid hand chiselled stone; there was not a trace of mortar to be seen. Even the bench she lay on was just a solid stone mass that had not been removed from the grey black rock.

As the memory of standing on the Common dripped back into her thoughts, she lifted her torso and eased her aching arm down to her now free left ankle. It still hurt, but it did not hold her attention long as she noticed the front of her cloak was torn in several places. The tears were long, reaching across her body and over her upper arms. She inserted her right index finger into one of the folds created by the torn cloth. As she drew her finger from the hidden space, she found it to be covered by rusty brown dried blood, mixed with a few fresh red drops. As her wound became apparent to her conscious mind, so did the pain.

The pain transported her back again to the green. She remembered the feeling of the arms of the unseen creature slowly closing around her, its claw like fingers pressing through the cloak into her flesh. She remembered the clammy hard body behind her, its naked torso briefly making contact with her neck. But the embrace was not her final memory. She only had a glimpse, but she was sure she could recall a sense of incredible motion. It had been pitch black and she had seen nothing, but the momentary memory of her body moving through space at a great speed was real. Everything after that moment was darkness. She assumed she had passed out.

Florence eased herself up off the stone bench and moved towards the oak door that broke the monotony of the black grey stone of the rest of the room. The door was large, several feet higher than Florence herself. The proportions of the height of the room's ceiling, though, did not match the door and the two nearly met. There was no handle on the door, but there was a grate through which poured the only light illuminating her cell. Despite the scraping pain it caused her skin, Florence pressed herself against the door to look through the tiny squares of the metal grate. Her endeavour revealed another wall made of the same stone as the cell. It seemed that there was a corridor beyond the door. Further than that, Florence could discern nothing.

When Florence returned her attention to her cell, she noticed that there was a stone basin full of water at the far end of the bench. She cupped a handful of the liquid in her hands, but decided not to take a drink. Even in the shallow pool gathered in her hands, it was possible to see the cloudy brown colour of the slimy water. She let the water trickle free through her fingers.

"This one's awake," said a voice though the grate.

Florence froze. A high pitch mumble replied to the unseen speaker. A key was inserted into a keyhole invisible to Florence and followed by a short, heavy clunk. The door swung open to reveal two tall men in silhouette. They lurched into the room and revealed themselves to be identical. They both had close cropped black hair, greasy pale white skin and small dull eyes. They wore long grey cloaks that trailed along the ground despite their height. So much material had been left to be dragged along the ground, the cloaks had ripped in several places, leaving only loose coarse threads at their bases.

The two figures stopped in front of Florence and seemed to look through her. She opened her mouth to ask where was, but before a syllable escaped from her lips a voice intervened.

"You'll have your chance to speak in good time," said a shrill voice from the doorway. "Gentlemen, please escort the lady to the room down the hall."

Responding to the order like it was their own will, the two glassy eyed men practically picked Florence up and moved her into the corridor. With Florence's feet only touching the ground on occasion, the three pressed on down the mist filled corridor at a brisk pace. Door after door, identical to the one on Florence's cell, flashed by as they rushed down the smooth black grey stone of the passage. Gentle moans could be heard all the way down and occasionally a whispered voice escaped from a black grate. However, due to the uncertainty of her situation and the speed that she passed by, Florence could make out nothing of what the other prisoners said.

At the end of the passage, the three arrived at a door that looked much the same as all the others. The only difference here was the smell. The rest of the corridor had been filled with the odour of musty damp, but here the air carried the aroma of grilled meat. Florence's stomach grumbled and brought the reality of her aching hunger to her mind. The two lumbering giants beside her giggled.

"Always the same," they said to each other.

The man to Florence's left retrieved a circular mass of keys from his pocket. With an ease that demonstrated much practice, the man quickly found the right key from amongst the many others. As soon as Florence entered the room, it was plain that it was not the smell of a sumptuous banquet that was torturing her; it was something more sinister. The key-less giant picked Florence up as if she weighed no more than a loaf of bread and gently placed her down on a stone bench in the centre of the room. He then proceeded to lean across her and hold her hands down to the surface of the bench. The other twin took hold of a number of thick leather straps bolted to the bench's side and secured Florence to the cold stone.

The whole action seemed to take place so quickly that Florence did not have time to struggle for her physical freedom. Even though the straps were already fastened, she attempted to test their strength. Through her effort to move, Florence could feel that straps had been placed across her knees, her stomach and just below her shoulder line. Her head was still free. She lifted it to find that by resting her chin upon the highest strap, she could see through the open door into the mist ridden corridor.

The twins disappeared from sight behind Florence's head and started to busy themselves with something. "What are you going to do?" she whispered. The only response she received from the twins was further giggles. Frustrated, she shifted her body from side to side in an attempt to loosen the straps. It was pointless. The thick leather was more than a match for her.

One of the men suddenly reappeared at her right side, towering above her. A churning fear grew within Florence's gut as she looked directly into his smiling eyes. The man moved quickly, defying the expected dexterity of someone so large. He cut into the top of Florence's sleeve with a knife. After making the opening, he disappeared for a further second before returning with a pair of scissors. He widened the tear he had already made by pushing one of the blades of scissors into the hole. He continued to cut down the arm of the sleeve until he reached the strap just above Florence's writs. Florence watched, perplexed by the man's action, anxious about what the man intended to do next. To her surprise and relief, he just walked back to the space behind her head.

As Florence looked up from her now bared right arm, she noticed that a small figure was emerging from the mist of the corridor. Florence knew it must be the owner of the voice who had given the orders earlier on. She watched as the little figure metamorphosed from a dull shape, to a silhouette, to a small woman with a limp in her left leg. Despite the growing ache in her neck and jaw, Florence kept her chin tightly pressed to the strap until she could clearly see the woman's tight curly brown hair and sharply pointed face. When their eyes finally met, the woman gave Florence a tight lipped smile and a nod. After dropping her head to the table, Florence heard the door of the room being shut. The woman hoved into Florence's view of the stone ceiling and introduced herself, maintaining her unprepossessing smile.

"I'm sure you have many questions," she said with a small shrill and quavering voice, "but we have a few we would like to ask first. Oh, I have not introduced myself, how rude. I'm Mrs Finch. Good, let us proceed."

Like the men before her, Finch vanished into the invisible space behind Florence. A few hushed grumbles and shrill whispers followed before the woman reappeared with a brown clipboard and pencil.

"What's your name?"

"Florence Watchmaker."

"Good," said the woman noting it down. "Where are you from? What town?"

"I'm from..." started Florence, hesitating only a moment before emitting a pain ridden scream. A scream that flowed over the sound of sizzling.

"What are you doing?" cried Florence with a cracked and croaking voice. She looked up to find the laughing eyes of one of the giants who had just pressed a thin, white hot length of metal against the bared flesh of her arm. The reason for the cooked meat smell that permeated the room and the men's odd giggles became clear. Florence gagged as the urge to vomit overtook her system, but her empty stomach provided nothing.

"I'll ask you again," continued Finch as if all was normal. "What town are you from?"

"What's this all about?" muttered Florence looking into the calm eyes of Finch. Finch nodded to her side and Florence watched as the still glowing metal bar was lowered towards her still burning skin once more.

"No!" she screamed. "Pendon. I'm from Pendon. I've nothing to hide."

"Very good," said Finch making another note. "And why do you think you're here?"

Florence looked blankly into the woman's face. Hot tears welled up in her eyes and flowed freely down her cheeks. The metal bar was brought down to her flesh once more, burning a line parallel to the one she had already received. Florence's body tried to scream again but only managed a gulping noise. The other giant appeared on Florence's left side with his knife and scissors. He held the knife in front of Florence's eyes until she regained her senses. For a moment, she had lost consciousness of everything except the pain. But the twin eventually caught her attention and she followed the knife as it was brought down to the top of her left sleeve.

"Wait!" she cried. "Wait..."

She started to tell her story from the beginning. She talked about her life in

Pendon when the mist arrived, her meeting in Hesik, her journey to Wellbridge and beyond to the mist free town. She talked about Sewan, the others she knew and the work of the traveller. Every word felt like it was hacking out a deeper hole within her, but once she started she could not stop their flow.

\*\*\*

"How fortunate for you to be from Pendon," said Finch. "His Excellency will see you in the course of time."

The two giants removed the straps from Florence's body. She was exhausted and felt like the mist that permeated all those towns had finally entered her mind, clouding her very thoughts. In shock from what had happened to her, she did not hear Finch's words. Indeed, she hardly even noticed as the two men gently picked her up off the stone stab and carried her back into the monochrome world of the corridor. The twins paused just outside the torture room. Finch joined them before calling out into the opaque air: "You can bring him in now."

Out of the mist emerged two bull necked men pulling along a man in a tattered red cloak. Florence, half-aware of her surroundings, looked up and watched how the figure in the middle was letting his feet drag behind him, creating a grating noise as his heavy toe capped boots skipped and scraped along the smooth stone floor. He possessed a mass of long black hair, which rose like a stormy sea over his head and flowed down the front of his face, obscuring everything except a single dancing eye. It came to rest on Florence and brought her out of her trance. Thinking of what she had just done, how she had betrayed Sewan and the traveller, she could not face the staring eye and jarred her head away.

"Return her to her cell, gentlemen," said Finch.

The two giants walked Florence back to her cell slowly. Only one of them had a hold of her, the other walked just behind to leave her injured right arm free. They had not got far down the tunnel before they heard screams from the room they had just left behind. The screams continued to come, echoing down the passage as they trundled along. The hidden prisoners in the cells around them mimicked the man's wails; a cacophony of noise filled the corridor. Time did not pass for Florence. All existence became reduced to the monochrome tunnel, the pain in her arm and the screams that crashed down from every direction of the grey black walls around her. Eventually, one of the guards broke the spell.

"Seems like there's another non-talker."

Florence was returned to her cell. As soon as the guards had left, she ran over to the murky brown pool in the stone basin to plunge her burning arm into the cool water. The water could have been many times more disgusting and she still would have done the same; all she could think of was to dull the pain. As the shock of her situation had dissipated, the pain had started to grow. Though she had received the hot metal to her flesh some time before, the pulsating, tingling burning seemed to be more intense now than ever. She fell to her knees beside the basin and let her arm sink down slowly, soothingly to the bottom of the slimy water.

For the first time since she received the branding, she found she could really think. The thoughts that came were almost as painful as the damage to her arm. How could she have given in so easily. She did not know if she had given her captors any important information. If they used the branding torture on everyone, and especially if they used other methods if that did not suffice, then the masters of the dungeon probably knew much more than she did. This consolation did not seem to matter. She had still betrayed the people who had trusted her.

The cell door half opened and a plate of food was pushed through the gap. Florence turned to see the boy who had deposited the plate. He could have been no more than twelve. He regarded Florence with an absent expression before leaving and locking her cell. Florence quickly retrieved the steaming bowl of something close to porridge and returned to the basin to dip her arm into the cool water once more.

# Chapter Two

From the amount of meals the boy had delivered, Florence guessed that at least three days had passed. In the time since she had been returned to her cell, sleep had come at irregular intervals and never seemed to last long enough to revive her exhausted body. Her arm now carried two purpling lines, scattered with blisters of varying size. Sometimes, the pain was still intense, especially when she discovered she had burst the skin of another blister while sleeping, but things had improved. The first time she woke up after receiving the branding had been the worst. She had found the fabric of her right sleeve stuck to open wounds along her arm. After slowly peeling the material away from her skin, she had removed the sleeve from her cloak. Three days later, the tatted cloth still lay on the floor.

A clunk of the lock and a burst of light denoted the entry of someone into her cell. Florence opened her eyes expecting to see the boy, but instead discerned two guards. They swiftly moved over to her bench and grabbed her arms, not taking any notice of her wounds. She suppressed a cry and looked with fury at the man who had seized her injured right arm. He gave a wry smile, leading Florence turn away from his empty grey eyes so she could suppress her anger and pain. His expression had told her he would be happy to make her suffer.

The guards did not wait a moment to see if Florence would resist or not. They just dragged her out of her cell and along the corridor to a square alcove with an open ceiling. Unlike the rest of the passageway, the floor of the alcove was made of wooden planks. In the middle of its floor was a single beam topped by a manacle. The guard who had beamed at her pain yanked Florence forwards with her injured arm and shackled it to the beam. He took hold of her wrist and shook it until he was happy the manacle was secure. He then gave Florence another sickening smile before returning to the corridor.

The other guard retrieved a clipboard from a table beside the alcove and jammed it into a crack between a couple of the wooden boards. He walked to the side of the alcove, and along with his partner, started to heave down on a thick chain dangling from the ceiling. The platform started to rise.

Florence ascended through a shaft, which like her cell and the whole dungeon below her, had been carved out of the dark rock. The shaft ended abruptly, but the platform continued to rise up into a vast chamber, which was pervaded by low level light. Though she could now see the boards below her, there was little else to take in as the whole space was filled with dense grey mist. Florence knew the chamber had to be large due to the distant echoes created by the lift's chains, which occasionally scraped against the rock far above as the platform swung gently from side to side.

Florence continued to climb, but the light started to dim. It got darker and darker until suddenly the light disappeared altogether. The ascent continued for another minute or so until the platform came to a sudden halt in the darkness.

Florence did not know what was going to happen to her. She could hear no noise, nor could she see anything. Fear welled up within her, but for a time there was no release. Was this another form of torture? Were they going to leave her in this pitch black space until she gave them the right answers? Perhaps they were happy with the information they had been given. This thing she was on was possibly just a crude apparatus for execution. Perhaps after a set time, the two men far below would release the chains and let the platform fall back through the open air of the chamber, to let it and Florence smash into hard black stone to become one.

Florence heard a loud clunk. She attempted to move to the side of the platform in a panic and yanked at her arm still caught within the manacle. She twisted and pulled, tearing and bruising her already injured wrist on the unseen metal. It was no use, she did not have the strength to pull away.

Light suddenly filled the air and she froze while still in the act of pulling away from her hold. A tall soldier stepped forwards and retrieved the clipboard still lodged in the wooden floor of the platform. As Florence's eyes adjusted to the light, which was only relatively bright, she slowly relaxed and found the first soldier to be accompanied by two others. They all sported large silver breast plates and grey kilts. The silver of the breast plates was adorned with gold patterning consisting of interlinking spirals of varying sizes, which spread all over the armour. As the soldier retrieved the clipboard, Florence also noticed that interwoven into the material of the kilts was a silver threat that danced in the light.

"Don't worry Miss Watchmaker," said the soldier after quickly inspecting the clipboard, "the platform will not fall. Parkin, please release our guest."

"Please follow us," said Parkin after he had released Florence. He turned and marched off into the corridor with the other soldier. Florence did not advance. A moment passed and she felt the hand of the remaining soldier gently come to rest on her back. She looked around to see his dimly lit neutral face. He nodded in the direction of the corridor. Puzzled at her situation, which was totally out of the realms of her expectations, Florence followed the direction to proceed.

The lift led out onto a high-ceilinged, well-furnished corridor. Unlike the dull cave-like dungeon below, the walls here were white and scattered with gold leaf patterns which shimmered in the light. Huge paintings of battles, vast cities and half-naked men and women also adorned the walls. Chemises, sofas and other chairs made of oak and covered in white and gold fabrics often sat opposite the pictures. A plush thick white carpet lay on the ground and large silver and golden chandeliers covered in clear gems, which scattered light all around the hallway, hung heavily from the ceiling. It was difficult to take in the extent of the display of wealth that filled the corridor as it was still full of mist. Nevertheless, Florence had never seen such grotesque wealth nor anything that approached the quality and variety of the paintings.

"It's something, isn't it," said the tall soldier, once again gently helping Florence to move forwards.

Florence walked slowly, finding it difficult not to stop and admire the paintings. Some of the battles seemed so real, she could almost hear commanders bark orders and wounded soldiers cry out; sumptuous quantities of fruit were so well rendered, she could almost smell their rich decaying flesh. So captivated was Florence by what was around her that she did not really pay attention to where she was being taken. She walked clumsily into chairs and chests of draws, only to notice that these were just as much works of art as the paintings. Everything surpassed the quality of artistry she had previously known.

Florence was so caught up with everything around her, such a contrast to the weeks she had spent travelling through the drab and dark towns of the lost territory, that she did not see the standing soldiers who slowly emerged from the mist as she moved forwards. Nor did she notice the open door beside them. As she reached the two soldiers, Parkin told her to enter the room. In a dreamlike state, Florence wandered in. The door was closed behind her and she woke up.

Compared to her cell far below, the room was bright. Otherwise, it was much the same. The same dark chisel marked stone made up the walls, a stone slab functioned as a bench and a basin of water filled a corner.

"So they got you," croaked a figure lying on the bench. Florence was still getting accustomed to her surroundings. It took her a moment to realise who owned the voice. She could not believe that she now had to face him so soon after her betrayal.

The traveller was obviously weary. With much difficulty and a great deal of anguish playing out on his face, he attempted to get up to his feet. It was clear from his pain that Florence was not the only person in the room who had visited one of the torture chambers. Unlike Florence, the traveller had obviously not talked on his first visit. The man was covered with scars, scabs, open wounds, blisters and large bruises of varying age and colour. His cloak had been torn to shreds in the process and his gracious hosts had decided not to provide him with another. So, as he finally got to his feet, he stood with only strips of cloth hanging over his damaged flesh. Some of rags had almost become part of his body after commingling with the secretions of his open wounds. He flinched whenever he moved as strips of fabric would be torn away painfully to become just cloth once more.

"What happened to you?" asked Florence.

"I guess you talked pretty quick," murmured the traveller, regarding Florence's single uncovered arm. "You don't need to worry. We all do in the end, or die. If you were dead, what use would you be?"

Despite the consolation, Florence felt a wave of guilt surge over her being. She turned her gaze away from the sight of the traveller, unable to accept what she saw as it evidenced the stark contrast between his will and her own weakness.

"What are they going to do to us? Why have they put us together?" said

Florence wanting to move away from the thoughts of betrayal that dominated in her mind.

"No idea," whispered the traveller. "I'd have thought we'd be dead by now."

Slowly, the traveller carefully sat down on the bench. Florence continued to stand by the door, unsure of what to do.

"What did you mean in the letter?" asked Florence hesitantly, wanting to breech the cold quiet that was falling between them. The traveller looked up into Florence's eyes, but otherwise did not respond.

"What did you mean when you said that the mist came from a town's leader and its people?"

"Didn't the village make that clear?" said the traveller in a tone Florence thought was needlessly judgemental.

"No."

"The mist comes from the people."

"But, you said in the village that the followers of the sorcerer spread the mist."

"Yes, of course."

"I don't understand. How can it be the people and those who say we have to follow the ordinances? I know in my town lots of people followed the ordinances eventually, but not at first. They only started to think it was right after the mist had already arrived."

The traveller leaned back slightly and closed his eyes. He was obviously in great pain and Florence worried her questions were just aggravating the pain of a severely injured man.

"We received a message," said the traveller in a barely audible voice. Florence moved closer. "A message from a Protector. It'd been given by the man himself to one of our travelling preachers, Fuller. The Protector handed it to him as he was being exiled. The leader told Fuller it held knowledge that could help our cause. Fuller had been imprisoned in the town, Wilsford I think it was, for some time and was dubious about the message. Eventually, he brought it to Sewan and our group. We were not in the habit of receiving letters from Protectors and some, such as Sewan's brother Fare, argued that we should just consign the thing to the flames without reading it: he thought it was a trap. Sewan was also doubtful. However, he believed that as our battle against the sorcerer was being lost, we couldn't disregard anything that might provide us with help, no matter what quarter it came from.

"We were in Hesik. At the time, the mist there was still not too dense. Who knows what it is like now. Fuller arrived out of the blue at one of the public meetings we have to update the local resistance. Usually, quite dull affairs, but still a little dangerous. A town spy could just turn up and discover the identities of almost all the opponents to the sorcerer in the area. Sewan insisted on them.

"After the meeting, Sewan, Fare, Fuller and myself retired to some dull dingy pub nearby to read the letter. When Sewan opened the thing our first reaction was amusement. It was strange enough to get a letter from one of those so called protectors, but what was more, it was on the town's official missive paper and addressed to us."

"The letter began with an apology for having kept Fuller imprisoned so long. The leader claimed he'd undergone a long internal battle. He was not sure if he should listen to his heart and tell us what he knew or follow his head and have Fuller killed.

"It was the next part that led us both here. The leader went on to say that he knew that the sorcerer had no real power. This was because it was the people, not the sorcerer, who created the mist. He claimed that it was formed through their hatred and fear of others. As these feelings grew stronger, more ingrained in the body, and as more people found these feeling take hold within themselves, the mist would start to form and then thicken.

"Of course, we didn't take the Protector's suggestions seriously. We'd heard so many theories on how the mist formed that it was difficult to believe another. Nevertheless, we read on. He claimed that the sorcerer had only one thing that enabled him to expand his personal influence over such vast distances, one asset to reinforce his control: his odd alliance with the creatures I believe we've both recently met. He claimed these beings only exist in the mist environs. But, more than that, he asserted their world only pushes into ours where the mist exists. This means that despite the great distances between the mist soaked cities in our world, for them the mists are one continuous expanse.

"He said he didn't know how, but the sorcerer had formed an agreement with these demons; he had given them something that had bound him to them and enabled him to expand his word over the lands that surrounded his own.

"The Protector concluded that he didn't expect us to believe what he'd written. He knew that many people had their own ideas as to how the mist is formed. However, the difference between their ideas and his own was that he'd not just constructed his theory a priori. He claimed his theory came from the sorcerer himself. The leader asserted he had visited this very fortress. Before coming to power, he'd rebelled against the ordinances himself and paid the price. But, a remnant of what he'd been burdened him with guilt and pressured him each day to do something to continue the fight. At the same time, he was afraid. He said he was a coward, he did not want to die. So, he'd provided us with the information to find some sort of internal peace.

"He also claimed he had proof. Proof that both you and I have already seen. You see, it was that very Protector who provided us with the knowledge of the mist free Besketh village. I went there and found that his theory was indeed backed up by what had happened there. It seems that the free Besketh village was once shrouded in a light mist. Only when a collective effort was taken by the locals to oppose the sorcerer and his ordinances did the mist entirely vanish.

"Why am I talking about this? None of this makes any difference now. Now we're both here, the fight's over."

The sudden dive in the traveller's mood and the meaning of his words struck Florence with another wave of weighty guilt. She had walked up close to the traveller as he talked, but his finishing sentiments drove her away. She retreated to the other side of the room. As she stared blankly at the many chisel marks on the wall, she started to feel angry. She had not asked for the responsibility to convey the traveller's message back to Sewan. She had not even known much of what the traveller had expected her to convey; not until now, when it was too late. Fury grew until she felt she had to expel it in any way she could. She struck out at the wall with the palm of her hand. Once was not enough, she did it again.

The tingling sing on her palm helped her compose herself. It was not the injured man behind her who was her enemy. He was just a defeated man. He had invested everything into his mission. At one time, he had thought that his last mission was a success; his vital information would find its way back to Sewan. Now, near his end, he had discovered that the very person he had commissioned to convey his message to Sewan had joined him in the sorcerer's captivity. He had failed completely.

The sound of iron scraping against iron brought Florence from her thoughts. Four new soldiers, all dressed in the same ornate armour the others had been wearing before, appeared at the door. Two of them swiftly fell on the traveller. They attached shackles to his hands and ankles before standing him up and marching him out of the room. Florence watched on as if she were an observer from afar. After the last shred of the traveller had disappeared from view, she looked over to her own escort fully expecting to receive the same treatment. They just continued to stand in the corridor.

Florence was concerned by the action of the two soldiers. She was more frightened than she would have been if they had manacled her just as they had the traveller. At least then she would have known were she stood; she would have been able to resist and demonstrate her solidarity with the traveller. She could redeem herself in the sight of her fellow prisoner before they died together. Instead, her expectations were cast to the wind.

"Please, follow us," said one of the two pale, broad shouldered soldiers. Without waiting for Florence to respond, the pair departed and headed in the same direction as the traveller had been taken.

Florence was left all alone. The cell was wide open. 'Perhaps I can just go the other way and leave,' thought Florence. But she did not want to escape. She needed to know where the soldiers were taking the traveller. She stepped out of the cell just in time to see the grey form of her escort merge into the mist.

Florence first walked, jogged, and then ran blind after the two guards. She sped past the many frozen faces that lined the walls of the corridor until suddenly the sound of her footsteps changed. She stopped. The white carpet had ended to be replaced by naked stone. She looked down to see a familiar pattern played out on the floor; the spirals that adorned the armour of the guards were replicated in black and white marble below her; intricately cut stone wound around itself, creating an optical illusion. It seemed as if the floor was moving, curling into itself. The pattern spread across the ground before her and out into the mist.

Florence looked up and realised she had lost the guards. There were no shapes to follow into the mist. What was worse, the walls and ceiling of the corridor also ended were the marble began. She was left alone to determine what direction she should take into the empty expanse. Florence took a few tentative steps forwards. Nothing formed in the grey mass before her except more marble curls. She continued on until the corridor behind her slowly faded into the opaque air. Soon she found it was impossible to say which way she was walking as the only thing she could see was the dense mist around her and the perplexing monochrome stone beneath her feet.

Florence felt a tugging panic in her chest. Perhaps this was the end; a journey into nothing. She walked on, but her panic continued to grow until it demanded her to act. She turned around, to face what she hoped was the direction towards the corridor she had left somewhere behind. She moved at a brisk pace that steadily increased into a jog. Nothing emerged out of the mist except more patterned marble floor. Reason started to desert her. She spun around again, but with no thought as to what direction she would go, she ran. Further swirls of white and black curled into existence, but nothing else. She changed direction again and carried on without slowing her pace until something appeared in the mist. She stopped running, but continued to move forwards. As it became more defined, the something took on the shape of a person. Florence halted. She looked down to the ground, something had changed. She had not noticed at first, but the previously wild pattern of the curls in marble on the floor had become more orderly. As she followed the white and black lines towards the unknown person before her, they gradually formed into a spiral, curling round as one until they converged at the spot where the figure stood. As Florence progressed forwards with tentative steps, the undefined layers of the man melted away until it became the traveller, attached by chains to a thick white marble column, which jutted out of the ground at the centre of the spiral.

"Don't worry," said a voice from behind her. "He's still alive."

She turned to see an elderly man with a shock of white hair. He stood more than a head taller than herself and was dressed in a long white robe. His green eyes smiled at her as he waited for her to realise who he was. She was standing before the sorcerer. She was paralysed by shock. He looked nothing how she expected him to look, but she was absolutely certain of who he was. The shock lasted only a moment, replaced by intense anger. She threw a fist towards him, it was all she could think to do. Without any effort, the sorcerer caught her flying hand and, with surprising strength, spun her round to face the traveller.

"Welcome to my home," said the sorcerer with Florence in his arms.

Florence started to mutter a word, but the sorcerer clamped his large hand over her mouth and throat.

"Hush," whispered the sorcerer. "We're here to see a demonstration, you and I."

The sorcerer released his grip and moved several paces towards the captive at the centre of the spiral.

"But first, let me introduce myself. But what am I saying, you know who I am. I'm the man who protects all the mist covered lands from chaos and disorder. I'm the one who helps spread the gift of the mist wide and far to protect men and women from their baser instincts; I prevent them from harming each other, even in your town which is so very far away.

"I know why you've ended up here, but I want to ask you for a favour, which will redeem yourself. I want to you to help me spread the protections I can provide to your town, to Pendon. I want you to guide your fellow citizens to accept the help only I can give."

Florence was dumbfounded. What help could he bring. He just wanted to spread his power, something that Florence thought was already well rooted in her town when she had left. Had something changed since she had embarked on her journey, had the town been freed?

"I know what you're thinking. It's not quite that. Rather, the council of Pendon, led by a most difficult man as I'm sure you'll agree, will not accept my offers of assistance. So, you see, I need a friend, a partner in your town. Who better than a true native citizen like yourself?"

Florence looked up to the form of the traveller as the sorcerer continued to speak. As his words washed over her, she wondered why the traveller had not moved the whole time they had been speaking. He stood with his head turned away, his tattered garments hanging motionless. As the surprise of the appearance of the sorcerer ebbed away, she started to wonder what sort of situation she had wandered into. Why was the traveller even present? Why was he chained down while she was allowed to roam free? If the sorcerer really was requesting her assistance, she just hoped that the traveller was not part of some terrible ceremony in which she would have to show her commitment to the cause.

"I hope you two got on well just before," said the sorcerer while placing his large hands upon the shoulders of his prisoner. "If not, it is of no matter."

The traveller slowly lifted his head until he met the eyes of the sorcerer with his own. It was the first movement Florence had seen him make since she had stumbled across him in the mist filled hall. As she studied his face, she could see that the light that had once shone so brightly within him had now completely vanished. Indeed, he was facing the sorcerer, a man he had dedicated the last years of his life to fight, with seeming indifference. He muttered something through his remaining teeth too quiet for Florence to hear. The Sorcerer responded with a full throated laugh and slapped the traveller on the back.

"Yes, that's quite true. Our friend here is telling me that you know the mist is not formed through any power of mine. You're aware then of how little power I possess. I am very glad of it. You should also know that it is not me who spreads word of the ordinances either. I just collected them together and presented them to the world. Was it my fault if the world happened to listen?

"I only wanted to create a small list of mandates that I thought could ensure a safe and harmonious society that anyone could join. A society achieved not through the content of its rules, but in what it allowed people to do. You see, in one way or another, the ordinances I created enable people to pinpoint those who don't adopt the life they prescribe. As more people join the growing society, objectors become more conspicuous. Pressure might start to grow on an individual from the rest of the town, but the good thing about this system is that all an objector has to do to join the rest of the society is follow the list of rules. So you see, the system eventually creates a life of harmony and though this, peace. The individuals don't even have to believe anything about these rules in their hearts. Therefore, it's plain that I've done no wrong, no matter what those who resist my ordinances have told you. I've only acted in a way I see as democratic and right. I provided a chain of ideas and was just lucky that people chose them as this produced what almost everyone, from this city to your own, really wanted.

"Before my words spread around the lands outside this city and across the world to the edge of yours, such places were stricken with wars, famine and unimaginable terror. My words brought a commonality to them all, enabled them to live and work together. Now they exist in peace and demand nothing of one another than to respect the rules that enable them all to go on living so well. This is also why I see myself as a protector. Indeed, this is why all those who lead their towns are called Protector. Through maintaining the order that the ordinances bring, we save countless lives.

"When a town chooses of its own free will to adopt the protection of the mist and the stable life that the ordinances can bring, I see it as my duty to them to send a Protector; if I can, one who understands what happens to those who choose to disobey the ordinances after their town has chosen to adopt them. One, also, who understands what will happen to them if they disobey the ordinances and find themselves brought back here through the mist. With this knowledge in mind, these Protectors often go on to enforce the justice of the ordinances like no one else can, to help their fellow citizens see that order and peace exist under the common bond of these rules.

"What happens then, when one town comes under a Protector, fully under the rule of the ordinances, but another town sees the order and harmony that exists within the protected town. Often, they then choose to join them under the protection of the mist as well. What follows? More peace comes into the world.

"The towns and cities under the mist are often so pleased with their new worlds that they even send me small tokens of their appreciation; some of which you have surly seen on your way to this great hall. Others have gone to fund the building of this great monument, a palace created to facilitate the continued spread of the mist and all the benefits it brings. Altogether, you must see that through our efforts, we work for the people of all the world to uphold the secure and protected life they deserve; a life that many have freely chosen together as citizens in town after town. I find it hard to believe that anyone could oppose such order, stability and peace, or the choices their fellow citizens have made for themselves. I just hope that you, Florence, can see sense and assist me to help your own people's cause."

The sorcerer continued to stand by the traveller throughout his speech. As he finished, he held his arm out to Florence, signalling to her that she should come to him and take his hand. She was stood on the edge of the monochrome spiral. She let him hold out his hand, she did not move. No matter what the sorcerer said, he was still profiting from the mist, from distant individuals whose pain he could not see. More than that, Florence knew it was fear, not want of security, which made people take up his ordinances. Once the mist had formed in a town, its people became fearful that his retribution would fall upon themselves. Therefore, they forced themselves and others to follow the ordinances to avoid the terror they imagined would come about if his will was ignored. She had seen this for herself in Pendon. Her fellow citizens had not had a real choice. To her, the ordinances and the mist had given a position to choose from; it was not something many had wilfully moved towards. So, she did not move.

"Now, as I said before," continued the Sorcerer, lowering his arm, "I've had you brought here for the purpose of a demonstration. First, I need to give a little explanation. I'm a firm believer in the idea that an ordinance, once accepted by a town's citizens, is nothing if it is not backed by the force of a weapon in the hands of a man. The man, of course, is myself and the weapon, well, I believe you've already met." As the sorcerer finished talking, he backed away from the traveller into the mist until he was nothing but a voice. "But, I do not think you managed to see them in their full glory."

To the side of Florence, a form appeared. At first, as it entered the extremity of her peripheral vision, she thought one of the soldiers had returned. However, the briefest of glances proved it to be considerably larger than any soldier. Slowly, she adjusted her gaze until she could see what so many had seen only as an indistinct shape in the mist. This was no distant form that eluded plain sight. The monstrosity stood so close to Florence, if she had reached out her hand just a little, she would have been able to feel its clammy, milk-white flesh. The human-like form towered over her, at least eight feet tall, staring straight ahead. Florence first took note of its porcelain skin, sometimes shrouded in thick curling blonde hair. She then followed the line of its long arms until they ended in its trotter-like hands, pierced by three long nails half a foot long. She watched with disgust as the yellowy nails twitched and moved in the meat of the hand, occasionally coming together at their ends with a small bony click.

"Behold my firm ally," announced the sorcerer from somewhere behind Florence. "Behold the keeper of peace. You may be disgusted by his form, but I see a hero that has brought tranquillity to people's lives. They are intelligent, quite capable of seeking out those who breach the ordinances. They watch from the mist patiently, looking out for those who dare to violate their fellow citizens by flagrantly brandishing the symbols of their rebellion on themselves. They listen out while watching from the shadows. They hear when those who strive to overthrow the peaceful lives others poison the air with words of revolt. They remove these infections from our towns and cities and in reward, Florence, we allow them to feast on flesh."

When the sorcerer finished, his last word acting like a trigger, the beast bore down on the traveller. As the latter struggled with his heavy chain, the beast sunk its razor sharp nails into his shoulder and the soft of his belly. The traveller screamed out, but his wail of pain was cut short. The beast opened the vertical line of its mouth, revealing the blood red interior filled with hundreds of tiny translucent teeth, and snapped it shut over the top half of the traveller's face, tearing away flesh and bone. Scarlet streamed down onto the white of the floor and the skin of the beast.

Unable to turn away from shock, Florence looked deep into the large black eyes of the beast. Nothing human stared back. Her now dead friend's blood continued to flow down the beast's ivory chest and clotted in its wispy blonde hair.

After the initial moment of terror passed, Florence felt as if she had awoken from a deep sleep. But the nightmare continued, the beast brought its foul mouth down again and tore chunk after chunk out of the man she once knew. Florence tried to get away; she could watch no more. But as she started to move, she was prevented from doing so. The sorcerer was standing behind her. Just as before, he swung her round and held her so she could not take her gaze away.

"How can you turn away from him who protects us from our baser selfish selves? Our ally here feasts on the flesh of those who refuse to change. Look, so you can see it is good. Don't turn away from the fulfilment of the wish of so many."

The sorcerer continued to hold Florence fast for several minutes. If she closed her eyes, he would squeeze her burned arm until she opened them once more. The beast continued to feast, ripping the traveller apart bit by bit. Eventually, little was left but his blood, shreds of his cloak and his chains. As the beast got down to lick the blood from the floor with its long grey tongue, the sorcerer let go. Florence fell to the floor and lost consciousness.

# Chapter Three

Florence woke up on a soft bed with a red satin sheet spread across her. Half awake, she brought her left arm to her right to scratch the skin, but found it covered in a bandage. It was itchy, but there was no pain. Drowsily, she took in that she was on a four poster bed surrounded by walls lined with mahogany panels. She swung her feet down to into the deep red carpet covering the floor and knocked over a pair of warm waiting slippers. Her cloak had been replaced with a silk nightgown adorned with patterns of roses.

Dazed from a sleep of unknown length, Florence unconsciously wandered over to some thick wooden shutters and threw them open. Through the window, she saw nothing but opaque grey. This sight brought back the events which made up her last memory and she suddenly felt violently sick. She threw herself about before finding a chamber pot beneath the bed. She let go of restraint. Tears poured down her face as she clung to the pot. She stayed on the floor, with the thing in her hands, until a knock was heard from the corridor.

A young plump maid appeared and discreetly separated the pot from Florence's hands. The maid busied herself with tidying the bed and dressing Florence's body without a word or sign of effort. Florence absently let the woman get on with her work while feeling as if the reality she perceived around her belonged to someone else. After the maid had dressed Florence in a set of new clothes, she gave a small curtsey and left.

"Our new Protector," announced an unknown plump man at Florence's door. "How good to see that you're up and looking so well." Florence did not respond. Instead, she just continued to stare blankly ahead. This did not phase the cheerful man one bit. "It's wonderful to finally meet you. My name is Karl. You'll be glad to hear that you'll soon be dispatched back home. How long has it been since you saw your father? I imagine it must be difficult to be away from a loving parent for so long."

"Unfortunately, there is still a little business to get through, but I assure you it'll not take too long. First, I would like to extend my apology to you for the burn on your arm. It's an unfortunate consequence of the system we operate here, but it's necessary to ascertain if those who end up in the cells below are from towns who have not yet adopted the benefits the mist provides. When a person such as yourself finds there way here, we soon send them home. Of course, anyone who returns here for a second visit, or who comes from a town that has already joined our federation, is passed over to our allies so they can be dealt with appropriately.

"Now, down to business. As you know, your town is not part of our collective, and I for one think that is a shame. Consequently, we'd like to ask you to help your town to join. You can do this by attempting to become the Protector of Pendon. It'll obviously take some time to gain such a position, we don't expect you to perform any miracles. Therefore, we'd be happy to provide you with the means to assist you in your effort. The people of your town may choose another Protector, but we like to give a hand to those who have been here and gained first-hand knowledge of the work we do. This is because we think it can be useful when a Protector really knows what will happen to those who breech the ordinances. Now of course, it is possible that you are still thinking of disregarding some of the ordinances when you get back to Pendon. So, I think I should make something clear. Unfortunately, if you are returned here, even if you have become your town's Protector, then we'll have to treat you like everybody else. Nobody is above the ordinances and a good thing too.

"I know this might come as a bit of a shock," continued Karl, pleased with himself, "but quite a few of the people who get to this stage of our process are in much worse shape than you are now. Therefore, we made the decision long ago to take acceptance of our proposals on tacit consent. Otherwise, the process could take quite some time. So, all I need to say now is that it was a pleasure to meet you, Florence, and I wish you all the best in helping us in our mission."

As he finished, a smiling Karl took Florence's limp hand and shook it heartily. He withdrew then as swiftly as he had arrived.

\*\*\*

When Florence woke up the next day, she found the maid had shuffled in once more and was opening the shutters. After she had finished with her other duties, the maid brought in a low table and placed it next to the bed.

It was covered with sweet breads, several fine selections of dried meat and an assortment of unknown delicacies. Florence did not want any of the food, but something else on the table caught her eye. In the middle of the array of foods was a note, on thick yellow paper, in a fine sweeping hand.

Dear Florence,

We all wish you well on your journey. Your coach will be ready at noon. But in the meantime, please make use of this fine breakfast which I assure you is the best Geissdon, our humble city, can offer. It is an example of the finer things in life you may come to enjoy if you succeed in becoming our newest Protector. I am so very glad that we got to meet and hope that I will hear from you soon.

Yours, etc.

Karl

P.S. Please give my kind regards to your father.

Florence was sickened by the letter; her feelings were plainly painted across her face. The maid, who was in the process of slipping a new pair of leather boots onto Florence's feet, looked up to her with disapproving eyes and expressed her feelings by pulling a little too tightly when fastening the laces. Florence responded with a forced smile and thanked the maid for the assistance she had given during her stay. Although part of her wanted to rebel, she did not want to suffer the same fate as the traveller. She decided she could not afford to upset anyone. In response to Florence's words of thanks, the maid gave a polite nod. It was clear to Florence that the woman had not been placated. Therefore, to further show her good faith, Florence reached out for a honey coated bun from the pile of sweet breads and took a bite. This action seemed to hit the right cord; the maid smiled with approval before standing up and leaving Florence alone to her breakfast.

Florence lay back on the bed, but continued to chew on the sticky bun. The release of its sweet flavour in her mouth made her realise she had not eaten the day before. Suddenly, hunger was upon her; she felt light headed and weak. She sat up too quickly, exacerbating the problem. Black spots formed before her eyes. She waited a moment for her mind to clear before grabbing the first piece of food her hand came upon and gulped it down. She took another and another, hardly chewing before sending the food to her stomach and without a thought as to its fine quality or its expense.

After she had satisfied her body's demand for food, she leant back on the bed feeling quite drowsy. She thought about going to sleep, but the sound of scuffing feet and the briefest of glances informed her that two soldiers had joined her in the room. Wearily, she sat up. Her coach was ready.

The soldiers escorted Florence down corridors as fine as the ones she had seen on the way to the sorcerer's hall. They descended an ornate wide marble staircase and finally left the palace by passing through a towering arched doorway decorated with depictions of the beasts Florence had seen the day before. Whoever had carved the figures had managed to capture their essence with such skill that Florence had to look away.

Outside, a cab of iron waited for Florence. It looked more like the transport for a prisoner than a future town Protector. Florence did not want to quibble. She jumped up into the cab. Inside, she discovered a red velvet interior and another ample supply of food waiting for her. As soon as she sat down, a soldier informed her that the journey home would be long.

"Consequently," he continued "you'll be invited to be the guest of many town leaders on your journey. As not all of these leaders have been as fortunate as yourself to visit Geissdon, we think it'd be best for yourself if you refrain from mentioning how you ended up visiting our city. As you are new to your position, I have no qualm in informing you that such discussions are seen as contrary to the norms of good manners. Again, we extend our many thanks to you for your visit and hope you have a fine journey home."

The soldier gave a low bow and then closed the thick metal door. Florence was not surprised to hear a clunk as the door was locked, but the measure was unnecessary. She was glad to be on her way back to Pendon.

Florence sat back and pondered over the efficiency of the operation of the sorcerer. It sought to take in those who were once ardent protesters against his project and transform them into ardent allies; except that is those who resisted his project from the towns already under his spell: these people were just eliminated. The scale of the palace suggested that the process had been performed many times, securing further the position of the sorcerer's power and the permanency of the mist. He had created a treadmill of expansion.

After a short delay, the coach pulled off. Florence peered through the gaps between the bars of the window as parts of the city near her rushed by before disappearing into the mist forever. The city was unlike any she had seen before. Like others under the mist, it had done away with colour. But, to make up for this loss, the citizens had adorned their white marble buildings with thousands of carvings. One particular carving was repeated again and again; one of a face Florence would rather forget. Carved into doors, window frames, walls and fountains was the open mouthed face of the creature that had ended the life of the traveller. She had held the memories of what had happened in the hall at bay for a while, but the constant reminders around her forced her to confront what she had seen; the teeth of the beast, like shards of glass pushed through blood red gums, coming down repeatedly on the crumpled dead body of her friend.

By the time Florence had pushed the memory down into the depths of her mind once more, the coach had reached the edge of the city. The mist was already starting to recede and the blue of the sky above was becoming visible. Soon, the whole of the mist shrouded city was behind her. As she looked through the bars, she could see it climb up the slope she had just descended until it ended abruptly on what must have been a cliff hidden by a grey white shroud. Due to the sudden end of the hill, the city looked like a great grey wave emerging out of the green fields and undulating hills in the countryside around. The slow descent of the mist down the hidden cliff face resembled a great white waterfall. Behind it was hidden the open hollow through which the slow climbing platform passed to take unsuspecting prisoners to their fate.

By following the turn of the road, the coach took the strange site of the city out of Florence's view. Uninterested in the passing fields and trees, she leant back and let her mind move on to home. How long it seemed since she had left. How long it had been since she had really considered the possibility of returning. If she was honest with herself, she was not even sure if she would be allowed back inside the walls. Andrillo might have further secured his power, making it possible for him to refuse her entry at the gate. This thought of Andrillo suddenly reminded Florence of his watch-case, the only thing she had arrived with in Geissdon from home. Her hand went down to her pocket and to her amazement, Florence found it was still in her possession. It must have been put there by the maid when she was provided with the new cloak. She did not take it out. She just let her fingers move across the polished stones and worked metal. She wondered to herself how many miles it had travelled. Slowly, she let the case drift out of her fingers and slip back down into its hidden home.

Thoughts of Pendon made her wonder if it was such a good thing to be travelling back. She had set out to try to find a way to help the people of her town escape from the mist. Instead, she was now returning with the consent of the very man who used its power. She felt she had failed. There was no solution for her town, and as for finding the man who had first made her really think about the mist, he was dead. Her thoughts started to centre on the life of the traveller. He had been killed to demonstrate to Florence what would happen to her and all those who opposed the ordinances. The memory of his death brought her a sickening mix of guilt and grief. The two combined with the movement of the carriage and clawed at her gut. She moved over to the grate to get some fresh air.

She attempted to remember what she could about a man she barely knew. Her few memories could not cover what she was trying to hide. If it had not been for her, the traveller might not have been killed in such an undignified and functional manner. If she had only been more careful and not been caught. Nor could the idea that the traveller would have been killed anyway alleviate her mind. If anything, it just made her feel worse. How could she dare try to dilute her responsibility. No, she had been part of his murder and she had done nothing to stop it. For a long time, despite her attempts to direct her consciousness to other things, Florence's mind turned on the point of this thought.

Eventually, she could divert her thoughts enough to ask herself what she should do after returning to Pendon. The idea that she could become a town leader fluttered as a possibility, but the rest of her being was utterly disgusted at even considering this as a potential course of action. The reaction was so strong she became resolved in that instant. She would resist the sorcerer in any way she could, even if it led her back to Geissdon. She would try to do something in Pendon; she would get the traveller's message back to Sewan.

# Chapter Four

Florence's resolve only grew as she made her way home. She passed through an array of scenery between the towns she visited, from mountainous valleys to flat planes that expanded to the horizon in every direction. But as she continued on, one thing was always the same. The towns and cities were always covered in a thick mist. She would pass through the muted streets that were often further obscured by oncoming darkness. She would be welcomed by the leaders of the different towns or their deputies and greeted as a peer: an honoured guest sent from the High Protector himself. She would be asked to stay, though she had no real choice in the matter, in their homes, which often turned out to be grand palaces. It soon became clear that Wellbridge, rather than Ramskirk, was the norm. She would be treated well, with unlimited fine foods piled before her. However, the contrast between the life the welcoming elite enjoyed and that of the city dwellers outside was often stark, and increased Florence's dislike of their kind. These supposed protectors selfishly used their power and denied their citizens from living a lifestyle equal to their own. They crushed the good life of their citizens by upholding the ordinances without compunction.

As the Protectors' positions depended upon the ordinances being maintained, they ensured these rules were enforced with a violent passion. Or at least, this is what Florence was told. As she visited town after town, she found the leaders never tired of telling how they managed their dominions, crushing those who dared disobey the ordinances. Florence knew why the leaders treated her so well and told these stories. It was impossible for them to know if she was going on to be a town leader herself or if she was a spy. Some of them tried to draw her story out, informing her with a wry smile that they had been on the same journey that she was now making. But, she never told them what she was, did nothing to shake their illusions. Instead, she remained quiet and tried to hide her disgust. She just listened to their tales and watched, taking in all she could learn to help her in her future fight.

# Part Four, Chapter One

After three months of constant travel, without any warning from the taciturn driver, Florence realised that she was descending upon the walled city of Hesik. A chance glance out the grate of a window revealed a peeling notice listing the local ordinances which bared the city's name. Florence shot over to the other side of the cabin in an attempt to see the mountains that held her home, but was too late. Hesik was upon her and its mist had already obscured the distant landscape.

The coach continued to trundle forwards, bouncing over the cobbled road, until it came to a gentle stop before a city gate. The pale driver unlocked the door and poked his head into the cabin. Despite the long journey, few words had passed between this man and Florence. Indeed, Florence struggled to remember anything of significance the driver had said to her during the course of the entire journey. Consequently, it came as a surprise whenever he spoke.

"Leave you here, Miss," said the driver in a quavering raspy voice.

"What?" replied Florence in a firm tone, out of shock more than anything.

"If it's all right," continued the driver with deep worry in his eyes, struggling with himself to carry on speaking, "will leave you here."

Puzzled and not wanting to perturb the old man any further, Florence reassured him it would be fine for her to make her own way home from where they were. As soon as Florence's feet had touched the ground, the driver jumped up to his seat on top of the cabin. The coach lurched forwards and jittered around in a slow arch across the gravel in front of a newly closed coach station. The driver kept his head down as he brought the coach around and ignored Florence's waving arm. As he faded into the mist, Florence dropped her arm, giving up on the attempt to tell the driver that in his haste to leave he had left the cabin door wide open.

Florence examined the gate. She trawled her memory to place it, but it remained unfamiliar. Indeed, everything around her seemed alien. Hesik seemed to have twisted its form in her absence, mutating slowly until it had changed beyond all recognition. Alone and lost, she realised she missed the presence of the quiet driver. She missed the presence of anyone. There was not a single person around her; all she could see was the empty road and a few silent buildings. Suddenly, the mist seemed denser and reminded her of what it could contain.

\*\*\*

Though it took her some time, Florence found her way to the other side of Hesik. As she passed through the unfamiliar streets, she considered looking for Sewan and his brother, but the desire to see her father won out. She was not sure how long it had been since she had last heard his voice, nor how much time had passed since she had even sent him a letter to let him know she was still alive. A dark idea emerged at the back of her mind, but she pushed it away. Now that she was so close to home, that was a possibility she could not face.

Florence knew she was on the other side of Hesik as she had discovered the coach station she had seen many months before when she first arrived from the inn. In her absence, a peace had descended over the gate. A fair number of people still filtered through, but it seemed like a faint trickle compared to the torrent that she remembered. Furthermore, the yard of the coach station was virtually abandoned; many dilapidated coach cabs stood empty and still on the gravel. It seemed the quiet life of the ordinances had finally made its way through the town. Florence had no doubt that Hesik would soon become another part of the lost territory.

Florence's concerns for the people of Hesik at that time were outweighed by her need to find a way home. She had dismissed her driver without really thinking how she would complete the last section of her journey. Travelling by coach was still her preferred option, but how could she pay. Her hand gravitated towards the watch-case in her pocket. It was the only easily tradable item of value she had left. She was reluctant to part with the piece, though. It had travelled so far with her that she had grown attached to it. The possibility of walking crossed her mind, but she did not believe her legs would carry her so far without a couple of good meals; something else for which she would have to stump up the cash. By coach or by foot, she needed to pay. She wandered over to the entrance of the inn, hoping she could locate a driver who would accept her word that she would provide the money in Pendon, and walked straight into the large form of Butcher.

"Miss Watchmaker, what a pleasant surprise. What are you doing here?"

***

Florence could not believe how fortunate she had been. Butcher had insisted that she travel with him as soon as she said she was travelling back to Pendon; she had not even mentioned that she was in need of transport. As the road to Pendon flew by, she wondered how much had changed in the time she had been away. Her thoughts were interrupted.

"So, where'd you go on your travels?"

Florence was a little wary to respond to Butcher at first. She knew that he had been on the Board of Edicts before she left, and that he had sought other offices of influence after the mist had opened new paths to power. She had to make sure that she would give nothing away to this man who might just use her as a pawn to gain some advantage back in Pendon.

She informed him, briefly, of the first towns she had visited and worked in, emphasising the long coach journeys in between and her work routines. Fortunately, it turned out the man was not too interested in her. He soon turned the course of the conversation around to his two main concerns, Pendon and himself.

"Andrillo has changed so much since you left. We're very fortunate to have such a man leading the way in our town. The ordinances have been sharpened significantly through his scholarly work. And of course, I do not hope you'll think ill of me when I say I had a little role to play in the bettering of the town myself. Yes, I've worked with the great man on a number of occasions now. For instance, I've assisted in the rearrangement of our trade relations with other authorities; hence the journey today. It's been difficult to do -- against the grain of what was going on you see -- with the economy of new grey cloth flooding in and all; but, the council -- with a little help from yours truly -- has resolved that problem. Now we buy the cloth in ourselves and sell it on to the local merchants. Andrillo's idea.

Great man.

"Talking of our cloaks, I'm glad to see you sporting fine number. A lot of us were very concerned for you when you left; worried that you might become a problem for yourself and even the town. Glad to see that was just a phase. It looks very fine. Where did you get it?"

Butcher lent forwards and took a pinch of Florence's right sleeve between his fingers. After all of Butcher's words, Florence wished that his great man had instituted a stricter enforcement of the reduced speech ordinance, but she did not comment.

"It was given to me. I'm not sure where it comes from originally."

"Shame," said Butcher leaning back disgruntled. "If we could get hold of such cloth as this, Pendon would be rich!"

"Yes, but unfortunately I can't help you there Mr Butcher. I got it in a place a long way from here, and I'm not even sure if it came from there."

"Oh well. Never mind. I suppose you must be glad to be getting home. You'll be glad to hear your father is well. Indeed, most things have improved in Pendon. Although, I should tell you before we arrive that it seems that the effect of that travelling speaker must have been worse than we imagined. The mist's continued to thicken despite Andrillo's attempts to prevent it. I suppose there's only so much even great men can do when such malicious types stalk the land."

Florence choked back a short sob as Butcher mentioned the traveller. She fought back against the urge to tell him that the man he blamed was a threat no longer. It would be no use to inform the fool. Butcher quietened down. He saw that he had upset the girl, although his common sense made him quite sure that her distress resulted from hearing about the thickening of the mist and the fate of her town. He felt a sense of pride for the girl in the way she responded to the plight of her home and became a little emotional himself.

# Chapter Two

"Let us in boys," shouted Butcher. "We've got someone on board who's desperate to get home."

Florence put her head out of the cabin. She saw the same guards that had marched her from the town now opening the door for her return. As the coach passed by, the guards gaped at Florence. It seemed that interesting events were just as few and far between as in the past. Butcher moved over to Florence's side and turned his eye to the gazing guards. They quickly responded by busying themselves with whatever they could.

The coach continued up the cobbled path to the market square. When they reached the open field of cobbles, Butcher got out. He told the driver that it was possible for him to stay at the Black Inn, but it would be better if he could make his way back. Florence had not paid much attention to the town as it passed her by. She knew what to expect. She alighted slowly, keeping her eyes shut for a moment to avoid seeing the grey before her. After releasing a sigh, she stepped down from the last iron step and joined Butcher near the horses.

"Thank you for letting me ride along with you. If you come over to my father's, I'm sure I can get you my half of the fare."

"No, no, Florence. Don't worry about a trifle like that. All is settled, isn't it my good fellow?" he said nodding to the driver. "No, it was a pleasure to have some company on the road. Give my best to your father. I'm sure he'll be more than pleased to finally see you've arrived home and safe."

Florence thanked Butcher once more before making her way to her father's shop. She moved over the familiar stones of the marketplace quickly, keeping her eyes to the ground to avoid the side glances from the few market stall holders and punters that were trading silently. She reached the alley that had been her home for nearly all her life; the time that had passed since she left seemed to fade away.

She placed her hand on the street door of the shop. She found it difficult to believe that she was even there. Despite having been on that spot so many times before, the moment seemed unreal. She entered her home and looked around. The bright space of the workshop was just as clean as ever. The smell of wax and polish, so familiar, brought a warmth to Florence's heart. But, one thing was missing; her father was not there.

\*\*\*

Unlike the meticulously clean workshop, the kitchen was quite a mess. Though Florence tutted at the semi-disaster her father had left, she smiled as well. She smiled because as disquieting as mouldy mugs and plates were, the mess was evidence of her father. She started to clean. As time wore on, she was glad that she had something to do rather than just have to wait in anxious silence for his return.

As she busied herself with cleaning the kitchen, she avoided thoughts that suggested her father had changed. It was impossible to know what had happened to the man during her time away, especially in a city that revolved around Andrillo. Many good people had changed their ways before she left. What would keep a lonely man from doing the same after his rebellious and selfish daughter had gone?

As Florence tidied the newly cleaned earthenware away, she heard a noise from the workshop. She paused, the short tower of miscellaneous plates in her hands halfway between the counter and the open cupboard. Another dull thump came from the shop. Slowly and carefully, she set the plates back down. They rattled a little. Florence glanced anxiously at the entrance to the workshop.

"What are you..." said her father in a gasp as he burst into the kitchen. "Florence, my daughter! How long have you been here?" He paused a moment and then smiled. "I see you've been busy."

Florence ran over to the old man and clasped her arms around him. She tried to speak, but she would not have been able to utter a word without bursting into tears, so she just clung on for a moment longer.

"How long have you been here?" repeated the watchmaker as he gently moved Florence away to his arm's length. "Let me see you. You haven't changed a bit."

Florence looked at her father. He looked a little older, perhaps a little thinner, weaker.

"I've lost your bag," said Florence, but regretted it straight away. It felt like a clumsy way to greet her father, but she could not think of anything else to say.

"Oh, don't worry about that old thing. I would've thrown it away years ago if I'd remembered I had it before you needed it."

Florence choked a laugh.

"So, tell me. Where've you been?"

She knew she could not tell him everything. Not yet. She did not want to scare him or put him in any danger. Instead, she stuck to the story she had told Butcher. He was clearly aware she was not telling him the whole story, but he did not press her. She was very grateful for this as she was sure she could not have held out for long. He just inquired about what she had learnt, and if she could supply him with any news of new techniques or advancements in the trade she had come across while away.

\*\*\*

Florence spent a pleasant evening with her father. Unlike the last time she had seen him, he did not seem to be burdened much at all. As the evening went on, he even seemed to lose a few of the worry lines from around his eyes and regain a little vigour. After darkness fell, an utterly exhausted Florence made her way up to her bedroom. She collapsed on her familiar old bed, still unmade, and decided she would set off for Hesik the next day. She would pass her message on to Sewan and then consider her debt to those fighting against the sorcerer paid. Despite her resolve to do whatever she could to resist the sorcerer's power on her journey home, now she had arrived, she saw things a little differently. She would leave the rest of the battle to others. She was too tired and homesick to carry on a useless struggle against such a strong, well organised foe. No, she would just give Sewan all the information she could and that would be it. She would tell him everything the traveller had said, all about the town leaders and about the sorcerer himself.

After these considerations were settled in her mind, she looked forwards to the coming months, working with her father in the quiet peaceful workshop downstairs. For the first time in as long as she could remember, she slipped off into a truly restful sleep.

# Chapter Three

"I know I've only just arrived," said Florence to her father "but I'll be back straight away."

"Travelling to Hesik isn't like going to the butchers."

"It's only a day or two's journey away. I know it seems a little hasty, to go off straight away, but I have important news for some friends I made there. I didn't have a chance to meet with them when I came back through Hesik as I wanted to get back here as quickly as I could. A friend of ours died in a distant land, and I'm the only one who can let them know."

Several obvious questions sat on the tip of her father's tongue, but with a heavy sigh he let them pass.

"All right, Florence, but please come back as soon as you can. You've been away such a long time, and we haven't had the chance to properly catch up."

Florence got up from the kitchen table and moved round to where her father was sitting to give him a hug.

"Don't worry," said Florence. "I'll be back so soon it'll be like I never even left town."

Florence set out for the town gate once more. Like the time before, she was going to walk the pass to the inn before taking a coach the rest of the way to Hesik. As she walked along the cobbles, past the green stone porticoes to her side, Florence smiled. She was happy to be home, even if the blue sky was still not visible above her. She had made it back after her situation had looked very grim. She also smiled as she felt vindicated. Her judgement of the sorcerer had been proved right. As she looked up towards the sun, a perfectly round sickly yellow circle on the otherwise uniform grey sheet above, she thought perhaps there was still a chance to do something to clear the town; but not yet. She reaffirmed her decision from the previous night. She would just get her message to Sewan. The memory of the traveller drifted into her mind and wiped her smile away. She could not be as brave as him, but at least she would survive.

As the gate came into view, Florence's pace slowed and her confidence ebbed away. It was shut. How could she have been so foolish to think she could just walk out of the town? Andrillo had only let her leave the last time because it was the simplest way to deal with a threat. Now his position was probably much more secure and who knew what travel prohibiting regulations he had passed in the time she had been away. Still, she had to try. Despite a desire to just go back home, she pressed on.

"Hello Florence," said one of the guards as Florence came up to the gate. "Where're you off to this time?"

The voice was friendly and Florence though it sounded familiar. She looked up to see that the young guard at the gate was Mark Willow. Mark was a boy her own age and the two of them had played together as children. They had not seen each other very often since Florence started her apprenticeship, but she still thought him a friend. Florence repressed a laugh as she approached. Mark had obviously only just become a guard: his uniform did not fit his thin, untrained body. She let the joy of seeing him again show and approached with a new smile.

"Hi Mark, I just need to go back to Hesik. Forgot to do something there."

"No problem. Just need to see your permission slip from Andrillo."

"Ah, I see. I don't have one, Mark. You couldn't just let me through could you? I'm only going for a day or so. I'll be straight back. I don't even think anyone even knows I've returned."

"I would if I could. But," said Mark, moving a little closer and lowering his voice, "that old ogre has made things impossible for everyone. You know what, he wouldn't even let Thomas Farmer back to his barn without a slip and it's just outside town. Tom had to go to Andrillo all the time as he kept losing the stupid slips. Last time he came here, he'd lost it again and Toby let him through. Someone must have said something as the next thing you knew the two of them were in court. Toby lost his job and Tom wasn't allowed out for a month. Luckily, his wife Julia could manage the animals without his help. So, I'd let you through, but it just doesn't make sense for either of us. Especially after what happened, well, you know. Best thing is to go to the old man. If he's in a good mood, he might let you through."

"Who you talking to boy?" screamed the voice of the Sargent from inside the gatehouse.

"No one, sir."

Mark gave a nod and a little grimace to show Florence she had to move on. He obviously did not want to get into trouble. Florence gave him a half-hearted smile. Disappointed, she returned to the alley. She would just have to seek permission to leave from the man who had previously forced her from the town and hope he would repeat his gracious act.

\*\*\*

As Florence approached the large main entrance of the council palace, she was concerned that the two guards flanking the passageway would stop her to ask what she was wanted before guiding her home. However, the guards did not even stir so much as to look at her as she crossed over the threshold. She had only taken a few steps into the building when she was met by a voice.

"And what do you want?"

Florence looked down to her left to see the disgruntled sitting figure of a council usher. He was squashed in behind a flimsy wooden table covered with several seemingly unordered piles of paper.

"I've come to speak to Andrillo."

"Oh, very good," said the usher in a sarcastic tone. He rummaged around in his papers and retrieved a slip before handing it to Florence. "Just fill this in and make your way down the hall to the waiting room. I'm sure he'll see you soon."

With that, the usher returned to his papers. As Florence was not sure where the waiting room was, she continued to stand on the spot. With his head bowed down close to the surface of the table, the usher proceeded to take pieces of paper from one of the piles before placing them on another. Florence tried to read what the documents said and work out what he was doing, but she could not discern any apparent rhyme or reason to his activity. He continued this unfathomable process in an agitated manner, moving the unsteady table as he worked, making one of its legs knock against the stone floor at uneven intervals.

"Excuse me," said Florence quietly.

"You still here," replied the usher, obviously frustrated at the continuous interruptions and Florence's apparent stupidity. "Look, go down the corridor and enter the first door on your right."

"The courthouse?"

"Yes, the courthouse, if you like. Now, if you'll excuse me, we can't all hang about disturbing others all day."

"Sorry, I..." replied Florence, before thinking better of it. She left the usher to his toil and walked down to the door. The faint sound of knocking soon started up again behind her.

\*\*\*

Florence entered the waiting room. It was a high ceilinged, but cramped and humid wooden panelled space, crammed with people. Florence knew many of the faces, but despite her being absent for such a long time, almost no one responded to her presence. A reason for this was that most of the occupants of the room did not even make the effort to look up as she came in through the door. Florence carefully made her way across the worn brown tiles of the floor to a desk near the courtroom entrance. Florence used the fountain pen and ink provided to complete the little slip the usher had given her and posted it through a slot marked 'Requests'.

She did not know how long she would have to wait, but with the number of people in the room she assumed it would be a while. She squeezed herself onto a bench between Mrs Donny, a friendly old widow dressed in a thin grey nightgown, and a young man Florence knew to be a cloth merchant. She looked around at the faces in the room. Most of the people were sitting in complete silence. A brave few were speaking, but only in a whisper, creating a bed of constant rustling which combined with the sound from people's cloaks as they adjusted themselves on the hard wooden benches that filled the room.

"Good to see you again, dear," whispered Mrs Donny, tapping her finger on Florence's leg. "I heard that you'd arrived back in town."

Florence turned to Mrs Donney's kind grey eyes and nodded her thanks for the welcome home. It was good to know that at least one kind spirit had not been lost to the fear created by Andrillo.

"How long have you been waiting?" asked Florence.

"Oh, a few days now. Maybe a week. Yes, it must be as I came before I last saw Mildred for tea last Wednesday. Time flies by these days."

"Over a week!" replied Florence a little too loudly, silencing the rustle of the room.

"Yes," continued Mrs Donney in a quieter voice after the hum of the room had returned. "You see, priority cases jump the queue. And a request like mine, to visit my sister in Hesik, just mustn't be important enough for Mr Andrillo."

"Are we all waiting to see Andrillo? Does every request go through him?"

"Yes, I suppose you don't know as you've been away. Mr Andrillo made a something, a declaration, that no one else can say what the sorcerer means except him. It's all very new and I'm sure I don't understand it all, but it does seem that very little has been happening over the past few months. This room seems to get smaller every day. Not that I think Mr Andrillo doesn't know what he's doing. Would you like some marzipan while you wait?"

Florence happily accepted the sweet and chose not to wonder where Mrs Donney had got the expensive treat from.

"Miss Florence Watchmaker," announced a burly usher who appeared at the courtroom door.

"Oh, how lucky you are, you're already through. Your case must be important. Well, go on then," said Mrs Donney as she delicately pushed the shocked Florence forwards. "And send my best to your father. He did such a lovely job on Freddy's watch."

Florence tried not to compare her own request with that of Mrs Donney's. She had only asked for permission to visit friends in Hesik and had already been granted an audience. She nodded slowly and got up, avoiding the envious glances that fell upon her.

\*\*\*

Florence had never been in the courtroom before. Like the waiting room, it was lined with plain dark wood and lit by two high windows. Indeed, except for the absence of benches and the supplement of a judging platform, the courtroom was a near exact copy of the room Florence had just left.

The platform was a wooden structure that sat incongruously in the middle of the otherwise empty space. It was about seven feet high and had space enough at its top for a narrow desk as well as three councillors. The height of the platform had come about to protect the judges from any belligerent defendants; it also provided the judges the opportunity to peer down on anyone who came through the courtroom door and establish their authority before proceedings began.

Andrillo sat in the centre of the platform, flanked by two other councillors. As soon as Florence looked up to him, she was struck instantly by something she should have realised long before. She let her eyes follow his scars, the very same sort of long thin burn scars that marked her own arm.

Florence was prompted by the usher, but she could not speak. Her mind was racing at the idea that Andrillo's actions now started to make sense. If he had also been through Geissdon and the sorcerer's process, it was no wonder that he was trying to set himself up as the leader in Pendon. Unlike her, he had been swayed by the sorcerer's arguments and inducement of fear. The only unknown for her was why he had not sought to do this in his home town.

"Miss Watchmaker," said of the two flanking councillors, "we do not have all day."

Florence shifted her gaze away from the steady eyes of Andrillo to look at the other councillor. He probably had to speak up as he only retained his place beside Andrillo due to the town's traditions. But when focused her sight upon him, she was taken aback again. Next to Andrillo sat his brother also clearly carrying the mark of the sorcerer.

"Miss watchmaker, if you please."

The comment snapped Florence out of her transfixed state. She took a moment to remind herself why she was there and composed herself to speak.

"I've come here to ask for permission to go to Hesik. I have a friend there who I need to inform about the death of someone they held close. I'll not be long, if that is an issue."

"Request denied," said Andrillo.

"But..."

"Not only is the request denied, but you also cannot leave the building. I hereby order you, on behalf of the council of Pendon, to be taken to the detention cells below this building and be held there until a trial can be convened to determine the extent of the threat you pose to us all."

As he finished, Andrillo signalled to the usher to take Florence away. The usher was obviously expecting a struggle from Florence as he positioned himself with open arms to catch Florence as she turned. Florence just mutely signalled for the usher to lead on.

# Chapter Four

Florence was taken down into the depths of the building until she reached what had once been the council's mediocre wine cellar. The musty damp space consisted of a wide rough stone walled vault with gently arching ceilings. Along its walls, where the few bottles of wine for the councillors' meals used to rest, eight small holding cells had been built. They were made of a dense wood and their ill-fitting appearance suggested they had been built as a hasty solution. The scent of sawdust and varnish mixed with the otherwise musty atmosphere to leave little room for fresh air.

"In you go Miss Watchmaker," said the usher after opening a cell.

"How long will I have to wait?"

"Difficult to say really. A small number stay for an hour, young Toby had to stay for a week."

"Can someone tell my father that I'm here?"

"I'm sure he'll know soon enough," replied the usher, but after recognising the distress his statement caused in Florence's features, he continued, "but I'll send someone to let him know."

The door was locked and the usher's footfalls soon died away. Florence inspected her new cell. The back wall was rough stone. It seemed the wood of the new cell ended as it reached the wall of the old cellar. Florence moved over to the hard wooden bench that acted as a bed and sat down. She felt queasy and had to hold back the urging of her stomach as her body reacted to the dense human smell that was all around her. Despite the cells being new, the still air of the underground space meant that the stale stench of previous occupants had already firmly established itself in the pens.

Florence was flabbergasted that she had found herself imprisoned again so soon. She had only just arrived home, hopeful that she could live a normal existence for a while; perhaps it was already too late. Too late to even go back to the reduced life she had once had under the mist. The door of the cell opened. Florence expected the usher to appear with a couple of guards.

Instead, it was the lone figure of Andrillo. Without a second of hesitation, Florence went on the attack.

"I know where you've been. I know you've visited the sorcerer: you have his mark. How can you live with yourself for bringing his power here and blame it on the innocent actions of others. How dare you turn my town into another prison, to be watched over by those things that lurk in the mist. How can you proudly sit in judgement upstairs and uphold his meaningless rules when you must have seen what I have seen."

Andrillo's first response was shock, but this was just because he was surprised to find that Florence's will had not yet been broken. He quickly recovered his composure.

"Heard stories from other fools have we?" said Andrillo with a condescending smile.

Florence marched over to Andrillo with such purpose that the councillor instinctively stepped back. As she got close to the man, she pulled back the sleeve of her cloak, revealing the long thin fresh scars on her arm. Andrillo visibly crumpled and turned away in an effort to avoid the truth of an inescapable memory etched into his own skin.

"If you've been there," said Andrillo, still looking away, "then you must know why I've had to act in the way I have. You've seen his power and the demons that follow his every whim. You must see that I've tried to protect the people of this town from those things."

Andrillo looked into Florence's eyes for the first time and found them burning with silent fury. She did not pose a threat, she was just angry and lost; much like himself when he first returned home.

"You have no reason to listen to me, I suppose," continued Andrillo in a whisper. "Maybe you think I meant to bring the mist to this town and become one of those Protectors, but that was never my intention. My brother and I, as you know, come from another town. It's completely lost to us now, much closer to Geissdon than here. It fell under the mist long ago, but I still remember the town being full of colour, diversity and life when I was a young man. We got to experience much of it as well, my brother and me, as we were the sons of a wealthy merchant. We'd often travel to the cities around with our father and enjoy the many delights that could be had in all those magnificent places. That was not to last.

"I was even younger than you are now when things started to change. I noticed it first only through a reduction in our trade and the number of journeys we made from home. Soon enough though, towns nearby transformed. Superfluous centres of culture and life were quickly reduced to grey, miserable and silent shells. Merchants like ourselves working in these towns were often expelled, or worse, as we were seen as a threat to their safety. Many, including my father, were hit hard. After his business failed, he soon faded away.

"Our town was so dependent on trade that unemployment soared; there were no ready jobs for my brother and me. We struggled on, but eventually we'd sold almost everything we could to sustain ourselves. My brother decided that we had to take ourselves and our mother to another town or starve. So, we sold the house that had been in our family for generations. This gave us just enough to travel to the home of our aunt; she promised us we could get work in her husband's business. We would still be merchants, but now we would trade in those ubiquitous grey cloaks. You see, my aunt lived in a town already shrouded in mist. The business was profitable, and we played our part through connecting our uncle with the contacts we knew from working with our father.

"I hated the job. Not the work itself, I enjoyed bargaining and making new connections. But, I felt like I was betraying my father by working in the towns that had given up on him and led him to his death. I argued with my brother almost every minute we were together. I wanted to go back to our home, or further if necessary, just as long as we didn't have to take money in those mist sodden towns. I became increasingly angry at everyone, especially my brother. I decided that if he would not let us move, I'd take matters into my own hands and force the issue.

"Under some pretence or other, I went back to my old home and managed to secure a large number of colourful cloaks; they were exceedingly cheap as the price had dipped due to the spread of the mist. I exchanged these for the grey ones we were about to dispatch to a neighbouring town.

"We were both put on trial, my brother and I. We were found guilty of breeching one of the ordinances. We were ordered to wear the bright red cloaks I had bought as a symbol of our treachery. I thought we'd got off lightly, but I soon found out how wrong I was. We were taken that very night as we were returning home.

"We both resisted telling them anything in Geissdon, even though we had nothing to hide. We were stubborn and young. It was useless really. We told them everything they wanted to know in the end. We were ordered to return to our town, our father's home, and start to implement the ordinances in any way we could. If we did not, we were told we'd suffer the same fate as the young woman who had been killed before us."

"We returned to our father's town in our new grey cloaks. In our absence, things had changed. They would not even let us in. The mist had fallen there too. They were trying to uphold the new ordinances they had established and had purged the town of anyone who rejected them. We were informed of this at the town gate. We were also told to move on quickly or suffer an arrow through the neck. Travellers, even those returning home, were not welcome.

"We stayed for a short while in a village not far from our old home. We knew it'd be impossible to go back to our mother; we were anathema in that town. Instead, we just sent word through a merchant friend to tell her we were not dead. We also promised we'd get a message to her as soon as we were permanently settled somewhere, but new travel restrictions had been imposed before the note even got to her. We never saw her again.

"We drifted for a number of years until we settled here by chance. My brother met his wife in Hesik while we were trading there and they married soon afterwards. Her family home was in Pendon; with her permission we moved in and made it our new business base. I wasn't really interested in starting a family myself; I just wanted to lose myself in work to forget. The image of that dying woman could not be washed from my mind. The reality her horrible death and the need to hide from those daemons haunted my every moment. I became obsessed with the distant mist covered towns. My brother would often jokingly chide me for wanting to leave when we were there, and how after we'd left, all I could do was talk about the place.

"As I was still travelling as a merchant, I found myself wandering ever closer to the cities that had already disappeared under the sorcerer's shroud. I talked to those few who ventured out of the mist covered cities. They were always reticent to share information. But, after a long time spent gaining their trust, I started to hear the same stories again and again: they told me that those who flaunted the ordinances soon disappeared; I had no doubt where to."

"As the years passed, it became clear to me that the spread of the mist was inevitable. I heard of some who tried to stop its progress; they all failed. I was determined not to be taken again: I had to change. Using the information I'd gained over years of listening to those from the mist ridden cities, as well as my own experience and reason, I established what the sorcerer wanted. If I fought to keep in the good faith of the sorcerer, I'd be left alone. If I fell into disgrace in his eyes, I'd pay the ultimate price. I adopted the grey cloak and tried my best to appease the sorcerer by conforming with the ordinances I'd heard about, as well as those I'd discovered through my own judgement. I also dedicated myself to help the citizens of the town that had accepted me as one of their own."

"I think you know the rest. I warned the people here that they had to change too, to prepare or suffer the sorcerer's wrath. To further this end, I took on the burden of public office. Few believed me at first, but those who travelled saw what I said was true. Slowly, many came around to my position. But, my work was not yet complete when that travelling mist spreader came to our town just over a year ago. An insufficient number had taken heed of my warnings and his words proved more damaging than I could've imagined. As the mist descended, I knew I'd failed to keep the demons from our home, but at least I could still attempt to save those who could see that to fight against his great power was useless. To help themselves, they had to change for both the town's sake and their own.

"I'm telling you all this to help you understand why I acted the way I did. More importantly, I've given you my story in the hope that you'll change yourself. I see you've taken up the grey robe, but I know this is nothing. I fought with myself for such a long time after seeing what you've also seen. I also decided to wear the grey to shield me from unwanted attention while I attempted to resolve my mind. I could've gone either way. In the beginning, I was still torn, thinking that perhaps it would be better to die fighting in a hopeless battle than succumb. Eventually, I saw the truth. Living is the greatest victory we can hope for.

"I hope this knowledge will guide you in the right direction, the one I know you cannot be sure of if you wish to travel off to Hesik again so soon. Please, learn from my experience and my mistakes. I came to see that to resist would not only lead to the loss of my own life, but through wishes of retribution and justice, through influencing those who know no better, the loss of others. So, now you've heard why I brought you down here, to speak in private about this issue, I have something to ask you: are you willing to help your town and yourself?"

While Andrillo had talked, Florence had slowly drifted over to the bench and sat down. She had realised Andrillo had been right in his own mind, but he had been missing a vital piece of information. His final question to Florence hung in the air. She did not want to respond. She was not sure if he could accept what she had to say.

"You're mistaken," said Florence after making up her mind. "You've acted blind. The mist was not brought here by the travelling speaker, it was not a sign of the sorcerer's wrath: the mist was created by the people of our own town. No one has to capitulate to that man's demands. All they have to do is give up their fear, their notion that those who do not follow those meaningless ordinances constitute a threat to their lives. Don't you see, it wasn't that poor man who brought the mist, it was you! Over years, you convinced a small number that the mist would come if they didn't change and force others to do the same. You prepared them to become mist spreaders themselves. The travelling preacher's arrival was just a catalyst for their fears. The mist descended soon after and others started to believe they had to amend their ways because of what they'd been told by you. Without even knowing it, while trying to help, you laid the foundations for the sorcerer's power in my town.

"But the cause is not yet lost. Despite the damage you've done and what you believe, Pendon can still be saved. I've seen a town, deep within the lost territory, free of mist. Its people live free and happy lives, reduced only by being surrounded by those who are still deluded. All you have to do is to tell everyone how you've been wrong. They'll listen to you. You must do this, before they lose faith in what you say. You owe it to everyone here.

You must repair the harm you've caused."

"No, no," said Andrillo slowly, shaking his head with disappointment. "I see I've failed again. I am sorry. Your tale is an intriguing one, but it's just as wrong as all the others. I've heard so many, so many plans of action, so many theories; their result is always the same. If you're set on a course to undo the work I've done here, then I have no option but to treat you as another threat to the town. I will ask you one more time, though: are you sure you'll not reconsider? You've seen many of the mist ridden towns and could help protect your fellow citizens by improving our knowledge, our ordinances and behaviour. I'd be very glad of your help in the council. But first, you just have to give up these silly notions."

"You're a fool! You can't even see that you yourself are the problem."

"Such a shame. I wish it wasn't so, but you leave me with no other option. You'll go before the council to be tried. If you continue believing the nonsense you've told me, we'll have to take measures to ensure you'll not poison the minds of anyone else. Please, reconsider if you can."

Andrillo was tired. He looked with care into the eyes of Florence, but the anger was still there. Knowing he could do no more, he stepped out of the cell and locked the door behind him.

# Chapter Five

Florence woke up early in the morning the next day. She did not know what time it was as the candles in the cellar had been left to burn down the night before, leaving it in pitch black darkness. As her mind took in her cool damp surroundings, and the stench of past and present occupants burned her eyes, she remembered where she was.

She fumbled her way out of bed and stood alone in the darkness. She tried to move on to other places in her mind's eye, but the loud snoring of another prisoner vibrated through her body and kept her firmly in the reality about her.

Time passed slowly until a burst of weak light illuminated the grate on the door. Florence followed the wall with her hand and made her way to the now dull yellow square. As she reached it, she could see it was light only relative to the total darkness of her cell; the illumination only provided enough visibility to make out broad shapes beyond her door. Murmuring voices could be heard from an unknown distance. She tried in vain to make out what was being said. By the time the sounds reached her, they consisted of little more than hushed hisses.

The scuffing of boots against unseen steps sounded out. The light in the old wine cellar started to increase. Further steps followed until the podgy face of the usher appeared before Florence. After her cell was opened, she could see the stout little man had come prepared for trouble. Two guards, with dark rings under their eyes and looking as if they had got dressed a little hastily, had come to assist him.

"Where am I going?" said Florence, the first hoarse words of her day.

"Turns out you won't be waiting long at all, Miss Watchmaker," said the Usher. "I've come to tell you that you'll have to follow these gentlemen up to our court." He paused for a moment as if considering something and then continued, "thought you'd be glad to hear that your father knows where you are."

\*\*\*

Unlike the day before, the waiting room outside the courtroom was empty. The door to the council's palace was still shut, the tapping table near the entrance unoccupied. So, as Florence was led into the courtroom itself, she was surprised to find all twelve councillors present.

Andrillo was once again perched at the top of the platform, but this time he was alone. Florence looked around at the faces of the other councillors. A few changes had taken place among their number while she had been away. Though Andrillo's brother was still among them, a few of the old guard had been replaced by the likes of Butcher and other former Board of Edicts members. Andrillo cleared his throat and started proceedings.

"You find yourself here today, Miss Watchmaker, as it has been suggested that you are a threat to the peace and wellbeing of our town and its citizens. You have wilfully asserted, in front of others, the dangerous idea that it is right to fight against sorcerer by actively opposing the ordinances which protect us all. Do you deny these charges?"

Florence examined Butcher, the man who had been so pleased to see her only a couple of days before. His eyes were now filled with hate and displayed no surprise at seeing her before him as a prisoner. Florence had to look away.

"I don't deny what you say about my wish to fight against the sorcerer. This is because I know such a struggle will not undermine the safety of anyone here; it will secure it. I'm aware you're all under the power of this man's words," said Florence to the councillors at the base of Andrillo's pedestal, "but if you can hear me, listen. The mist does not come from the sorcerer, it comes from us. It develops out of our fears, our hatred of others. It then intensifies them and through this, strengthens itself."

"Enough," said Andrillo to Florence, while his fellow councillors muttered to one another about the impudence of the girl.

"I know this as the sorcerer admitted as much to me himself. I've visited Geissdon, the seat of our distant enemy. I implore you to believe me when I say we can resist him and the creatures that live in the mist by just realising that we are in control. We must do this before it's too late and you forget how we used to live. This man before you," said Florence, pointing to Andrillo, "has been to the sorcerer as well. He only acts out of fear. All that he has told you and made you do has resulted from his cowardice. All because he knows what awaits for him if he returns."

"I said enough!" shouted Andrillo, shooting up from his chair. He silenced both Florence and the rest of the room. He stood for moment with all their eyes upon him. The fire in his eyes slowly died down. After carefully retaking his seat, he continued to talk.

"I see you've decided not to repent from the wild and dangerous illusions you have about the situation we're in. I'm not sure why you persist in these unfortunate stories."

Andrillo finished the sentence by trailing off into silence. He wanted to consider the situation of the poor girl before him as rationally as he could. Florence, meanwhile, thought that after she had not apologised for what she had said the day before, she would be exiled. She was resolute it would have been impossible for her to live in her town under the yoke of this man. His misunderstanding of the power of the sorcerer could only lead Pendon into further darkness. If she was exiled, at least she could meet up with Sewan and tell him everything she knew.

"This is a very difficult decision we have to make today. A young citizen stands before us, one whose family is well respected. But, fellow councillors, you can see what Miss Watchmaker is. Just like the others before, she is a mist spreader; worse, a threat to our very lives. We need to mark her out so that others in our town will not be swayed by her dangerous lies. We also need to protect others, away from this town, from suffering the same fate that has befallen us. In short, gentlemen, I think that only one course of action is due. All those who disagree with me should make their voices heard now." Andrillo paused only a moment before continuing. "Very well. Miss Watchmaker, I hereby revoke from you the right to the protection this town grants its true citizens. You will, in sight of this court, be sown into a red cloak which you will never be allowed to remove. You will continue to wear this colour to remind you and those around you about the evil in your words. Furthermore, to protect other towns from such poison, you will remain at all times within the walls of Pendon. That is, until a time when the sorcerer determines you should be subject to his will, or when this court can be shown you have renounced your erroneous ways."

Florence knew she was effectively being handed a death sentence. She would not be able to leave Pendon after all. With a nod of Andrillo's head, the guards behind Florence stepped forwards to remove Florence's cloak. Though she did not fight or resist, they forcefully tore the cloth away from her body, pulling and pushing her without any thought to the violence of their action. As the tattered cloak was finally pulled from her shoulders, a clattering sound echoed around the otherwise silent room. Most of the councillors did not pay attention to the sound, they just looked at the prisoner passively while an usher brought in a tailor to fit the new, well deserved red cloak.

Andrillo's brother, Illarno, had listened with incredulity to the girl. He was surprised to hear about her illusions of visiting the sorcerer. He knew that she had been travelling and supposed many tales of Geissdon had now spread from those who had suffered like himself. It was plain from her face that she had never been near the place. He had also ignored the metallic clatter; such things were normal when a prisoner's cloak was removed. But, as the tailor went down to measure Florence's leg, he noticed the watch case on the floor. He tilted his head to the side, puzzled by what he saw. He advanced towards the girl.

"Brother, where are you going? Do not approach the prisoner!" exclaimed Andrillo, but the man kept on moving. "I demand that you stop! What do you think you are doing?"

"Where did you get this?" asked Illarno in a soft voice, full of confusion.

"Your brother gave it to my father, he considered it too ornate. My father gave it to me."

"How funny, this was the only thing we had left from our own father. It shows the towers of our city, built long ago when it was still rich."

For the first time, Illarno considered the girl before him. He looked her up and down until his eye was caught by a familiar mark.

"Where did you get those scars?" he said after taking hold of her arm.

"The same place as you."

By this time, Andrillo had made his way down to the pair and attempted to wrestle the watch case from his brother's hands.

"You knew about this?" said Illarno looking despairingly at his brother as he held the watch aloft.

"What do you think you're doing, Illarno? Don't be a fool!"

The tailor stopped what he was doing to watch the two middle aged men play out the childish game where an older brother holds an item just out of reach of his younger sibling. Andrillo kept trying to reach for the watch, but his taller brother had the upper hand. Just like when they were children, Andrillo would not give up.

"Stop, Marcus, stop. Its time they all knew," Illarno turned to the rest of the councillors. Andrillo's blood drained from his face and he stepped away from his brother. "What this young woman says is true. Marcus and I visited Geissdon ourselves. This was long ago, before we came here. Before we even knew Pendon existed. In that city, we received these scars, where this girl claims she acquired these scars of her own. We got to know of the torture the sorcerer meets out first hand. But it was his promise of death that affected us even more. We have acted on our fears all this time; the girl was right. But I'm fed up of sacrificing everything. If this girl has travelled to the sorcerer's castle and experienced what we went through, but still believes there is a way to resist, then perhaps we should listen to what she has to say.

"Marcus, we always wanted to seek solace for the death of our father, for our family being torn apart. Let us not throw away a chance to act if we have one. Fellow councillors, this girl has as much knowledge as we do about the mist: if she has travelled all the way to Geissdon, perhaps more. If we listen to her and what she tells us just leads to the further thickening of the mist, what difference will it make? Brother, even you must admit that since you started your campaign, the mist has only thickened."

"Illarno, have you gone mad?" exclaimed Andrillo. "How can you seek to undo all we've achieved? Ignore my brother, fellow councillors. I think sentimentality over this old scrap of metal has made him lose touch with his senses."

"Perhaps, Mr Andrillo," said one of the elder councillors, "but what your brother says is true. The mist has got worse during your time of office. We need not be hasty, but maybe it is time to try another path."

# Chapter Six

"Are you sure you have to leave again so soon," said Florence's father. "You've been back barely a month."

Florence brought her new bag up to her shoulders before giving her father a kiss on the cheek.

"As I said, I'll not be away too long. Anyway, I need to get a new tool-kit to replace the one I lost. I can't keep borrowing your things; it slows you down and while your account book is full, you don't have time to spare."

"Yes, yes. Well, don't spend too long with those friends of yours."

Florence gave her father a frown and a smile; she was still not sure if she should have told him she was going to visit Sewan. It was too late now.

"I'd better go, or I'll not make it to the coach station in time."

Florence left her father at the workshop door and was welcomed by the summer day outside. She wandered a few paces over the cobbled street before turning back and waving to the old man. As she did so, two running children bumped into her leg, almost toppling her over.

"Sorry Florence," came their call as they disappeared into the buzzing hum of the market. She looked up to her father and they both laughed.

"Don't worry," she called. "I'll be back soon."

Florence made her way to the town gate. She was annoyed to find her path blocked by the Andrillo brothers and a few of the other councillors.

"Ah, Florence," said Andrillo moving up to her. "We just wanted to wish you a good journey and to thank you for the work you've done."

"Give the girl some space, Marcus," said Illarno twisting a gold chain between his fingers: one that disappeared into his new deep blue jacket and led to his father's watch case, neatly fitted with new workings by Florence's father. "But my brother is right. Thank you for helping the town, for helping us all, see what we had been blind to for so long; especially me and my brother."

This sentiment was met with a murmur of approval from the other councillors.

"Thank you gentlemen," said Florence. "It was a bold decision you took yourselves that led to today. You could've just as easily ignored what I said and fought on along the road you had thought right for so long."

Florence looked directly into the eyes of Andrillo as she finished. She noticed for the first time how old he seemed; much more so than his elder brother. He gave a half smile then looked away. It was plane that he was still fighting with himself.

Florence bid farewell to the councillors and made as quick an escape as she could, claiming she needed to leave straight away, otherwise she would not reach the coach station before dark. After shaking the final councillor's hand, she wandered through the open gate and nodded a smiling farewell to Mark and Toby. A couple of carts heading to Pendon trundled by her as she made her way up to the pass. They were overflowing with colourful garments that would be sold cheaply in the market below. One was being driven through the muddy track by a couple of men; a familiar old woman was sat on top. She gave Florence a warm smile of greeting as she passed.

Just before her town would be obscured from view by the curve of the road, Florence looked back over her shoulder to see her town completely clear of mist under the summer sun. She returned her attention to the path. The mist covered town of Hesik lay ahead.

Printed in Great Britain
by Amazon.co.uk, Ltd.,
Marston Gate.